**The last notes of the seductive song
finally faded away.**

At the first drum riff, pulsing and fast, Kerry was more than ready to let the music take over again. The small dance floor quickly got crowded, but that was fine with her. Lost in the anonymity of the crowd, she moved and swayed, enjoying the occasional brush of a stranger's body against hers. This time it took more effort to lose herself, but finally everything but the music faded into the background. Yeah, this would do it. Once the song ended, she'd go home to sleep like a baby.

She danced, loving the slide of muscle under her skin, the fluid feeling of her bones bending with the rhythm of the song. Her soul was soothed. This was what she'd come for.

Then the night was shattered by a woman's terrified scream. "Fire! Oh God, fire!"

Kerry's eyes popped open. Everyone stood frozen in horror, their faces reflecting the crimson flicker of flames. Smoke burned her lungs as she struggled to remain calm in an ocean of incipient panic, caught up in a scene straight out of hell.

This title is also available as an eBook.

DARK PROTECTOR

DARK DEFENDER

Also by Alexis Morgan

Dark Warrior
UNLEASHED

ALEXIS MORGAN

Pocket **Star** Books
New York   London   Toronto   Sydney

Pocket Star Books
A division of Simon & Schuster, Inc.
1230 Avenue of the Americas
New York, NY 10020

This book is a work of fiction. Names, characters, places, and incidents either are products of the author's imagination or are used fictitiously. Any resemblance to actual events or locales or persons, living or dead, is entirely coincidental.

First Pocket Star Books paperback edition August 2008

POCKET STAR BOOKS and colophon are registered trademarks of Simon & Schuster, Inc.

For information about special discounts for bulk purchases, please contact Simon & Schuster Special Sales at 1-800-456-6798 or business@simonandschuster.com.

Illustration by Craig White; design by Lisa Litwack

Manufactured in the United States of America

10 9 8 7 6 5 4 3 2 1

ISBN-13: 978-1-4165-6342-6
ISBN-10:   1-4165-6342-3

Acknowledgment

I want to thank all the ladies who keep D.J. company on his blog on my website. You keep him out of trouble (mostly) and never fail to inspire me with your insight into his world.

No book is ever created in a vacuum. I don't know how I'd ever manage without the support of the people who help keep me sane.

I'd like to dedicate this book to my favorite Canadian, Bonnie Spidle. Since that fateful day when our paths first crossed up in Victoria, B.C., you've become an important part of my life. Thanks for being my sounding board, my confidante, my roomie, and, most of all, my friend.

Alexis

Dark Warrior
UNLEASHED

Chapter 1

*D*arkness flowed in, washing over him in relentless waves. Closing his eyes, Ranulf drank in the shadows with his other senses. Evil always felt the same, but the taste and smell and sound of it were different each time. Even here in his remote mountain home, the violence from the cities below tainted the air.

Who had dared to disturb his isolation? Ranulf traced the web of his protection wards, testing each one to locate the intruder. The sticky triggers of his protections were silent but effective, for the more someone struggled against them, the stronger the bond became.

It didn't take long to locate the snarl in his trap. Ranulf released the mental coils that held the man enthralled and let him approach the front door. The intruder was human, with very little of the Kyth in his blood, but then the blood of Ranulf's kind had become diluted over the centuries, lost in the wash of mankind.

He triggered the door to open but left the man cooling his heels on the porch. Bracing himself for the assault on his senses that always accompanied his return to society, Ranulf stepped into the doorway.

"You have something for me?"

The messenger jumped at Ranulf's sudden appearance, but he recovered quickly. With a courtly flourish he produced a heavy velum envelope. "The Dame sends her regards."

"I'm sure she does, Josiah." Ranulf reluctantly accepted the envelope.

The handwriting on the outside was the same spidery scrawl that had been issuing him orders for far too long. A millennium had passed since he'd first sworn fealty to the Grand Dame of their kind. Months ago she'd promised him a respite from killing, but he hadn't really expected it to last. They both knew that if she had need of his special talents, he would go. Duty was the one thing he understood.

As he cracked open the old-fashioned wax seal, he noticed the messenger still hovering in the doorway, neither in nor out.

"What?" Ranulf demanded, already weary of the man's presence.

"I'm to wait for you."

Ranulf bit back a curse; a lackey didn't deserve to lose his head just because Ranulf's instinct was to attack first and answer questions later—and then, only when he was forced to.

"Tell her to expect me when she sees me."

"But she said it was an emergency," the fool sputtered.

"It always is," Ranulf snapped, his temper boiling close to the surface. It wasn't as if he could simply lock the door and follow the man back to civilization. For him, travel took preparation.

He forced a compromise. "I will be there as soon as I can. I can't be more specific, but after all these years, she knows that. Now get the hell out of here, Josiah. Every minute we spend arguing is a minute I could put to better use."

The man started to say something else. When Ranulf took one step in his direction with his fists clenched, the messenger backed away with a reluctant nod, then fled toward his car. Ranulf slammed the door shut and threw the dead bolt.

Delays were pointless; it was time to start packing. That wouldn't take long, because clothing had never been a priority for him. Not like some other Talions he could name. The Grand Dame had Old World sensibilities about such things, but bloodstains were a bitch to get out of silk and wool.

After packing his duffel, he zipped it closed and

set it down by the front door. Then he walked over to a glass case and pondered its contents. After a few seconds, he lifted the lid and picked up his talisman by its leather thong. The bright shine of the gold sparked and flickered with power. The talisman felt to him far heavier than it looked.

He settled the centuries-old image of a god's hammer around his throat and tucked it inside his shirt collar. The cool metal absorbed the heat from his skin, reconnecting him with the Grand Dame. Once again, he was a warrior preparing for battle.

The small cache of energy he kept stored in the talisman soothed his cravings enough to maintain control, but it wouldn't last long. He could've used the Dame's messenger for a quick fix, but she wouldn't appreciate his sending her man back damaged, even just slightly.

Retrieving his duffel, he headed out to the garage, where his dark mood immediately improved. It was early summer and definitely time to take the dustcover off the Packard. The car, a creamy white 1940 convertible, always drew a crowd—a drawback in his line of work. But as a six-foot-three, blue-eyed Viking with fiery red hair, he wasn't exactly inconspicuous anyway. If he had to drag himself back out in the world on a mission for the Grand Dame, at least he could do it in comfort and style.

He'd owned the car since it had first rolled

off the lot back in 1940, and it still looked brand-new. He put the top down, then brushed a hint of dust off the elegant curve of the fender, enjoying the smooth feel of the metal and the comfort of the buttery soft leather seats. On the outside, the Packard hadn't aged any more than he had. Inside, where it counted, he felt every one of his thousand years. He turned the key and the car purred to life, the 160 horses under the hood just begging to be unleashed on the mountain roads.

Ranulf ripped down the familiar curves, wondering why the Dame needed him. Most of the time she used the other Talions at her command, preferring to use diplomacy rather than Ranulf's brute strength to impose her will on their people. If she was worried enough to send for him, she must suspect that one of their kind had crossed the line and needed to die. He flexed his hands on the steering wheel, feeling the harsh scrape of raw energy under his skin. It had been a long time since he'd fed on a renegade, and he didn't relish the thought of doing so again.

Killing was rough work, and messy. It always had been, from the very beginning, when blood had flowed for the glory of his people. But he was a Talion, a group named for the eye-for-an-eye principle that ruled their kind. Ranulf served the Kyth as executioner and was the acknowledged best at what he did. He had few regrets, even if every life he'd taken had chipped away at his soul, leaving him cold and grim.

In recent centuries the Kyth had grown more civilized, and now most feared rather than respected the Talion class. Maybe rightly so. The ability to kill without remorse was a rare gift, but one he took no pride in.

On the way, he'd look for a crowd to get lost in long enough to harvest sufficient energy to last him for a day or two. That way he'd be better prepared to face whatever had the Dame worried enough to unleash a Viking warrior on the streets of Seattle. A growing sense of dread urged him on, his foot pressing down hard on the accelerator as he charged down the mountain and prepared to do battle.

The music was alive, pulsing through the dancers. The concussive beat vibrated through the club's walls, the floor, and the very air until it became just another note in the symphony. The melody flowed out in waves, reaching the farthest corners of the club.

Closing her eyes, Kerry Logan lifted her hands high in the air and gave herself up to the fierce beat, her hips swaying, her head gently rolling from side to side. For the first time all day, her skin didn't hurt from the demands and expectations of others. She'd ditched her coworkers and her friends for a night out alone on the town.

Right now the music was all there was, and that was enough. She'd spend the evening lost in the crowd of dancers, letting the music take control. After a few hours she'd head home, her soul replenished.

Lost in the anonymity of the packed dance floor, she moved and slowly spun, enjoying the occasional brush of a stranger's body against hers. She was dimly aware of the weight of voices and the crush of bodies, but finally everything except the music faded into the background. *This* would heal her weary spirit.

The city lay sprawled under a blanket of bright lights as Ranulf followed Interstate 90 into the heart of Seattle. Just before he reached the turn-off to the Dame's home, the song on the radio was abruptly cut off by a news flash about a fire raging out of control at a nearby dance club. There was nothing unusual in the few sketchy details, but Ranulf's gut instincts had him riveted to the story. Without hesitation, he drove past his exit and into the downtown area.

The blaze might have been caused by any number of things, from bad wiring to a careless fool with a cigarette, but if a Kyth had set the fire, Ranulf wanted a head start in hunting the bastard down. No matter how careful an arsonist was, he'd leave enough of a trace for Ranulf to detect. The unique flavor of his energy would identify him as clearly as a fingerprint would.

Screaming emergency vehicles were converging on the scene, so Ranulf parked a block away to approach on foot. The scent of smoke and the faintest tang of burned flesh hung heavily all around, and he could hear the screams from a block away. Drawing in a deep breath, Ranulf tasted a bitter darkness in the air—the familiar flavor of evil. He ran toward the burning building, determined to snatch as many away from the grasping fingers of flame and death as possible.

Kerry was dancing, loving the slide of muscle under her skin, her bones no longer solid but fluid and bending with the rhythm of the song. This was what she'd come for.

Then the night was shattered by a woman's terrified scream. "Fire! My God, *fire*!"

Kerry's eyes flew open. Everyone stood frozen in horror, their faces reflecting the crimson flicker of flames. As terror swiftly turned the crowd into an ocean of panic, Kerry fought to remain calm in a scene straight out of hell. She glanced at the ceiling to the silver glint of a sprinkler system, praying it would kick on to drown the roiling smoke and terrified voices.

How had the room filled up with so much black smoke and flame so quickly? It didn't make sense. Ignoring the chaos, she struggled to get her bearings. Access to the front door was already cut off by a lethal combination of too many people and the fire itself. The intense heat drove the crowd back, sending a solid wall of mindless bodies flooding right back toward her.

There had to be another way out. She wiped her eyes with her sleeve to clear away the sting of tears and smoke. Keeping close to the wall, Kerry darted toward the hallway at the back of the club. The power failed as she turned the corner, plunging the narrow passageway into darkness, leaving only the dim glow of the red emergency lights to guide her.

She tried door after door, including the bathrooms, but found no windows. No access to the outside. Spying an Exit sign at the back of a storage room, she ran straight for it. The heavy door resisted opening, but she gathered up her strength and shoved one more time. Blessedly cool night air poured through the opening and kissed her skin. She filled her lungs, shaking with relief at having made it to safety. But before she could step outside to freedom, the screams and agonized shrieks back in the club brought her up short.

She couldn't save herself and let the others die. Fear and common sense argued she was making a mistake, but her conscience wouldn't listen. After jamming a box in the door to keep it open, she drew one last breath of clear air and resolutely turned back toward the hell inside.

The fire had engulfed one entire side of the club, herding its victims back into nooks and crannies to consume at its leisure. Kerry grabbed two women by the arms and dragged them toward the hallway. Once they were headed in the right direction, she returned for more.

With smoke burning her lungs, she made trip after trip out of the inferno, leading some people, herding others, helping as many as she could. Once the able-bodied were moving in the right direction, she looked for anyone who didn't have the strength to make it out on their own.

Ignoring the stench of burned flesh, she lifted a man who was struggling to breathe. Wrapping his arm around her shoulder, she staggered under his weight as they shuffled step by step through the heavy smoke, half carrying and half leading him toward the exit.

A tall male figure suddenly loomed up in front of her through the smoke. The haze was too thick for her to make out his face clearly, but she was sure he hadn't been among the dancers. She would have remembered someone that size. He seemed to be the only other person who'd managed to keep his head in the face of such terror.

She shoved the injured man at the tall stranger, shouting over the chaos, "Get him out of here while I go back for another look."

Before she'd gone two steps, his hand snaked out to catch her by the arm. "I'll be back to help."

"Fine."

With a renewed burst of energy, she made another foray back into the club. The dim hallway was no longer clear of smoke and fire, and heat licked its way along the ceiling, rolling in blue and red waves. Dropping to her hands and knees, Kerry crawled and coughed her way back into the dance floor, where she spotted four people huddled behind the bar. Were they waiting for an engraved invitation, for God's sake?

"You've got to get out of here!" she shouted, frustration and a growing fear threatening to overwhelm her.

When they didn't respond, she tried again. "Come on, get moving! I'll take you to safety."

A boy who looked far too young to be in a bar shrank back farther into the corner, his eyes huge with panic. "NO! We're waiting for the firemen to come get us."

"You won't live long enough for them to find you." Running out of time and patience, she gave his arm a solid yank. "Now get moving, all of you!"

"You heard her, boy. Move or we all die."

Kerry jumped at the deep voice barking orders from right beside her. The stranger was back, just as he'd promised. With him standing beside her, the fear that had been lapping at her control faded to a manageable level.

He shoved the boy and his friends back toward the exit, then leaned in close to yell over the roar of the fire, "Better get out of here. The rest of the roof is about to go."

"I'll be right behind you."

"You better be." Then he was gone.

Dimly aware of the shouts behind her, she realized that the fire department had arrived and was sending in the troops. At last.

Before she'd gone more than a few steps toward the exit, she heard a sound that chilled her despite the boiling heat surrounding her.

Closing her eyes to listen, she hoped to hear nothing but the mad cackle of the fire's fury. But there it was again—a whimper coming from off to the left. Common sense told her to leave any more rescues to the pros. But she had to live with herself, even if that meant dying right along with whoever was still trapped inside the inferno. Praying for deliverance or, failing that, a merciful death, she worked her way farther into the room.

Part of the ceiling crashed in, sending up a shower of sparks as the front door of the club was axed open and the first spray of water hit the flames. A rush of steam hissed and boiled through the room, and she instinctively flattened onto the floor. If the fire didn't finish her, the superheated water would.

From the floor, she spotted the source of the agonized moans. A woman lay curled up on her side a few feet away, cradling her badly burned arm. From the unnatural position of her foot, it looked like she also had a broken ankle. Kerry lurched to her feet, then muscled the woman up off the floor and over her shoulder. She wasn't sure how far she could carry someone who was both taller and heavier than she was; hopefully that huge guy would reappear.

The smoke had too much substance now for her to see clearly, so she was forced to trust her instincts. Through the darkness, she fought her way toward the exit one last time. It felt like it took an eternity before she finally staggered through the door.

Outside she was dimly aware of the crush of people and the scream of sirens as ambulances pulled into the parking lot. She turned in their direction, going only a few steps before EMTs were there to relieve her of her burden. As they gently settled the woman on a gurney, she grabbed Kerry and held on tightly.

Squeezing her hand lightly, Kerry offered what comfort she could. "You'll be fine. They're going to take you to the hospital."

"What's your name?" the woman rasped, her voice damaged by the smoke.

"Kerry. Kerry Logan."

"Thank you. Without you, I'd be dead." A tear streaked down the woman's sooty face.

"We'll take her now, miss." The EMT wheeled the gurney toward a waiting ambulance.

Kerry stared after the flashing lights long after the ambulance streaked out of the parking lot. The adrenaline rush left her buzzed and unable to concentrate, with no outlet for the energy coursing through her. Where was that tall guy? She wanted to thank him for his help and make sure he'd made it out of the fire safely. Odd that just his presence had helped her remain so calm.

Before she could spot him, a uniformed man approached her. "Miss, I'd like to talk to you if you wouldn't mind."

Kerry blinked several times, forcing her eyes to focus. "Yes, Officer?"

"From what I've been hearing, a lot of folks are alive here because of your efforts. So far it looks like no one died, in large part thanks to you. Tell me what happened in there."

Kerry shuddered as images of flames and fear flooded her mind. "There was music and dancing, and then suddenly there was fire everywhere."

He looked up from his notebook. "Can you describe it in more detail? I'm the arson investigator for the fire department—Maynard Cooper, although most folks just call me Coop. I'll be in charge of the investigation."

"I'm Kerry Logan, but I don't know how much help I can be. Most of it's just a blur." She shoved her hands in her jeans pockets. "Right now I just want to go home."

"You'll get there, but first I need your contact information. Then you need to get checked out by the EMTs before we can release you. You took in an awful lot of smoke tonight."

She was reluctantly following him across the parking lot when Coop abruptly steered her back the way they'd come.

"The vultures have landed." He glanced over his shoulder. "Listen, unless you want to be grilled by a mob of reporters, why don't you wait by my car over there? I'll send one of the techs to check on you."

"Thanks." The last thing she wanted was to face the flash of cameras and a bunch of stupid questions.

While Coop fended off the press, she watched the firefighters swarm the club, pouring on more water and checking for hot spots inside the remaining walls. Had anyone been left inside? God, she hoped not. What a horrible way to die! Visions of that fiery hell would terrorize her dreams for weeks to come.

As she waited, she could feel the weight of

someone's gaze. She looked around, at first seeing no one, then spotted a man standing back in the shadows of a nearby alley. Though she couldn't see his face, she could feel him staring directly at her. She tried to ignore him but found it impossible to look away.

As if sensing her interest, he stepped forward into the glow of a streetlight and met her gaze head-on. His mouth turned up in a predatory smile that chilled her to the bone. Glancing toward the door to the club, he held out his hand. With a quick flick of his thumb, he lit his cigarette lighter, then lifted it up as if he'd been making a toast.

His smile broadened and he bowed, then faded back into the shadows as quickly as he'd appeared. Kerry stood frozen, unable to move, grasping for words to describe what she'd just seen. Only one fit.

Death.

There wasn't a doubt in her mind that this man was responsible for the fire. Closing her eyes, she did her best to recall every detail about him, then ran straight for Coop.

He was still fielding questions from the reporters. She caught his eye and gave him a pleading look. Abruptly he cut off the interview, promising the reporters an update as more information became available. Kerry waited impatiently for the press to start moving off.

When they were out of hearing, she leaned in

close to the arson investigator and whispered, "I need to talk to you, but not here."

After one look at her face, he nodded and took her arm. "Let's get in my car."

There, he asked, "What's up?"

Bracing herself, she met his gaze head-on. "I know who started the fire."

The investigator jerked upright, all signs of exhaustion gone. "What makes you say that? Where is he now?"

"Gone." Her teeth began to chatter, and cold chills raced through her body. "Can I borrow your notebook and a pencil?"

He handed them over.

With trembling hands, she started sketching the face she'd seen, closing her eyes periodically to remember more detail. It took her several attempts to get the mouth right, but finally she was satisfied.

And scared all over again.

Coop leaned over to look at the picture. "Who is he? And what makes you think that he's the one?"

"While you were talking to the reporters, I felt someone staring at me." She pointed toward the alley. "He was standing in the shadows between those two buildings. As soon as I spotted him, he smiled and held up his cigarette lighter and flicked it. As if he was making a toast to celebrate the fire."

She shivered. "His smile was the scariest thing I've ever seen."

Coop merely nodded. "How come you draw so well?"

"I'm a graphic artist. That's a pretty rough sketch, though."

He studied the picture. "Looks pretty damn good to me. And it's a helluva lot more for my team to work with than we had a few minutes ago. I had one of my guys taking pictures of the crowd. Maybe we'll get lucky and find him in one. I'd like to take you into headquarters to make a statement."

She ached all over, but she couldn't find it in her to refuse. "If you think it will help."

He pulled out a cell phone. "I need to let my men know where I'm heading. Do you need to call anyone?"

She shook her head. No family, few friends, and she'd told her boss that she was going to work at home tomorrow. Glancing at the digital clock on the dash, she realized that it already was tomorrow. She'd been up for almost twenty-four hours straight and felt every minute of it.

As they drove out of the parking lot, Coop opened his mouth briefly, as if to say something but then closed it when he thought better of it. Whatever it was, she'd be better off knowing what he had to say, especially considering the worried look on his face.

"Tell me, Coop. I'd rather know."

He gave her a sidelong glance. "I didn't give the

reporters any information about you back there, but they're bound to interview some of the people you saved tonight. If any of them know your name, the media will be on your trail, wanting your story. Your name and picture will end up splashed across tomorrow's headlines."

It didn't take a genius to add two and two and come up with a scary answer. "He'll find out who I am."

Coop nodded grimly. "I can request some protection for you, but until we get a fix on who this guy is . . . Hell, he could be anybody, anywhere. I won't lie to you, Miss Logan. It could be dangerous, because so far you're the only one who can place him at the scene."

"How mad will he be that I screwed up his plans?" It was a hard question to ask, but she preferred to have all the facts, no matter how grim.

Coop stared out the windshield as he considered his answer. "It depends. Chances are he loves fire like most men love a woman. If that's the case, he might be happy with burning the place to the ground. But if he wanted more than that, then he's crazy as a bedbug and there's no predicting what he'll do."

"Either way, I have to do this. I couldn't live with myself, knowing what I saw and not doing anything about it."

"You're a brave young woman, Miss Logan."

She laughed shakily. "I'm not so sure about that."

"Like they say, being brave is being scared and doing it anyway." He gave her a reassuring smile. "And a lot of people are still breathing today because you kept a cool head in that fire, Miss Logan." The respect in his voice came through loud and clear.

She managed a small smile. "Thank you, Coop, and call me Kerry. I suspect we'll be seeing more of each other."

"Yeah, and I'm truly sorry about that." Coop patted her on the shoulder just before turning into the fire department parking lot.

"Me, too, Coop. Me, too."

"Son of a bitch!"

Ranulf kicked a rock, sending it skittering down the street after the car disappearing down the block. He'd been too busy trying to trace the elusive scent of the renegade to realize that the woman was about to be whisked away by someone in a uniform. For her sake, he hoped the man really was part of the fire department. The renegade Kyth's scent had faded away at about the same time, so it was possible that the bastard's fun wasn't over for the night.

He turned back to where the fire crew continued battling the blaze. Soon there'd be only charred wood and a few nightmares for those who had lived through it. Which brought him right back to the woman in the fire. She was *Kyth*. He hadn't known that until he'd grabbed her arm.

His hand still tingled from the burn of energy that had arced between them. Had she recognized him for what he was? Probably not. She'd been too intent on hauling that human's sorry ass to safety to notice anything else. How many of those trapped in the renegade's fire party owed their lives to her cool head and clear thinking?

The Dame would want to hear about the woman's exploits in the club. Thanks to the fire and smoke, he couldn't provide many details about her other than she was on the small side and had dark hair. And that she'd displayed far more strength and courage than anyone he'd met in a long time.

The renegade would be hunting for her, but Ranulf wasn't going to let him get to her. Not on his watch.

With the fire department and police still crawling all over the scene, there wasn't anything else he could do now. First thing in the morning, he'd return to study the scene and start tracking down his target. He'd do better after he'd rested and fed.

After one last look at the smoldering ruins, he walked back to his car. Time to report to the Dame.

Chapter 2

*T*hough the shower had washed the lovely scents of smoke and burned flesh from Bradan's skin, it hadn't taken the shine off the fun he'd had watching the dance club burn. In tomorrow morning's paper, there would be an accurate count of how many had died screaming as the bright, dancing flames had consumed them.

It had been his first effort at arson on such a scale, and it had been an overwhelming success. He slid between the sheets of his king-sized bed, relishing the feel of the cool, clean cotton against his skin. Closing his eyes, he relived each moment, from the first screams right up until the moment the firemen turned off the last hose.

The only fly in the ointment was that little brunette who'd led the charge out of the back of the club. If there'd been more time, he would've figured out how to block that door, too. Oh, well, live and learn. When he'd first seen her carry out a burn victim he'd been seriously pissed.

But when she'd done it again, he'd become curious. Who was she? Whenever a human did something extraordinary, they always assumed that the adrenaline coursing through their bodies was responsible. But no amount of adrenaline could account for how much she'd accomplished.

When everyone else had been choking on all that luscious smoke, she'd barely noticed it. Could she possibly be one of his people? After all, the Kyth thrived off of human life force. The heady perfume of fear and pain had rendered the night air an elixir fit for the gods, but ordinary humans lacked the ability to utilize it.

Which meant she had to have Kyth blood in her veins, even if she didn't know it. His body stirred in response. Once the newspapers got wind of what she'd done, he'd know her name. From there, it was a short step to finding out where she lived.

The two of them would have a lovely time together. If she was as pureblooded as he suspected, she would make a perfect mate for him. And if she didn't like that idea, she'd make a good plaything until she broke like all of his other toys did, bleeding and screaming for mercy.

Maybe he'd keep her alive long enough to bear

him an heir. His brains and good looks, combined with hers, would definitely create a superior product. A son to follow in his old man's murderous footsteps, or perhaps a daughter who liked the joy of pain as much as her dad did.

A huge yawn surprised him. He'd meant to wait up for the early morning news, but his body was demanding rest. He needed sleep to allow his body to process all the energy he'd taken in, otherwise he'd lose most of it.

When he woke up, he could buy the daily papers. The coverage on the afternoon news wouldn't be as extensive, but it would have to do. Once he had the girl's name, he would make plans.

Thinking of her big dark eyes, he slid his hand under the sheet, imagining her in his bed, under him as he rode her hard. A few strokes was all it took to have him arching off the bed, his body shuddering in release. Someday he'd be spilling his seed into his future mate. But for now, it was the perfect ending to a perfect day.

Judith impatiently listened to the clock in the hallway tolling the hour. "Where *is* that man?"

Sandor shrugged and poured himself another brandy. "Ranulf thinks he is a law unto himself. Perhaps we cater a little too much to him."

Dame Judith was well aware of the animosity

between Sandor and Ranulf, and rarely asked them to work together. This time she had no choice.

"I don't coddle the man, Sandor. His needs are different than yours and mine." She sipped her sherry, missing the strength and support of her beloved late Consort, Rolf.

She glanced up at his portrait hanging over the fireplace. Rolf's eyes seemed to watch her no matter where she stood in the room, as if he'd been keeping an eye on her from the afterlife. It was a silly fantasy, but she drew comfort from the knowledge that he was there, waiting for her to join him when her work here was done. That time was coming soon. She knew it, even if those around her didn't want to see it.

Some nights the burden of her many years weighed her down, and tonight was worse than most. Once Ranulf appeared, she would give him and Sandor their marching orders, then retire to the sanctuary of her rooms.

Josiah, who served as both her butler and messenger, appeared in the doorway.

"Yes, Josiah, what is it?"

He approached, stopping a few feet away to bow slightly. "Talion Thorsen just pulled in and is getting out of his car."

"Please ask him to come straight here."

Josiah frowned. "Considering his attire, madam, I would think he would want time to change first."

Sandor laughed, and not kindly. "Why? Is he dressed in animal skins and a horned helmet, like the barbarian he is?"

Josiah drew himself up and shot Sandor a disapproving look. "Not at all, sir. However, I'm sure that Master Thorsen would want to pay the Dame the respect due her, and dirty jeans are hardly the appropriate attire for that."

"That's quite all right, Josiah." Judith hid her amusement at her butler's ability to look down his nose at someone who towered over him by at least six inches. "Please ask Ranulf to come directly here. Waiting for him to change will only delay matters."

Josiah left, and almost immediately she heard the front door open and close. Josiah spoke first, answered by Ranulf's deep rumble in disagreement. She couldn't hear the particulars, but she was willing to bet that Ranulf would prevail. A few seconds later, Josiah reappeared to announce her guest's imminent arrival.

"Dame Judith, Talion Ranulf Thorsen asked me to say that he'd be joining you in five minutes."

"That's fine, Josiah. Would you put together a meal for him? I suspect he'll be hungry after his long trip." A Talion of his power would need food to counterbalance the energy feeding he would have done on his way to answer her call.

Josiah nodded, then glanced at Sandor. "And you, sir, would you like a small repast as well?"

Sandor set down his glass. "If it wouldn't be too much trouble. I'm guessing it's going to be a long night."

"Yes, sir. I will serve you all in a few minutes."

When Ranulf appeared in the doorway, Dame Judith could see why Josiah had thought he'd want to change. Very few of her people would have dared appear before her wearing dirt-streaked jeans and an equally filthy flannel shirt that reeked of smoke. Interesting. Where had he been? To give the man credit, his shoulder-length hair had been recently combed and his face freshly washed.

She held out her hand, and his huge one engulfed her fingers as he bowed and brushed a kiss across her knuckles. No matter what Sandor thought, her Viking warrior knew how to behave— when he wanted to.

"I'm glad you've made it, Ranulf. It has been a long day and promises to be even longer. Josiah should be along in a moment with something for you to eat. I trust you are otherwise well?"

Among the Kyth, asking if another had recently fed was considered rude. But however delicately she couched the question, it was important to know the answer. His bright blue eyes narrowed as he straightened up. The lines bracketing his mouth spoke of tension, but he seemed in control of his emotions.

"I am well, my lady. Out of necessity, I made a couple of stops on the way here."

He stepped away and she noted that he was careful to stand near the door with his back to the wall. A lifetime of fighting made a man understandably cautious.

She picked up the folders full of articles she'd clipped from the local newspapers. "Why don't we adjourn to the dining room? Once you've eaten, we can decide what steps we need to take."

She led the way across the hallway and sat at the head of the table. Sandor automatically sat on her left, while Ranulf took the seat on her right. Josiah immediately entered from the kitchen, carrying a tray laden with sandwiches, sliced fruits, and cheeses.

Both men reached for the folders she held out to them. "I'll give you some time to eat while you read over the information I've gathered. I've called you both here because I suspect we have a renegade in our midst."

It would be interesting to see if her Talions came to the same conclusions she had. Her instincts screamed she was on the right track, and if a renegade was running rampant in Seattle, leaving a trail of death and pain that could lead straight to her front door, that could spell disaster for them all.

It didn't take long for both men to read through the material. Sandor frowned as he closed the file, but Ranulf looked especially grim.

"It's a renegade, all right." He tapped his fore-finger on the stack of papers. "But these were only his opening moves."

Sandor frowned. "And you know that why?"

"Because he set fire to a dance club downtown tonight and did his damnedest to kill a whole lot of people." The calm announcement didn't disguise the fury in the Viking's eyes. A shimmer of hot energy danced over his hands as he shoved the file back toward the center of the table.

"On my way here, I heard about the fire on the radio and thought it was worth checking out. I don't know who the son of a—" Ranulf stopped, glancing at Judith. "Uh, I don't know who was behind the fire, but he's definitely one of us. There were too many people and too much smoke for me to be able to track him through the crowd, but I could taste his presence. First thing tomorrow, I'll go back and try again. There won't be much left to look at, but I should be able to pick up traces of his energy signature. Once I have that, he won't be able to hide for long."

"How many were killed?" Judith grasped the talisman that hung around her neck and prayed to the gods that the number was small.

Ranulf's grim expression softened. "Near as I can tell, none. They hauled a few off in ambulances, but no one was seriously hurt. Not like you'd normally expect from a fire that size."

Sandor looked puzzled. "But from what you said, the place must have burned to the ground."

"It did. But there was a woman who managed to get everybody out of the club before the roof caved in." Then he smiled. "And, Judith, she's one of us."

Kerry was so tired that her hair hurt. Coop had kept her sequestered for hours with a sketch artist while he wrote a report. Finally he'd sent out for breakfast for everybody. The wonderful combination of salt and grease went a long way toward improving her mood, but if she didn't get some sleep soon, she wouldn't be responsible for her actions.

Coop appeared in the doorway so silently that she had to blink twice to make sure he was real. He looked even worse than she felt.

"You sure you don't want to go to a hotel, at least for today?" His voice was rough with exhaustion.

"No, I'll be fine. I'd appreciate a lift home, though."

He gave her a wry smile. "Did you think we'd boot you out the door and let you fend for yourself?"

"Sorry—it's been a long twenty-four hours."

"For all of us." He stepped back. "Come on, I'll give you a lift, and then we can both get some rest."

As she followed him down the hallway, she noticed he had a death grip on a folded newspaper. When they reached the elevator, she braced herself and asked, "Did the reporters find out about me?"

He nodded and shoved the paper at her. "Evidently one of the women you carried out of the fire gave them your name."

Kerry sighed. "She asked for it after I carried her out of the building. It won't take the reporters long to find me, will it?"

"Probably not." Coop ran his fingers through his sparse hair as the elevator bumped to a stop. "Look, the idea of your staying at a hotel room really makes good sense."

She considered her options as they went to his car and got in. She never slept well in a strange bed, but she doubted she'd sleep at all if a gaggle of reporters decided to camp out on the sidewalk outside her apartment.

"Maybe that would be best for today. Eventually I'll have to face the press, but I'll do better after some sleep." She leaned her head back.

"Duck down. I'd just as soon no one outside of the department knows you're with me."

He slowed the car to a crawl until she slid down out of sight. The last thing either of them needed was to lead a parade to her temporary sanctuary.

Darn, now she was uncomfortable as well as tired. It was hardly Coop's fault, but she was having a hard time keeping a lid on her temper. Finally, she poked her head up and looked around. "Is it safe?"

"I think so. I'm going to take you to a hotel on the east side, where a friend of mine works. He'll let me register you under a fake name, and supply you with some of the basics from the gift shop."

"I appreciate everything you've done."

"It's the least I can do. Your quick thinking saved lives, and that picture you drew might help us catch the bastard who lit the match."

It was only luck that had prevented anyone from dying, Kerry thought. Coop had checked with the hospital, and most of the victims had been treated and released. The only admission had been the woman with burns and an injured ankle. Although the doctors were at a loss to explain it, the burns had already visibly improved and her ankle was only a bad sprain. Kerry would have sworn that ankle was broken, but she'd take all the good news she could.

Was the bastard who set the fire disappointed? She shivered. Of course he was. And whom would he blame? Her. The danger would only get worse when it became public knowledge that the authorities had a sketch of his face. She stubbornly shoved the fear aside, concentrating on just staying awake.

A short time later, Coop turned into a hotel parking lot, checked his rearview mirror, then parked the car.

"Okay, lady, let's get you checked in."

"Yes, sir." She executed a mock salute as they headed into the hotel.

An hour later, she was showered, fed, and sound asleep.

Ranulf skimmed the morning papers over a late breakfast. They pretty much all said the same things about the fire, which wasn't much. Obviously the reporters had submitted their articles to meet a deadline before they'd known many details. At least now he knew the mysterious woman's name: Kerry Logan.

But reading between the lines wasn't hard when you knew what to look for. Or rather, *who* to look for. There were definitely two different people involved in the fire who would require Judith's attention: the arsonist and Kerry Logan.

"Was the Logan woman treated for any injuries?" He looked up from the clipping to find Dame Judith watching him.

"Not as far as we know. Miss Logan disappeared right after the fire was out, and no one has seen her since." She pushed her plate away. "I've made inquiries, but there is only so much I can do without drawing undue attention."

"He may have already gotten her." Sandor closed his file and reached for his coffee. "May the gods help her, if he has."

Ranulf went with his instincts. "I'm sure that was her I saw leaving the scene in a fire department vehicle, but you're right to be concerned. Even if the culprit was an ordinary arsonist, he'd be angry at her interrupting his fun. But since he's one of us, he'll also find her extraordinary reaction to the fire as intriguing as we do. He might forgive the interference if it brings an unschooled Kyth into his crosshairs. We can't let that happen. I won't let it."

Judith gave them both a satisfied nod. "So, gentlemen, your orders are simple. Sandor, find the girl and ingratiate yourself using that abundant charm of yours. Ranulf, do what you can to help keep Miss Logan safe, but bring this arsonist to justice. *Our* justice."

Ranulf met the old woman's sharp gaze. She was ordering him to carry out an execution, just as he'd known she would. It was the best use of their talents, logical, cold, and brutal. Ranulf didn't enjoy being the messenger of death for the Kyth, but he knew his duty and he would do it. He closed his eyes, seeing his life stretch from his past to his future filled with nothing but an endless line of violence meted out for the good of their kind.

Judith seemed to be waiting for some response. What could he say?

He grasped his talisman and met her gaze head-on. "By my honor, the renegade will die."

• • •

Half an hour later Ranulf was on his way back to
the club, his blood singing with the joy of the hunt.

Back when he'd been a boy, the warriors had always enjoyed the choicest bits of the game they'd
brought back to the village. Now, for him, it was the
spicy, hot taste of the black energy a renegade had
fed on. Even the smallest taste of human joy could
keep a Kyth electrified for days, but the dark end of
their emotional spectrum had the richest flavor and
the most power. Ranulf had consumed so much of
it in his job as enforcer that it had extended his life
for centuries beyond the norm.

And that was why the Dame's other chief Talion, Sandor Kearn, didn't trust Ranulf.

Maybe the pup was right, but Ranulf didn't like
to think so. Not once in all of his centuries of service had he ever been tempted to harvest the dark
energy straight from the source. Renegades went
after humans with cold cruelty, wallowing in the
pain and misery and terror they drew from their
victims. They took pleasure in the unspeakable.

The law of the Kyth demanded that punishment
match the crime, and it was the job of the Talion to
carry it out with no hope for appeal. When a Kyth
turned renegade, destroying a human's mind and
soul, Ranulf hunted the bastard down and stripped
him of every bit of energy he'd stolen and then his
own life force as well, leaving only a dead husk behind.

That made Ranulf the stuff of Kyth nightmares, the horror whispered about in the dark of night.

He parked the Packard half a block away from the club. The charred bones of the building jutted up against the sky, giving mute testimony to the violence that had consumed it. It was a miracle that no one had died in that inferno.

He wondered if the owners had needed the insurance money, but he rejected the idea. His gut feeling was that the people inside the club had been the target, and the building just collateral damage. It all added up to the perfect menu for a renegade's banquet: terror, pain, panic, and death. The bastard would be riding high for days from the dark energy he'd have gotten. Except that one woman's unexpected heroics had shortchanged him by keeping the death toll to zero.

Kerry Logan was one gutsy woman, and Ranulf hoped that her courage didn't cost her too dearly. If the renegade found her before Sandor did, there'd be hell to pay, so Ranulf would work with the devil himself to save her life. It was the least he could do to reward such bravery.

He climbed out of his car and headed down the sidewalk to the club. Closing his eyes briefly, he listened for the sound of heartbeats but heard none. He circled the building, studying the details. The fire had started in the front near the door, convincing him that he'd been right about the arson-

ist's intent. Block the exits and people would die—
horribly.

The stench clogged his mind and senses. The air
tasted acrid with the tang of burned human flesh
and ashes. It was as if pain was a memory, forever
burned into blackened bits and pieces of wood that
surrounded him. He'd tasted the savory energy
often enough, but only secondhand from a renegade's cache. This was too recent, too direct.

Clasping the Thor's hammer amulet at his
throat, he felt its power thrumming and burning.
He forced himself to walk forward until he came
full circle around the building. He moved closer to
the outer wall, seeing everything and focusing on
nothing. His mind roamed freely as he processed
the scene on multiple levels: scent, taste, and
sound. Echoes of the event still hovered in the air
for someone able to hear them.

Ranulf cocked his head to one side as he traced
the path of the back hallway into what had been the
dance floor. He closed his eyes and listened to the
fading notes of music as they were drowned by a
rising crescendo of panic and screams. He only saw
faint traces of the events as they'd played out. Sight
was the weakest of his senses, but he could hear
and he could feel.

A single column of wood still stood, holding
up the remains of the roof. He trailed his fingers
along the ebony surface, soaking up the memories

held in the charred remains. Heat. Flashing lights. A woman. Not just any woman; Kerry Logan had stood right there. His pulse sped up, keeping time with the driving rhythm left behind by the music.

Oh, yeah, she was Kyth, with nearly pure blood flowing through her veins. Anything less and her impression wouldn't have remained so strong. He followed her essence, the trail somewhat confusing because she'd crisscrossed the room multiple times last evening. In one place he could feel where she'd knelt and then walked away, burdened with something heavy. Perhaps one of the victims she'd snatched from the licking tongues of fire?

Now that he'd tasted her scent and her essence in its purest form, the urge to find her and keep her safe intensified. His hands flexed, ready to protect the woman he'd only met briefly, the strength of his reaction a surprise. If just her echo affected him this strongly, what would she do to him in person? Damned if he didn't want to find out—and soon.

As swiftly as the thought crossed his mind, he rejected it. It was Sandor's job to bring the newly discovered Kyth into their society, Ranulf's job to take out the arsonist. Sandor was the light; Ranulf, the dark. The younger Talion wouldn't appreciate any interference in his duty—but maybe that was just too damn bad.

Ranulf dug out his cell phone and hit Sandor's number on speed dial. It rang half a dozen times.

"What?" Sandor sounded distracted.

"I was right. Kerry Logan is definitely Kyth, and close to a pureblood."

"Have you found her?" There was a definite excitement in Sandor's voice.

"No, I'm at the dance club. The fire has been out for hours, and I can still feel her here."

"If she's that strong, how have we missed her all these years?"

"A good question." To find a Kyth of this strength was a valuable gift to their dwindling race.

"I'll let Judith know. Thanks for the heads-up. I appreciate it," Sandor said, sounding as if he really meant it.

Would wonders never cease? Ranulf shook his head as he hung up. After another trip through the ruins looking for a trace of the arsonist, he returned to the club's parking lot. The firebug would've wanted a front-row seat to watch the entertainment. The question was, where? Several buildings were close enough to give him an unobstructed view without the risk of being seen. Ranulf turned slowly, studying the windows staring down at him like so many blind eyes.

No. It felt wrong to him. Fire was no good unless you could feel its heat and smell the smoke. The arsonist would have needed to be close to ground zero to get the most bang for his buck. This time Ranulf studied the various possible vantage points at ground level. His eyes drifted past an alley but were immediately drawn right back to it.

He headed straight for it on instinct, and after reaching the mouth of the alley, he stopped and looked back toward the club. Yeah, this felt right.

Placing one hand on the brick wall and the other on his talisman, he closed his eyes and slowly entered the alley. Filth and lust and fury burned along his nerve endings, making him queasy and sick to his soul. Oh, yeah—the arsonist had stood right here, cheering on the fire and soaking up the pain and suffering from a safe distance. Ranulf couldn't wait to get his hands on him.

And judging by the strength of the emotional stain the killer had left behind, the bastard wasn't only Kyth but a Talion as well. One of Dame Judith's personal warriors had started this fire to watch humans die—may the gods help them all.

The knowledge would hit her hard. He'd like to keep that little bit of information to himself until he stripped the culprit of his stolen energy and safely watched him breathe his last, but he couldn't risk it.

It was time to go. He'd learned all he could from the scene.

Chapter 3

Sandor logged off his computer and stood up to stretch. Normally at the start of a new mission, his energy ran high as plans and ideas swirled through his brain. Right now, all he felt was anger.

Why in hell had the Dame called in that Viking berserker for backup? She knew they could hardly stand to be in the same city, much less the same room.

Sandor would do as she asked, of course, but Ranulf was a loose cannon. The man had probably raped and plundered his way across half of Europe before Judith had found him and brought him to heel. And no one fed off the dark energies for centuries and remained stable. But their Dame had a blind spot when it came to Ranulf. Why?

A soft knock on the bedroom door interrupted his silent tirade. He crossed to the door and opened just as Josiah was preparing to knock again.

"What?" He grimaced, knowing how surly he'd sounded. "I'm sorry, Josiah. What can I do for you?"

The butler nodded slightly, accepting the apology. "Dame Judith is holding lunch until you are ready to join her, sir. Shall I tell her that you'll be down momentarily?"

"I was just coming. Please tell her to start without me." He started to close the door.

"Mr. Thorsen and I both suggested that exact thing an hour ago, but she insisted on waiting."

Josiah kept his face carefully blank, but there was a glint of censure in his eye that Sandor didn't appreciate. Hell, it wasn't as if he'd been holed up in his room twiddling his thumbs. He pinched the bridge of his nose, trying to ease the headache he'd gotten from growing frustration and hours spent staring at the computer screen. At least he had some answers to show for it.

He headed into the dining room, where the combined scents of coffee and food had his stomach rumbling. Dame Judith once again sat at the head of the table with the afternoon paper spread out before her. Ranulf stood looking out the window, his back to the room, but Sandor knew that the Viking was fully aware of him. The man hadn't survived for centuries by being careless. As Sandor crossed to the table and took his usual place, Ranulf followed suit. Judith put her paper aside.

She smiled at Sandor. "How has your morning been?"

"Very productive. I've been digging into Kerry Logan's life. I have her home address and where she works, so later this afternoon I can see if she has reappeared."

"Was there anything more about her on the noon news?" Ranulf leaned back in his chair to give Josiah room to place food on the table.

Judith frowned. "Not much. The reporters are all describing her as 'heroic, but elusive.' They won't give up until they find her."

Which would make Sandor's job harder. She'd definitely be skittish if the press succeeded in running her to ground. "I'll let you know when I find her."

Ranulf threw in his two cents' worth. "I visited the site this morning. Next I'll check with the authorities to see what they know about the arsonist."

"Good. I'll feel better once we start getting some answers." Judith poured herself some coffee. Hopefully we'll be able to identify the renegade quickly, though I haven't found anything specific to point us in the right direction yet. I try to read all of the area newspapers, but with everything else I have to do, I often only have time to skim the headlines."

Ranulf gave her a rare smile. "And here I thought ruling the Kyth was a piece of cake."

"Show her respect, Viking!" Sandor clenched his fists in his lap. The Grand Dame deserved to be treated with the same formal courtesy as a member of high royalty. Ranulf never failed to make him crazy.

Ranulf's eyes burned hot with energy. "And how are you going to make me?"

"Enough, you two!"

Sandor needed to leave before he lost complete control. Rising to his feet, he said, "I'm sorry, my lady. If you'll excuse me, I'd like to get back to work. As soon as I know anything more, I'll let you know."

"Thank you, Sandor." Judith smiled up at him as she patted him on the arm. "Having you here has eased my mind."

As Sandor walked away, he tried to hide his shock. When had she gotten so thin? Her hand felt way too frail. No one knew the Dame's real age for certain, but she was older than Ranulf, and the Viking remembered events that had happened close to a thousand years ago.

Dame Judith had always been a force to be reckoned with, but the loss of her Consort had been hard for her. When Rolf had died, Sandor hadn't been the only one to worry that they might lose Judith, too. Slowly, she had picked up the pieces and moved on, but it clearly had been a struggle.

Back inside his room, he booted up his laptop.

He'd start with Kerry Logan's finances and go from there, looking for a way into her life. One way or another, he was about to become her new best friend.

Ranulf watched Sandor leave. He didn't really hate the man, but his presence was a constant itch under his skin. The other Talion had much in common with the knights of the Crusades—too damn noble for his own good. It was a shame the pup had been born too late to be one of the Knights Templar, because he had all the makings of a martyr. Idiot.

"Stop baiting Sandor!" Judith snapped. "He serves me as well as you do. It would be better for everyone concerned if you two could find some common ground."

"We have. He hates me and I hate him." He knew he was treading on shaky ground, but he couldn't help himself.

A sudden jolt of high-powered energy flattened him back in his seat as Dame Judith held her hand out toward him. "That's enough, Ranulf Thorsen! I will have peace in my home!" She kept him pinned for several seconds before easing back on her control. "I am well aware of how hard it is for you to be around crowds anymore, which is why I allow you far more leeway than I do my other Talions. Do *not* mistake my understanding for weakness."

"I have never failed you, Grand Dame Judith, and I have given you my oath yet again," he growled, falling back on formality to express his own displeasure. "But I grow weary of Sandor's constant questioning of my control and my honor. I will do my best to work with him, but if he continues to push me, I *will* push back."

Judith finally released him, her shoulders sagging with the effort it had taken to hold him. "I will speak to him, too. And I know your honor is my own. I believed that was true when you first swore allegiance to me, and I believe that today." She held out her right hand, where she wore the heavy signet ring of her office.

Ranulf leaned forward and kissed the ring, just as he had centuries ago. "Don't bother yourself with Sandor, my lady. You can trust him to do his job, and I'll do mine. With luck our paths won't cross any more than is absolutely necessary." He softened the remark with a small smile. "Now, unless you have further need of me, I will see what leads I can find on the arsonist."

"Thank you, Ranulf. Do you have your cell phone with you?"

Most of the time he hated the intrusive nature of technology in all its forms, but he accepted the necessity of it when he was on a mission. "Yeah, I've got it."

She followed him toward the door. "And you

understand how it works?" The laughter in her eyes belied the stern look she gave him.

Judith was the only person who had ever teased him; he would miss that when she was gone. Feeling daring, he leaned down to kiss her cheek. "I'll promise to keep in touch if you promise to get some rest. The Kyth can get by without you at the helm for one day."

She wrapped her arms around her waist and allowed that straight spine to sag a bit. "It's a deal."

Her easy acquiescence worried him. He would've offered to share his energy with her, but his own control was too shaky.

"Tell Sandor that you need to feed," he told her bluntly. "He might as well make himself useful before he leaves the house."

"Ranulf, I've already warned you about talking that way." She shooed him out the door. "I'll be fine."

But she wouldn't be, not for much longer, and they both knew it. He grieved for the eventual loss of his one friend. For their people, the world would be a far colder place when Dame Judith drew her last breath. Once she was gone he would retreat from society, ending his thousand years of service with the solitude of his mountain home. Not exactly freedom, but as close as he was likely to get.

Outside, he decided to pay a cold call on the man in charge of the investigation. Thanks to the

Dame's many connections, Ranulf had an almost endless variety of credentials that would convince the man to share information with him. This time he'd be an independent adjuster for an insurance company. Any number of people could be making claims for damages arising from the fire, making it impossible for an overworked arson investigator to double-check everybody that approached him about it.

In the Packard, Ranulf rummaged through his briefcase for his stack of business cards, and soon had everything he needed for the part. For the first time, he regretted bringing the Packard instead of his four-wheel drive. How many insurance company employees could afford such a car? But it was too late to worry about it.

The important thing was to find the Talion renegade and eliminate him as a threat. Just thinking about the man's betrayal had Ranulf holding the steering wheel in a white-knuckled grip, his fingers burning with the need to fight. With considerable effort, he drew upon the dwindling supply of energy stored in his talisman to regain control. He'd have to replenish himself soon, if he had any hope of passing as normal when he met with the investigator.

Glancing up at the sun, he prayed to the gods for a quick resolution. Considering the strength of the stain the renegade Talion had left behind in that alley, Ranulf was up against the most powerful opponent he'd faced in centuries. Success would require all of his considerable concentration and control, two things that he was in short supply of and had been for far too long.

Adding in the temptation of a certain Kyth woman, he was seriously screwed. When the stoplight changed, he peeled out as if the hounds of hell had been on his heels, concentrating on the sweet taste of speed and fresh air. Maybe if he didn't think about Kerry Logan, he could stay focused. He downshifted and headed downtown.

Once again Kerry found herself riding with Coop. "Thanks for picking me up, but I could've taken a cab."

"It's no bother. Besides, I needed to talk to you." He jerked his head toward the file laying on the seat between them. "Take a peek in there."

She opened the file—and found herself staring right into the face of the man from the alley. Next to the picture was the sketch she'd provided to Coop and the police.

"It's him."

Coop kept his eyes on the road. "You sure nailed his likeness, right down to that small scar on his chin. We enlarged that from one of the crowd shots we took."

She studied the picture. How could someone who looked so normal have such crazed eyes without anyone around him noticing? He'd been hovering on the outside of the crowd when the picture had been taken. Even in the grainy photo she could feel the sick intensity of his interest in the fire, as if the flames fed some need inside him.

"Got any leads on who he is?" she asked. He'd played far too prominently in her dreams last night. She'd sleep much better once he was locked up.

Coop slowed for a stoplight. "No, but we'll find him." He looked over at her. "Sure you don't have someone you can stay with for a while? I'm afraid you'll be a sitting duck in your apartment."

"I can't live my life hiding, and I won't put my friends in danger by bringing them to his attention. Besides, if you run his picture in the paper, *everyone* will know who he is. That will eliminate any need for him to come after me."

Coop shook his head. "Don't think for one minute that we can predict what a psycho will or won't do. Running his picture in the paper is a crapshoot. Someone might recognize him and come forward fast enough for us to net the bastard before he runs, but he's just as likely to be watching to see if we're onto him. At the first sign that we're closing in, he could go on the attack. And if he was willing to murder a whole club full of people, he won't hesitate over killing one."

"Well, thanks for scaring me spitless, Coop. But I *won't* allow this man to take my life away from me. I worked too long and too hard to get where I am, to go into hiding." Despite her bravado, she felt cornered. She yanked on her shoulder restraint, trying to loosen even its small hold on her.

"Shit." Coop pulled to the curb a block away from her apartment.

Parked outside her building was a van from the local news channel. They'd found her. Oddly enough, Kerry felt relieved. No more trying to hide. The longer she evaded them, the more determined the reporters were likely to become.

"Is there a rear entrance? I could drop you off in back and then circle around," Coop offered.

She patted his shoulder. "Don't worry. I've faced worse things than a few microphones. It's time to get back to real life, and I can't do that if I'm playing hide-and-seek with them."

"You've got guts, young lady." He pulled back out into the street. "A word of advice, then: don't volunteer anything, keep your answers short, and don't let them push you around."

Kerry nodded as he parked in front of her building. Drawing a deep breath, she stepped out of the car and walked over to the van.

She knocked on the driver's window. When he rolled it down, she smiled and asked, "Are you looking for me, by any chance?"

The startled look on his face made her laugh as three people scrambled out of the van. She stepped back to give them room, then realized more reporters were pouring out of cars up and down the street.

Feeling exposed, she waited on the sidewalk for the reporters to get set up. Coop hovered off to the side, staying close enough to step in if she needed him.

"Okay, Ms. Logan, on a count of three the camera will start rolling."

Her heartbeat ticked off the seconds, and then the inquisition began.

Sandor watched as the last of the reporters finally drove away. He'd studied her from his parking spot across the street, learning what he could from her body language.

So far, he was impressed. The press was obviously eating up whatever she said. At first glance there was a fragile air about her, due to her slender build and dark eyes that looked too big for her face, but her looks were deceptive. Even with the crowd of news-hungry reporters surrounding her, she stood ramrod straight and calmly answered all of their questions.

Finally, she held up her hand to signal she'd had enough. Even from a distance, he could feel the shadows in her eyes and her growing need to bolt for the safety of her apartment.

An older man who'd been hovering at the edge of the crowd started forward, but when Kerry glanced in his direction and shook her head, he immediately retreated.

Once the reporters had backed off, Kerry smiled and waved at the unknown man, then headed to her apartment, her head held high. Sandor was willing to bet that she'd collapse as soon as she was inside with the door locked. The amount of energy she'd burned maintaining control in front of the reporters would have left her drained and shaken.

She was strong, but if she didn't learn to tend to her body's needs soon, she was going to go down in flames. And it would be a damn shame to let a woman that beautiful, Kyth or not, go to waste. This assignment was suddenly a lot more interesting.

Now all he had to do was plan his approach. He'd hacked into her financial records and made an interesting discovery—the woman liked to dance. Her credit card bill showed charges from a variety of local clubs two or three nights a week. She'd also purchased season tickets to a couple of the local sports teams. Interesting.

She appeared to be unaware of her Kyth heritage, but judging from her predilection for crowds, she'd learned how to meet her physical needs pretty efficiently. The life energy she needed from humans would be thick in the highly charged atmosphere of sporting events and crowded dance floors. Had someone taught her that trick, or had she stumbled upon it on her own?

A movement at the end of the block made Sandor sit up straight and curse. What the hell was Ranulf doing prowling around here? His assignment was the arsonist, not the woman. Sandor wanted to remain inconspicuous, and Ranulf was anything but, with that red hair and shoulders that would do an NFL linebacker proud.

It didn't take long for the Viking to reach Sandor's car. He slid into the passenger seat, taking up way too much room as usual.

"I see she made it home safely." Ranulf's gaze was pinned on the second-floor window of her apartment. "I made a cold call on the arson investigator, Maynard Cooper. He blew me off until later this afternoon, so I staked out his car and followed him to the hotel where he'd stashed her last night, then here." He turned briefly in Sandor's direction. "She handled the reporters well, but I'm betting she's pretty strung out by now."

Sandor nodded. "I know. She was burning energy like crazy, and her reserves have to be low. From what I can tell, she spends a lot of time in dance clubs and baseball games."

Ranulf continued to stare out the window. "That'll be your in with her, then."

"How about your end of things? Any news on the arsonist?" If he hadn't been looking straight at Ranulf, he would have missed the sudden tightening of Ranulf's jaw.

Ranulf turned his ice-blue eyes back toward Sandor. "He's definitely Kyth. I'm hoping to learn more when I meet with the investigator."

Ranulf was holding something back, but Sandor knew from long experience that pushing wouldn't accomplish anything.

"When are you going to introduce yourself to her?" the Viking asked.

"As soon as possible. After being cornered by all those reporters, she's probably feeling a bit skittish. Kerry never goes more than three days without going out clubbing, so I'm betting she'll bolt for one of her favorite hangouts about sundown. Once she does, I'll ask her to dance."

Ranulf snorted. "And do all women simply fall into your arms, or do you have to exert yourself?"

"Jealous, Viking?" Sandor taunted. "Maybe if you didn't spend all your time hibernating up in the mountains, you'd have better luck with women."

Suddenly Ranulf had a fistful of Sandor's dress shirt, and he shoved his face up close and personal, his eyes glacial cold. "Watch your step, Talion, because it's Kerry Logan's life on the line—not yours. If you spend all your time sniffing around her, she might end up dead. That would not please me. Not one bit."

He shoved Sandor back, yanked open the passenger door, then stomped down the street.

What the hell had brought *that* on? Sandor watched him until Ranulf disappeared around the corner. Couldn't the Dame see how unstable that son of a bitch was? Somebody needed to yank his leash—but if Sandor went after him now, he wouldn't be doing his own job.

He settled back in his seat, fighting to restore his own self-control as he waited for Kerry Logan to make her move.

Chapter 4

*R*anulf was seriously pissed off, but mostly at himself. It had been foolish to blow up over the image of Sandor holding the delectable Kerry Logan in his arms on a crowded dance floor.

It was none of his business how Sandor did his job, and it made sense for the handsome Talion to approach her in neutral territory. Knocking on her apartment door and announcing that she wasn't really human would only convince her that Sandor was insane.

Sandor was the perfect one to acquaint Kerry Logan with a subculture that she still didn't know existed. He'd use charm and tact to gently introduce her to her newfound family, the Kyth. And despite his glossy exterior, the man was a warrior in his own right, fully capable of protecting her while Ranulf hunted down and killed the renegade.

He walked back to the Packard and called the arson investigator's number.

"Cooper here." He sounded overworked and short on patience.

"Mr. Cooper, I'm the insurance adjuster who stopped by earlier. I still would like to talk to you about the dance club fire."

"And which company do you work for?"

"I'm an independent. I've been asked to check into the circumstances of the fire." Hopefully the man would buy the story without Ranulf having to fabricate an elaborate cover.

"I've got a couple of stops to make before heading back to the site. Should be there in about thirty minutes. If you want to talk, that's where I'll be." Cooper hung up.

The man's attitude was infuriating, but Ranulf needed Cooper's cooperation more than he needed to rip the man's fucking head off.

Ranulf checked the time. If he hurried, he could pick up something to eat at a drive-thru. Living up on the mountain meant never having fast food, and he had a real weakness for it. Two or three cheeseburgers with the works, an extra-large order of fries, and a chocolate shake should hold him until dinner.

Forty-five minutes later, Ranulf parked three blocks away from the club to keep the investigator from seeing the Packard. Grabbing his briefcase, he headed down the street and was just about to turn the corner to the rear parking lot when his mental alarms went off big-time. He reached inside his bomber jacket for his Glock and stopped to listen. The ruins were ominously silent. *Too* silent if the arson investigator was inside poking around.

Ranulf tasted the air and gagged on the smell of hot blood and cold death. This wasn't an echo of the injuries from the fire; this was fresh and pungent and raw.

Moving cautiously, he eased around the building and through what had been the back door. It didn't take long to find Maynard Cooper's body—or what was left of it. The man's face was contorted, giving silent testimony to how much he'd suffered. Judging by the number of gashes on his arms and legs, his murderer had played with him for a while. Then the killer had gutted the poor bastard and left him to die in a pool of blood, the deep red standing out in stark contrast to the soot-blackened carpet of the dance club.

Ranulf cursed until he ran out of words. He stepped back, careful not to disturb the scene. If he called the police, he would lose countless hours answering needless questions. At this point, all he could do was tell them how he'd found the body. And while his credentials would hold up at first glance, they might not if the police looked at them too closely.

The investigator deserved better than to be left lying there, but Ranulf couldn't afford to get entangled—not with a murderous Talion to be brought to justice.

One thing struck him as odd: it would appear that Cooper had walked into the site empty-handed. At the very least he should have had a notepad or a camera, or some other tool to help him evaluate the crime scene.

So the killer had walked away with whatever Cooper had brought with him—which meant that Cooper had known something that would identify him.

Ranulf started cursing again. If he hadn't stopped for junk food, he might have gotten there in time to save the human. He might even have had a shot at taking out the renegade Talion and ending this whole mess.

Just as he was about to turn away, he noticed a small piece of paper sticking out of Cooper's clenched fist. Ranulf carefully teased the paper free and unfolded it.

It was a pencil sketch of a man's face—one that he immediately recognized. Cold rage churned in his gut. This particular betrayal might just be the killing blow for their fragile leader. For Bradan Owen was one of Judith's most trusted Talions, and Sandor's closest friend.

After murmuring a prayer for the dead, Ranulf

left, vowing retribution against the vicious animal who'd stolen another life and might be on his way to take another.

Ranulf reached Kerry's street just in time to see her step outside to pick up her mail. The sense of relief that washed over him surprised him with its intensity. She was safe. He'd still keep watch, though. Where the hell was Sandor? He was supposed to be keeping an eye on her.

To find out, he hit Sandor's number on speed dial. When he got routed to voice mail, he disconnected and tried the Dame's number.

She answered on the first ring. "Ranulf? Where are you? I had expected you to report in person."

"I'm parked outside of Kerry Logan's house—right where I expected Sandor to be." He let a little of his temper show.

"We both thought that Miss Logan would be safe enough during daylight hours, while he followed up on another lead. Sandor will be back in place in time to follow her if she does go out for the evening." She paused. "The real question is why you are there instead of tracking down our renegade."

He hadn't planned on breaking the news to her about Bradan over the phone. But then, he hadn't been thinking about much of anything except making sure Kerry Logan was safe. "I went back to the club to talk to the arson investigator. I found him all right, but he was dead. He'd been murdered."

There was a sharp intake of breath over the phone. "Dear God! I hope he didn't suffer."

Ranulf had never lied to Judith before and wasn't going to start now. "He did, but that's not the worst of it. The arsonist isn't just a Kyth; he's a Talion."

He braced himself to tell her the rest. "I have reason to believe it was Bradan Owen who started the fire and then killed the investigator."

It took Judith a few seconds to respond. "What is your proof?"

"I'm sure the killer took the investigator's records, but he missed a pencil sketch in the man's fist. It's a picture of Bradan, and I can't think of any other reason why Cooper would have had it. He died protecting it."

The silence from the other end of the line was painful, as he waited for his leader to cope with such a betrayal.

"Find him." The terse command was steely.

"I will. Bradan will make another mistake, and then we'll have him. He's already made a couple. He let himself be seen and recognized on the night of the fire, and then he missed that drawing."

"Shouldn't we return that drawing to the authorities?" Judith asked. "It's always been our policy not to interfere with their investigations."

"We couldn't even if we wanted to, because my fingerprints are all over the paper. There would be no explaining that without having to admit that I stole evidence and also failed to immediately report Cooper's death."

"I don't like it."

"Neither do I—but at least now we know who we're looking for. It was worth bending a few rules to speed up our investigation. If they found Bradan first, it would only complicate things. He needs to die, not rot in a human jail."

"Yes, he does. This is going to be very hard on Sandor when we break the news to him. And Ranulf, I want you to find a way to get Kerry Logan to accept you as a bodyguard."

He sat up straighter. "That's Sandor's job."

"And now it will also be yours. Even Talions must sleep sometime, so it will require both of you. Bradan's going to be hunting for Kerry because she messed up his plans. And if he has any idea that she's one of us, he'll be brutal if he finds her."

"What about Sandor?"

"If he has a problem with my orders, tell him to see me."

"Okay, but we both know he won't like the change in plans."

Not that it would stop Ranulf from marching up and knocking on Kerry's door. Honesty made him admit that he'd been looking for an excuse to meet her ever since he'd touched her arm last night during the fire. Tasting the afterburn of her energy in the empty shell of the dance club had only whetted his appetite for more.

"Aren't you worried that we'll overwhelm her? If she feels trapped, she might reject both of us," Ranulf said.

"Judging by what I've uncovered on Miss Logan, she's off the scales bright. Once she understands the facts of the situation, she'll accept them. And once we've taken Bradan out of the picture, she'll be free to do as she likes."

"Then I'll go introduce myself now."

"I'll be interested to find out if I'm right about her. Report to me here after you've spoken with her."

Right about what? The line went dead, so he shoved his cell phone into his pocket and reached for his briefcase. It was showtime.

A sharp rap at the door startled Kerry out of her concentration. She'd been sitting with her eyes closed, trying to chase down an idea that hovered just out of reach, one that she knew would pull the entire ad campaign together. Now it was gone, maybe for good. Muttering under her breath, she marched to her front door, ready to rip into whoever was on the other side.

She yanked the door open. But as soon as she got an eyeful of the mountain of a man standing there, she scrambled to slam the door shut, to get the chain back on, to put every possible barrier between them.

But his big foot was already in the door, keeping her from barricading herself inside. Where was her cell phone? Was there time to call 9-1-1 before he broke in?

"Miss Logan, please forgive me. I didn't mean to frighten you."

The behemoth made no move to come any farther, and his voice was calm, even soothing. She backed away far enough to snatch her phone off a nearby table and keyed in the emergency number, keeping her finger poised to hit Send.

"What do you want?" Her voice cracked, but she held her ground.

He looked like one of those warriors on the covers of the historical romances she liked to read. She'd always thought they made for a good fantasy, but this guy was all too real. It was very easy to imagine him with a sword in his hand, ready to charge into battle. Or to save a damsel in distress.

Oddly enough, she suddenly realized that despite his size and fierce appearance, she didn't feel threatened by him. Snapping her phone shut, she set it down.

"Can we try this again?" She offered him a small

smile as she opened the door wider. "You obviously know my name, but we've never met." She let her eyes travel from his face down to his scuffed boots and back up again. "I would have remembered someone like you."

He looked mildly insulted, but he stayed where he was. "Actually we have, although under the circumstances, I'm not surprised you don't remember. My name is Ranulf Thorsen. I was there last night. At the fire."

She started to shake her head, but then images of the mysterious stranger looming up out of the smoke to help her flooded into her mind. With them came an odd buzzing sensation on her arm, right where he'd grasped it the night before. Rubbing the spot, she forced a smile.

"Oh, yes, I remember. I apologize for not recognizing you, Mr. Thorsen. With all the smoke, I never got a clear look at your face. What can I do for you?"

"Under the circumstances, I'm amazed you remember even that much." He lifted his briefcase to bring it to her attention. "If you don't mind, I have some questions I'd like to ask you."

Disappointment flooded through her. She'd hoped he . . . well, she wasn't sure what she wanted from him. "I've answered all the questions for the press that I'm going to, Mr. Thorsen. Now, if you'll excuse me—"

"I'm not from the press, Miss Logan."

"Then take your questions to Maynard Cooper. He's the one investigating the fire, and I'm sure he can answer them better than I can."

An odd expression flickered over his face, and when he spoke again, there was a trace of an accent that hadn't been there before. Northern Europe, perhaps?

"I'm sorry, but it's you that I need to talk to. I promise that it's important."

Nothing short of a bulldozer would move him out of her doorway, and she sighed. "All right, you may come in for a few mintues. I was working when you interrupted me, and I need to get back to it."

She gestured toward the couch. "Make yourself comfortable. I'm going to get something cold to drink. Can I get you something?"

"Whatever you're having will be fine." He sat down on the far end of her oversized couch, yet took up most of it.

She escaped to the kitchen, glad for the brief respite. She wasn't used to men invading her space. On her rare dates, she'd never invited the man inside her home. Most of the time she met her escort at the theater or restaurant, preferring to keep her home as a refuge. The sooner she answered this man's questions, the sooner she could send him on his way.

After popping the tops on a couple of longneck

beers, she filled a bowl with some tortilla chips, opened a container of humus, and set it all on a tray. After adding two small plates and napkins, she picked it up and headed back to the living room, feeling a bit foolish. Since when did she do the happy hostess routine?

"I hope you like dark beer. It's all I have."

"I like it just fine." He took a long pull from the bottle before reaching for a handful of chips. "I didn't mean for you to put yourself out, Miss Logan."

"That's okay. I was ready for a break. Now, Mr. Thorsen, why are you asking questions about the fire? Maynard Cooper is in charge of the investigation."

That pained look was back in his eyes, and in an instant he went from relaxed to full alert. Her open and airy home suddenly closed in on her, the air seeming too thin to breathe. He knew something, something so terrible that he was reluctant to share it.

"Well?"

He looked past her toward the workstation in the corner. Sketches littered the counter and the wall surrounding her computer.

"Sometime during the fire, you saw someone— someone who frightened you." His blue eyes came back to focus on her. "You drew a picture of him for the investigator."

Wrapping her arms across her chest, she shivered at the memory of the arsonist's sick smile. "He was in the alley watching the fire. But if you already know that, why are you asking me about it?" That look was back on his face. "What's wrong? You *have* talked to Coop, haven't you?"

His gaze shifted past her to the wall behind her. "Yes, I talked to him very briefly."

"Then what's the problem?" There *was* one; she would have bet her life on it.

"I'm sorry to be the one to tell you this, Miss Logan, but Maynard Cooper is dead. He was murdered this afternoon, I suspect by the arsonist— the same man you saw outside the dance club last night."

The seconds ticked by as he watched her process the bomb he'd dropped in her lap with no finesse. Sandor would have found a way to soften the blow, but this woman had already proven herself to be surprisingly strong. She could handle the news.

She stared down at her hands for a long time, a statue carved out of living flesh. Her high cheekbones stood out in sharp relief from the soft curve of her lips and the heartbreaking beauty of her dark eyes.

When at last she spoke, her voice had an edge, high emotion coloring each word. "Who are you, Mr. Thorsen? And don't lie to me. I can tell."

"I wasn't lying about having questions about

what happened during the fire." He chose his words carefully. "I am hunting the man who set the fire and killed Maynard Cooper."

"Are you with the police?"

"No, I'm not. I am an investigator in the private sector. My people prefer to operate out of the public eye." To the point of being paranoid about it.

"So what do you want to know?"

"I'd like you to start when the fire broke out and tell me what happened. The more detail you can give me, the better. If you noticed anything odd, don't hesitate to tell me."

As she forced herself to replay the evening's events, her growing agitation hammered at his senses. Closing his eyes, he reached out to bathe her with a pulse of calming energy, putting her in a trancelike state. It took more effort than he expected, more proof of the purity of her Kyth blood.

If necessary, he could force himself into her mind to watch a replay of the fire and its aftermath, experiencing it as she had. But as strong as she was, such an invasion could very well do permanent damage. Besides, his personal code of ethics prohibited such an intrusion except in the most dire situations.

She recounted the nightmare with an artist's eye for details. When she reached the part where she was safely tucked into Maynard Cooper's car, Ranulf gradually withdrew the trickle of energy he'd been feeding her. When she stopped talking, Kerry shook her head as if to clear it.

She glared at Ranulf. "Tell me again who you work for."

"A private party."

Judging by the stubborn tilt of her chin, she wasn't going to accept that answer. How much of the truth could he tell her? "I am not at liberty to reveal the name of my employer. However, I've been instructed to offer you my services as bodyguard until the arsonist is apprehended."

"And if I don't want a babysitter?" She slammed her bottle down on the table with enough force to rattle the bowl of chips.

He cocked an eyebrow and looked at her with narrowed eyes. "You don't look stupid."

That did it. Kerry was up and out of the chair, marching straight for the door. She threw it open in a clear signal for him to hit the road.

"Leave, Mr. Thorsen. Now."

When he didn't immediately move, she said, "Leave or I'll let you explain to the police just who you really are."

She'd do it, too. His lips twitched with the need to smile, but for now he'd allow her the small victory, then hang around outside until Sandor reappeared. Wouldn't his fellow Talion get a kick out of knowing this slip of a woman had successfully vanquished Ranulf?

As he walked past Kerry, he allowed himself a small taste of her scent. His body stirred to life with almost painful intensity as he fought the urge to kiss that frown off her face. It was definitely time to put some distance between himself and temptation.

"We'll talk again soon, Miss Logan."

She slammed her door closed. Ranulf turned away, grinning at the show of temper. Despite everything that had been thrown at her, Kerry definitely had spirit. He liked that about her. He liked it a lot.

Kerry hesitated briefly before entering the club. Maybe it would have been smarter to stay home, but she'd been pacing the floor ever since Ranulf Thorsen had dropped his bombshell about Coop. She'd watched the news until she'd confirmed his story; only then had she allowed herself to shed a single tear. After the torrent had finally slowed, she'd known that she'd either have had to get out of the apartment to go clubbing or start screaming. Craving the catharsis of music, she'd fled.

She smiled at the woman collecting the cover charge, then handed over her money. After getting her hand stamped, she headed straight for her favorite corner and absorbed the pounding rhythms with a sigh of relief. The music felt like warm honey pouring over her skin and soaking into her soul.

For the first time since the fire, she could breathe without feeling as if she had to force her lungs to work. After a few seconds, she was ready to join the throng on the dance floor. As the music warmed her up, she let loose and let it all go. Swaying, spinning, losing herself in the moment.

When the song ended, she took a break at the bar and ordered a drink. If she wasn't careful she'd run out of steam after the first few songs, and she wanted the evening to last as long as possible. All that waited for her at home was memories of the night before. As she sipped a glass of the house red, she watched the ebb and flow of the crowd.

She was dimly aware of a large male body sliding onto the stool next to hers. When she gave him a quick glance, he smiled at her before trying to attract the bartender's attention. The place was busy, so it took a couple of minutes for the bartender to work his way down to their end of the bar.

"While he's here, do you need a refill?"

Kerry had been watching the dancers, especially one couple with particularly dazzling moves. Their intricate, fast-stepping dance patterns bespoke a lot of practice and hard work, even if they were making it look easy. She wished she'd been a part of a couple who looked at each other with such intensity. It was obvious they were having fun with the dance, but it was the passion in their eyes and the way they touched that made it special.

She realized that the stranger next to her was still waiting for her answer. "I'm fine, but thanks."

He nodded and told the bartender, "A beer. Whatever you have on tap."

Once he had his drink, he turned to watch the dance floor. "They're good."

"Yes, they are. I'll be sorry when the song ends."

Normally she would have resented his interrupting her private time, but somehow it didn't feel as if he was intruding into her personal space. As he watched the dancers, she studied his profile. He was handsome, but good looks weren't everything. And there was something beyond his good looks that drew her interest. How odd.

She finished her drink and set the glass on the bar to rejoin the dancing. Would he follow her? For some reason, she wanted a partner tonight. Or at least she wanted him. She turned back after taking only a few steps.

"Did you come here to dance?"

If he was surprised by her invitation, he didn't show it. "Sounds like fun."

He followed her onto the floor but made no effort to take her in his arms. Good. The DJ could have been reading her mind as he played song after song with a fast beat and heavy rhythm. Her partner was as lost in the dance as she was.

Then the music changed, slowing way down with lots of sax and softness. Without hesitation she stepped into the stranger's arms, feeling a surge of warmth and peace as he pulled her close. She didn't question her body's unusual response and allowed herself to enjoy the four minutes of solace.

Kerry felt damn good in his arms. She was a great dancer, but that wasn't all. Was she aware of the flow of energy between them? Probably not—or at least she didn't recognize it for what it was. Luckily, the humans around them were giving off plenty of their life force for him to feed from.

The song was ending, which was a damn shame. The tough part of his job would start when he had to turn this woman's world upside down and inside out. Most newly discovered Kyth reacted in a predictable manner: fear, denial, anger, and finally acceptance. It was hard to suddenly wake up and find out that the reality you'd always known was flat-out wrong.

He suspected Kerry was stronger than most, which made it difficult to predict what she would do. She might reject his claims outright, or she might embrace her newfound kin with exuberance. The only thing he was sure of was that it would be anything but dull.

The lights came up, and couples all over the dance floor separated, him and Kerry included. She seemed a bit hesitant about what to do next.

He made it easy for her. "I'm going to have another beer. Can I get you anything?"

"I'd love something cold and nonalcoholic." Her smile was grateful.

"Why don't you grab a table and I'll fetch the drinks."

He walked away, leaving the final decision up to her. When he returned, she was perched on the edge of a chair at a table on the edge of the dance floor. Her body language made it clear that if he pushed too much, she'd be off and running.

As he set her drink down, he smiled and took the chair opposite her. "I just realized that I never got around to introducing myself." He held out his hand. "I'm Sandor Kearn."

She accepted the handshake and looked startled at the small jolt of energy that surged between them. Pretending nothing had happened, Sandor gave her a questioning look.

"What? Oh, I'm sorry. I'm Kerry Logan." Her dark eyes slid past him to watch the dancers again.

"I'd ask if you come here often, but I'm afraid that would sound too much like a pickup line." He sipped his beer and joined her in watching those still out on the dance floor.

Her dark eyes twinkled. "Yes."

"Yes, you come here often, or yes, it's too much like I'm hitting on you?"

Kerry only laughed as she set her drink down

and headed for the dance floor. He was about to follow her when he saw a familiar figure standing across the room. What the hell was that damn Viking doing there, and how had he found them? As soon as Ranulf knew Sandor had seen him, he jerked his head in the direction of the restrooms and disappeared into the crowd.

Rather than head straight for the Viking, Sandor made his way to where Kerry had staked out a spot in the middle of the dance floor. She immediately turned her back but eased closer to him. Talk about conflicting messages. He leaned close enough to make himself heard over the music. "Kerry, I didn't want you to think I was abandoning you, but I need to make a quick call to my boss. I'll be right back, if that's okay with you."

Without missing a beat, she nodded and let the music sweep her away. Sandor dodged between the dancers to follow Ranulf into the men's room, where they could talk without Kerry seeing them together.

Chapter 5

*R*anulf leaned against the wall by the sinks and waited for Sandor to show up. It didn't take long, and the Talion wasn't bothering to hide his irritation over Ranulf's interrupting his move on Kerry Logan. Too bad.

"I see you've already gotten chummy with her." Ranulf was proud of how calm he sounded.

"That's my job." Sandor's eyes narrowed. "Look, Viking, I'm tired, so don't fuck with me. What are you doing here? And how did you find us?" He splashed water on his face and reached for a paper towel.

How could Ranulf explain that he'd happened to drive by the club and had felt Kerry's proximity? He didn't understand it himself. Her energy signature was resonating with his in a way he'd never experienced in all his years. He ignored the question and said bluntly, "We know who the arsonist is."

"We do?" Sandor straightened up. "Who is it?"

Ranulf held out the small sketch he'd taken off the dead investigator. Sandor didn't miss the splash of dried red-brown droplets, but it was the face he reacted to.

"Bradan?" he sneered with a bitter laugh. "You're saying Bradan set the fire? That's bullshit! I've known him my whole life. He's the last Talion I'd believe would go renegade."

He'd never hidden the fact that he thought Ranulf would be the first, and he was wrong about that, too. Ranulf took the paper back and tucked it into his shirt pocket. "Believe what you will, but I got that from Maynard Cooper, the arson investigator."

"I don't know where he got that sketch, but if it was part of his investigation, he sure as hell wouldn't have given it to you." Sandor started to walk away.

"I didn't say he gave it to me. I took it off his dead body." Ranulf waited until Sandor turned back around. His eyes burned bright with fury as he continued, "He'd been gutted and left to die. Whoever did it took pleasure in the act, and most likely took all of Cooper's files with him."

Sandor swallowed hard. "How did he miss that picture?"

"Cooper had it in his hand and died protecting it. Judith and I both believe it had more meaning than just a random drawing."

Ranulf understood Sandor's pain, but now wasn't the time for grief. That would come later, when Bradan was dead and buried. Ranulf would give Sandor another few seconds to snap out of it, or he'd have to take over protecting Kerry himself.

The music outside changed pace again, and Sandor jerked. "Hell, we're standing in here talking, and Kerry's out there alone!"

"Make sure she gets home safely. I'll stand watch tonight." Anything to get Sandor away from her for a while. Even now, *he* wanted to be the one to charge out to the dance floor to hold her close.

"I'll relieve you at first light. She's pretty damn skittish, so I may not be able to press her about her plans for tomorrow. I'll call you with whatever I find out."

"Fair enough." Ranulf braced himself for another explosion. "Just so you know, when I called Judith about Bradan, she sent me to check on Kerry myself since you were busy elsewhere."

"Son of a bitch! She knows Kerry is my half of this deal." He glared at Ranulf, a surge of energy dancing darkly in his eyes.

"Yeah, well, if it's any comfort, Kerry didn't like it any better than you do. She threw me out, and I can't see her welcoming me back anytime soon."

"Figures. Stay away from her, before you screw this up for all of us."

Now wasn't the time to get into a pissing contest,

though. "Look," Ranulf interjected, "I'm not planning on getting in your way, but I thought you should know. Go distract her, so she won't see us together."

"Fine." Sandor started to leave, then abruptly stopped to check his appearance in the mirror. Under other circumstances Ranulf would have ribbed him about it, but he saw the real grief in Sandor's eyes over Bradan's betrayal. If Sandor needed a little time to gather himself, Ranulf would give it to him.

After the younger Talion left, Ranulf waited several minutes before leaving the men's room. His intent was to head for the nearest exit, but his steps faltered. Kerry had worked her way to the edge of the crowd, her back turned in his direction. She moved so well that it was as if the music had been hardwired right into the heart of her.

He'd always preferred his women tall, buxom, and blonde. Kerry was the exact antithesis, but his body didn't seem to care. His nostrils flared, trying to draw in her scent from across the room, his pulse stuttering with a hot rush of hard-driving need.

He wanted to go claim her right there on the dance floor. Maybe he was still a barbarian at heart. After all, he'd been born a Viking and raised in a time when warriors roamed the world taking what they wanted. Dame Judith might have taught him civilized manners, but obviously those old urges were merely buried, not dead.

He stood mesmerized by the woman he was supposed to protect, his mind filling with erotic possibilities, until he noticed Sandor glaring at him. The handsome Talion immediately moved to block Ranulf's view of Kerry. With some effort, Ranulf shook off his testosterone stupor and shoved his way out of the club. Outside, he sucked in several deep breaths of the damp night air to clear his head.

Bradan paced the floor, then returned to the stack of papers on the dining room table. With an angry jerk of his arm, he sent them flying up in the air. Kicking them as they landed, his temper reached a full boil. There was no use in asking how the investigator had picked his picture out of the crowd. Even if it had been his own damn fault for showing off in front of that woman, he didn't regret the human's death. Spilling the investigator's blood and then licking the knife clean while the bastard had breathed his last had almost made up for no one having died in the fire.

That was Kerry Logan's fault, too. If she'd been human, he would simply have tracked her down and killed her—horribly, painfully, gleefully. But she was Kyth, so he wouldn't rush into anything. Now that he knew her name and address, thanks to the dead man's detailed report, he could plan his next move. Right now she'd be looking over her shoulder, watching for his attack. She had to know that he'd be coming.

The only unknown was whether or not Dame Judith's intelligence network had picked up on the fire. He hoped so. Taking out her beloved Talions one by one would enhance his pleasure. Sandor would probably be the first one on the scene, and he wouldn't be much of a challenge. By all reports, the Viking had retired, which was too bad. Matching wits and strength against Ranulf would have been a challenge worthy of them both.

Bradan had been playing bloody games with humans for years on a small scale, but he'd grown weary of having to hide his particular tastes. Why should he have to operate under the radar of humanity when he was their superior in every way? Sure, they outnumbered the Kyth a million times over, but Mother Nature always made sure the prey far outnumbered the predators.

Picking up a newspaper from the stack he'd accumulated since the fire, he studied Kerry Logan's picture. Despite her bedraggled appearance, there was a lot of strength in the way she met the camera's eye head-on. The press had practically bowed before her, all because she'd saved a few worthless lives. They should have been focusing on *him*.

It was rather irritating, but no matter. He had bigger and better plans. Kerry Logan could bask in her fifteen minutes of glory, because that was all the time she had left. Once he had her, life as she had known it would be over.

He cut her picture out of the paper and taped it into his scrapbook. He flipped through several pages of clippings, smiling at each memory of pain inflicted and the satisfaction it had brought him. Pleased with the start he'd made, he poured a glass of wine and settled into his favorite chair. Reaching for a pen and paper, he wrote down all of his plans for Kerry Logan. Lord, he loved making lists.

Kerry kicked off her shoes and sighed with pleasure. Though she'd had fun at the club, it felt good to be home. For a few hours she'd forgotten about the fire, although the specter of Coop's death remained fresh in her mind. At least Sandor had turned out to be an enjoyable companion, attentive but not pushy. She'd surprised herself by giving him her phone number and address when he'd invited her out to dinner. Normally she wouldn't have done that without knowing a man far longer than an evening of dancing.

She wasn't nearly ready to turn in for the night, so maybe she'd spend some time on her latest work project. Her boss had been most understanding about her wanting to avoid the office for a few days, as long as she kept up with her assigned projects.

And though she didn't want to admit it, she was afraid to turn out the lights and close her eyes. At the hotel she'd been able to sleep, since the arsonist didn't know her name or where she lived, but the headlines had ripped that security blanket to shreds. She felt exposed and vulnerable.

She picked up a small blown-glass dragon she'd found at a local street fair and traced its curves. The smooth, cool surface helped soothe her as she stared out her bedroom window into the darkness. Was he out there, watching and waiting?

No, he wasn't. Looking up at the stars, she got the strangest feeling that a guardian angel was watching over her. In that instant, for no discernable reason, she went from being fearful to convinced that she was safe for the moment. Maybe it was just exhaustion, but a sense of well-being and warmth that had been missing since the fire stole over her.

At last, her bed was calling. Tomorrow she would concentrate on getting her life back to normal. For now, she would sleep.

Standing in the shadows of the trees, Ranulf stared up at Kerry's bedroom window. He could just make out her silhouette, but his mind supplied all the details: the burnished silk of her hair, those huge dark eyes, and her body that moved with a dancer's grace. Kerry had come to the window, her fear of Bradan keeping her from going to bed. Ranulf had never experienced such a strong emotional connection with anyone, but he didn't question the truth of what he was feeling.

He sensed her fear, tasted her worry, and reached out to offer comfort. Had she felt it? Maybe this was all in his head, his loneliness reacting to the first woman of his kind he'd encountered in such a long time. He closed his eyes and once again sent a burst of energy in her direction to soothe and reassure her.

She disappeared from view, and one by one, the lights in her apartment blinked out. If she was still frightened, she would have left one burning in order to hold the shadows at bay. Satisfied that Kerry knew on some level that she was safe, he resumed his patrol.

Dawn was but a few hours away. When Sandor returned, Ranulf would retire to Dame Judith's house. Once he was back at full strength, he would resume his hunt so Kerry and the rest of the world would be safe from Bradan Owen.

Sandor took a sip of wine. "How was your day?"

Kerry didn't even look up to answer. "Fine. I worked at home."

Conversation had been strained between them

all evening. Kerry didn't seem upset, but she was definitely distracted. This was his third attempt to draw Kerry out, so he gave up and ate the rest of his meal in silence. He'd hoped to find an opening to explain his real purpose in asking her to dinner, but that hadn't happened. If an opportunity didn't present itself later tonight, he'd have to force the issue.

"Did you two leave room for dessert?" The waiter hovered beside the table, the check in his hand.

"Not me, but would you like something, Kerry?" Figuring he already knew what her answer would be, Sandor reached for the check.

She perked up a little. "We should split that."

"Nope, my treat." He grinned at her. "You can pay our way into the dance club."

As the waiter departed with Sandor's credit card, she said, "I wasn't aware that we were going dancing."

"Let's just say I was hoping." He gave her his most winning smile. "Otherwise I'm stuck spending the rest of the evening in my hotel room."

"Poor baby," she teased, but at least she was smiling. "Okay, we'll dance."

An hour later, the two of them were firmly ensconced in the center of the dance floor. If not for the occasional worried look, Kerry appeared to be enjoying herself. And him. That was a good thing. If he hadn't been here on business, it would have been a very good thing.

But he had learned the hard way not to mix pleasure with the business of indoctrinating a newly discovered Kyth. It had resulted in a messy entanglement that had taken a long time to get over. So while he enjoyed Kerry Logan's company, that was as far as their relationship would go.

He was about to ask if she'd like to get a cold drink when she got a puzzled look on her face and then froze, staring at someone or something behind him. He instinctively reached for his weapon until she uttered two words that had him cursing, but relieved.

"Ranulf Thorsen," she repeated with a frown. "What's he doing here?"

Great. For the second night in a row the big lummox was standing on the edge of the dance floor, not even bothering to try to look inconspicuous. As if a six-foot-plus giant with flaming red hair could ever hide, anyway.

The real question was, how was Sandor supposed to react? As far as he'd been told, he and Ranulf weren't supposed to know each other.

"Someone you know?"

She nodded. "He came by my apartment yesterday. He's investigating the fire." Kerry's eyes filled up with tears. "The fire investigator who helped me was murdered by the arsonist, so Ranulf wants to protect me."

That much was true. However, it was also true that Kerry had kicked the Viking out of her apartment. So what was he doing here, interfering again?

Sandor quickly led Kerry over to a table in the corner. "I'll go order us a drink, then I'll go talk to this guy."

"That's all right. He's not bothering us."

He sure as hell was bothering Sandor. If their orders had changed, he wanted to hear it from Judith. After catching the waitress's eye, he ordered two beers and then headed straight for Ranulf.

The Viking shifted his stance, planting his feet apart and crossing his arms over his chest as if declaring he'd taken root and wouldn't move, come hell or high water. Well, they'd see about that. Sandor pulled out his phone and hit Judith's number on speed dial.

"Yes, Sandor? I assume there's a problem if you're calling at this hour." There was enough chill in her voice to make a brass monkey nervous.

"I'm at a club with Kerry Logan. Why is Ranulf here, too, instead of out tracking down Bradan?" He kept his voice civil, but his jaw ached from the effort it took.

"Have you asked him that question?"

"No, I wanted to hear it from you." He considered turning his back to Ranulf, but that smacked of cowardice. The man had to know that Sandor was talking to Judith and didn't care, which meant she had changed their orders without telling Sandor.

"Hear what?" Her voice said she already knew the answer to that particular question but wanted him to say it.

"That you don't trust me to do my job." And that betrayal hurt on a gut level.

The silence on the other end of the line dragged on for several seconds. When Judith finally spoke, there was a world of weariness in her voice. "Sandor, although I knew you didn't like working with Ranulf, I also thought you'd have enough faith in my judgment to accept that his presence is needed. I've already had this argument with him after Kerry threw him out. My orders stand. I apologize for offending you. If it's any comfort, he's not happy about intruding on your part of this operation."

"Fine. I'll talk to him and we'll decide what to tell Kerry. I assume that will be satisfactory."

"Yes, Sandor. Divide the work as the two of you see fit and let me know your plans. But I want at least one of you watching over her at all times." She paused briefly, then added, "Tomorrow morning after breakfast will be soon enough for a report."

"I'm sorry I woke you, Judith." She worked too hard and needed her rest.

"That's all right, Sandor. And you're right: I should have called you myself." The phone went dead.

He closed his cell and stuck it in his pocket. Ranulf stood staring at him, waiting for Sandor to speak first.

"Judith thinks we can work together."

"I take it my presence here came as a surprise. I thought she would have called."

It wasn't exactly an apology, but it was as close as he was likely to get. For Judith's sake, Sandor pushed his simmering anger aside.

"What did you tell Kerry about me?" Sandor responded. Damn, he hated improvising in the middle of an operation.

"Nothing. She thinks I'm investigating the fire."

"So what do we tell her?"

Ranulf looked past Sandor. "I suppose the truth is out of the question. You do what you do best, and I'll tell her that in light of Cooper's murder, I was assigned the job of bodyguard for the time being. We'll just keep it a little vague about who sent me."

"Fine. Go get yourself a beer to give me a chance to talk to her before you join us. Maybe she won't feel so overwhelmed."

"If you think she's easily overwhelmed, you're underestimating her. Remember what she managed to accomplish the night of the fire." He met her gaze across the room and nodded. "I have the strangest feeling . . ."

His words trailed off, leaving Sandor wondering what the big man had been about to say as he disappeared into the crowd. Sandor headed back to the table to tell her that the Viking was going to join them.

Something was definitely up between the two men. Normally Kerry preferred to sit alone at a club, if she even bothered with a table. Now she found herself flanked by two men, each of whom was remarkable in his own right.

Sandor was all sleek moves, dimples, and charm, but with a surprising amount of muscle for a man who claimed to be a computer jockey in town on an extended business trip. His eyes saw too much, constantly sweeping their surroundings. Although he pretended to only be out for a good time, she didn't buy it. The signals he was sending her were confusing, but he hadn't made any moves on her.

If he was out to enjoy himself without entanglements, why focus all his attention on just one woman? And if he wasn't interested in taking Kerry to bed, why had he acted like a jealous lover when Ranulf Thorsen had shown up?

Speaking of which, she should be demanding an

explanation from Ranulf about why he was there and how he'd found them. Instead, all she felt was relief that he was there.

Normally she would have felt claustrophobic with two males crowding her space; right now, she felt . . . what? She felt soothed.

How odd. If one of them had asked her to dance, she would have, but her usual compulsion to be out on the floor, lost in the crush of anonymous bodies, was gone.

Ranulf shifted slightly. She was aware that when his restless gaze wasn't sweeping the room, he was watching her out of the corner of his eye. As different as he was in looks from Sandor, there were some startling similarities in the way they moved and in the way they were constantly watching and assessing their surroundings.

She was convinced they knew each other, despite the way they'd exchanged names when Ranulf had joined them at the table. She wasn't sure why she knew that to be true; she just did.

Acting on impulse, she announced, "I want to dance." Rather than wait to see which of them would stand to follow, she headed out onto the dance floor alone. This could be fun.

Where was she? Bradan had been lurking outside Kerry's apartment for hours now.

She must have gone out dancing; it was the only explanation that made sense. Pretending to be a reporter, he'd interviewed the woman whom Kerry Logan had carried out of the fire. She'd told him that thanks to Kerry's quick thinking, her injuries had turned out to be much less severe than originally feared. No shit! Without Logan's interference, the woman would have died. She *should* have died. And if he had a chance to go back to the hospital unobserved, she would die. It was only fair.

But it hadn't been only Kerry's timely rescue that had saved the woman from more severe injuries. If his suspicions were right, Kerry had actually healed the woman, even if neither of them was aware of it. That particular talent was rare among the Kyth, almost to the point of extinction. The only one he'd ever met who had that power was Dame Judith.

Maybe his suspicions were wrong, but he'd learned to trust these leaps of logic, since they'd kept him undetected among the Talions for a long, long time. He'd know for sure soon enough, once Kerry Logan realized that she belonged *with* him. And barring that, she would belong *to* him.

But he was getting tired of waiting. Before giving up, he'd give her a few more minutes to return home. But when he got home, he'd add her inconsiderate behavior to the list of crimes she'd pay for, either with her body or her blood. Or both.

Chapter 6

*J*udith stared out the window, unable to sleep after Sandor's call. She thought back over the long centuries of her life, to when she'd first met her beloved Rolf. He'd been such a brash young man, handsome and too full of himself. Her father had tried to prevent the match, claiming her royal blood was too good for a lowly commoner, even one who'd earned a reputation as a fierce warrior. Despite her father's disapproval, she'd taken one look at Rolf and her heart had claimed him as her own.

His strengths had complemented hers, and she'd helped tame his wilder nature, turning his energy to the protection of their people. In the end, even her father had admitted her choice for *her* Consort had been a wise one. Together, she and Rolf had ruled over the Kyth in this ever-changing, ever-more-dangerous world.

Which brought her thoughts back to the present. What did Kerry think of Ranulf and Sandor? The well-being of their race might very well depend on the answer. Judith was a strong believer in fate: that when you most needed something, it would appear. For the past two centuries, she alone had held the power to transmute human energy into the ability to heal.

It appeared that Kerry Logan might have inherited that same ability from some unknown common ancestor; Judith would know for certain when she met the woman. It would be good to have some younger shoulders help bear the burden of ruling their people.

Not that she'd admit that to Ranulf or Sandor. She could only imagine their reactions if they thought she was playing matchmaker. A smile tugged at her mouth. Sandor would get all haughty and resentful, but he'd do his duty if Judith ordered him to court Kerry Logan. Ranulf would be more likely to tell her to kiss off, then retreat to his mountain refuge as soon as he'd hunted down Bradan and carried out Talion justice.

She walked away from the window, feeling saddened and chilled to the bone. She had no regrets about ordering Bradan's death. The one she had regrets about was Ranulf. He'd been ordered to carry out Kyth justice far too many times, at such a cost to him. When was the last time he'd really enjoyed himself or simply laughed? There used to be a time when he'd enjoyed the company of his own kind and even that of humans, but no more. He'd withdrawn, finding what solace he could in his self-imposed isolation.

She grasped the Thor's hammer at her throat and made a solemn vow. A surge of power tingled her fingertips as she vowed that this would be Ranulf's last job for her. As soon as it was over, she would release him from his vow of fealty. He deserved to live out his life in peace. She just hoped he wouldn't live it out alone.

Kerry knew without looking that it was Sandor who had followed her out onto the dance floor. Disappointed, although not sure why, she deliberately chose the least populated spot on the dance floor to ensure he couldn't crowd her.

He didn't push it, though she was aware of him watching her. Ranulf always managed to be looking somewhere else every time she turned in his direction, but he wasn't fooling her. He was on full alert, watching the crowd for any hint of trouble. If someone made a move on her, he was poised for attack. He'd already managed to scare off one potential dance partner by glaring at him so fiercely that the poor guy had fallen all over himself to get away.

If Ranulf had been anyone else, she would have resented his interference. But the truth was, she did feel safer with him around. The arsonist hadn't made any move yet, but he could be waiting until she felt safe.

Like he had with Cooper. Her eyes burned, stinging with the need to mourn the fire inspector's senseless death. She'd only known him a short time, but he'd gone out of his way to be kind to her and keep her safe. She shivered despite the heat of the bodies on the dance floor.

Sandor seemed to sense her growing unease, because he shoved his way closer to her, ignoring the dirty looks of the other dancers.

"Are you all right?" he asked, lightly touching her shoulder. "Do you want to go home?"

She did, but she wasn't going to let fear of the arsonist dictate her life. "Not quite yet, but I'd like another drink. Bottled water would be good."

Sandor nodded and disappeared into the crowd.

Kerry hovered in the same spot, torn between returning to their table and staying out on the dance floor. The song was coming to an end, so she waited to see what the DJ would put on next, letting the music itself make her decision for her.

Ranulf watched Sandor walk away from her and gritted his teeth, cursing him for leaving Kerry alone on the dance floor. Of course, he'd also been cursing Sandor for being out there with her. He knew his feelings were contradictory, but his mood had started off bad and had grown steadily worse.

When the song changed again, Kerry swayed gently from side to side, gradually turning in his direction. He tried to avoid being caught staring, but Kerry did a quick spin and nailed him with a sharp look and a knowing smile. Busted.

She held up her hand and beckoned him with her fingers. He pretended not to notice, which only made her look more determined. She probably thought he didn't like to dance, and she would be right about that.

Still, he got up and headed for her. It had nothing to do with his duty to protect her, and everything to do with how it would feel to spend some time alone with her. He brushed right past Sandor, who was coming back from the bar with drinks for the three of them.

Sandor followed right after him. "Where do you think you're going?"

Ranulf kept going. "Where do you think?"

Kerry grinned up at Ranulf in victory over coaxing him onto the dance floor. Just as he reached her side, the tempo of the music changed radically, to a slow song.

Kerry looked up at him, her dark eyes sparkling as she dared him to retreat. Sandor was smirking, also clearly figuring that Ranulf would do that. Ranulf wasn't sure which of them was more surprised when he held out his hand and pulled Kerry into his arms.

The second Kerry laid her delicate hand in his, a powerful surge of energy burned up his arm. She felt it, too. Her eyes widened in surprise as she looked up at him in confusion. Realizing she had no idea how to manage her need for energy, he fought to establish enough control for the both of them. Once he had the burn tamped down, he took pleasure from the small buzz of current bouncing back and forth between them. Among their kind it was a kind of foreplay, though in their case, it would go no further than the dance floor.

Even if Kerry didn't know what the unusual tingling meant, she was gutsy enough to charge ahead, stepping into his arms, the curves of her body fitting too well with his. Her head rested against his chest just below his shoulder, as she raised up on her toes to twine her hands around his neck.

Ranulf leaned down slightly, filling his senses with the scent of her skin and the lemony tang of her shampoo. Despite the difference in their sizes, they fit together perfectly. As they swayed to the music, his wayward mind imagined other activities where they could test how well their bodies fit together.

Oh, yeah—a certain part of his anatomy sat up and applauded that idea. He tried to put a little space between them, hoping she wouldn't notice, but she resisted his efforts. He then tried not to think about how warm she felt, or the sweet crush of her breasts against his chest, or the way her fingers tickled the back of his neck as she toyed with his hair.

But nothing worked—not thoughts of duty, or Dame Judith, or even the waves of disapproval coming from Sandor. The sweet torment of holding her would end shortly, so he gave in and allowed himself to enjoy it. Wrapping his arms around her even more tightly, he cupped her neck with his hand to trace the pattern of nerves that were concentrated along the spine. He brushed his thumb back and forth in time to the music, sending small pulses of hot energy from his body into hers.

Kerry moaned softly, clearly enjoying the soft friction as well as the small buzz the sensation gave her. She snuggled in closer, looking up at him with a siren's smile and smoky heat in her eyes. He wasn't the only one enjoying the dance more than he should.

Once again the music changed, this time to a fast Latin beat. Shifting his hold, Ranulf led Kerry right into a salsa. She laughed with delight and followed his steps as if they'd been dance partners for years.

With a flick of his wrist, he spun her out and then back into his waiting arms. Dipping her over his arm, he was caught by her gaze, locked on his mouth as if she was thinking about kissing him.

Should he give in to the temptation? Hell, yeah. He pulled her upright, twirled her in close, then leaned down to claim her lips.

Her eyes flared wide, then drifted shut as she opened her mouth to invite him in. Their tongues touched and tasted in a rush of bright, clear energy that lit up his soul. If he wasn't careful, he'd drag her out into the night to find someplace private to finish what they'd begun.

Before matters could get out of hand, he spun her out again, letting the music lead them through a series of intricate turns. He grinned down at her, enjoying himself more than he'd thought possible. It wasn't just the sensuous movement of the dance or the kiss but also knowing that for a few minutes, he'd chased the shadows from her eyes.

The dance left them both a little breathless, and the DJ played another slow number next. He should step away and politely thank her for the dance, but he couldn't let go of her. If Kerry needed to dance to find balance, who was he to deny her?

Unfortunately, his pleasure lasted only a minute. He ignored the first sharp tap on his shoulder; the second one irritated the hell out of him. When Sandor tried it a third time, Ranulf growled, "Go away, Sandor."

Sandor's voice was low but insistent. "I'm cutting in."

"No, you're *not*." Ranulf spun Kerry around and turned his back to Sandor. Had the selfish bastard forgotten how long he'd had Kerry to himself on the dance floor?

Kerry planted her feet and glared up at him. "Is this a slow dance or a race?"

He looked around and realized that he'd all but dragged her halfway across the floor. "I'm sorry," he apologized as he slowed down to a rhythm more suitable to the music.

Unfortunately, Sandor had followed them. Ranulf was about to rip into him again when Kerry said, "Sandor, if there's one thing I hate, it's a possessive man. I came here with you, but you don't own me. Go sit down or leave. The caveman tactics don't work with me."

"Yeah, Sandor, go sit down like a good little boy," Ranulf sneered.

Kerry jerked free and glared at them. "That's it! Both of you go sit down. I'll be back when I'm good and ready."

She stalked off, leaving both of them staring after her and feeling stupid. She was headed straight for the ladies' room, and Ranulf knew that if she caught either one of them hovering by the door when she came out, there would be hell to pay.

Ranulf retreated to their table and took a swig of his beer. Sandor joined him after a few seconds, taking the seat in the middle if Kerry returned. From what Ranulf had seen of her so far, she was just as likely to pick another table or even try to leave without their seeing her.

But he had her energy signature now. He could sense her presence over short distances, and the ability would increase as they spent more time together.

Right now Kerry was still inside the restroom. Judging by the taste of her energy, she was still mad at them and having a hard time deciding what to do about it. There was a touch of fear in her aura that might keep her from rushing off into the night. She clearly didn't like her independence being curtailed by the very real possibility that Bradan might be waiting for her outside the club.

Suddenly she was on the move, slinking out of the restroom on the far side of a group of women who'd had enough to drink to not notice that their numbers had increased by one. Where was she going? He glanced toward Sandor, who didn't seem to be aware that their charge was on the move.

Ranulf drained his beer and stood up. "She's leaving."

Sandor's head jerked around, his eyes narrowing as he searched the crowd. When he spotted Kerry nearing the exit, he cursed and started for her.

Ranulf caught his arm. She's already mad. If we both chase her down, she's likely to explode. I'll meet you at her apartment."

Sandor shook his arm free. "If you hadn't crowded her—"

"By the gods, Sandor, grow up! Go after her. Use that endless charm of yours to calm her down. I'll get to the apartment ahead of you, in case Bradan's waiting there."

Sandor started after Kerry and Ranulf soon followed, kicking himself for letting Sandor be the one to take her home.

The cool air outside went a long way toward soothing Kerry's temper. It was foolish to charge off alone, but for the first time in days she felt more like herself, temper and all. At that moment, she wasn't sure if she was madder at Sandor or at Ranulf.

She decided it was pretty much equal. Sandor had had no right to try to run Ranulf off. Those few minutes in his arms had been the most soothing ones she'd felt since the night of the fire. In Ranulf's arms, she'd felt safe and warm and desirable.

The look on his face when she'd beckoned him to join her on the dance floor had been a hoot, though, as if she'd been a dentist with a dull drill in her hand. She didn't know why she'd coaxed him into dancing, since she usually avoided slow dances. With Ranulf, though, it had been intimate rather than invasive.

Her good mood restored, she turned back to the club and saw Sandor a few steps behind her. He stayed where he was, as if pretty sure he wasn't welcome. When she didn't immediately bite his head off, he came closer.

"I was out of line," he said, although the reluctance in his tone made it a pretty suck-worthy apology.

"Yes, you were." Crossing her arms over her chest, she prepared to wait him out.

Finally, he gave her a rueful grin. "All right, I was a jerk, and I'm sorry."

She looked past him, but the sidewalk was empty. "Where's your friend?"

Some of his good humor disappeared. "He's not my friend."

Having watched the two of them together, that was probably true. "But you knew him. Before tonight, I mean."

Sandor's dark eyes slid to the side, as if he'd been considering how much of a lie he could get by with. "We've met."

She couldn't help it; she giggled. Saying he and Ranulf had met was like claiming the Union and the Confederacy had had a mild disagreement. "You want to try that again, Sandor?"

He paused. "You're right. Ranulf and I know each other through our job. And you can trust me, even though it was no accident that I met you. It's time we had a talk, but right now we've got to get you safely home. We're too exposed out here on the sidewalk."

Since she'd been feeling the same way, she agreed. But what did he think they needed to talk about?

After parking his car in front of her apartment, Sandor followed her to the door. "Come on in. Would you like tea or coffee?" she asked as she pushed open the door.

"Tea. Herbal, if you have any." Looking tired, he dropped onto the couch.

She put the kettle on to boil while she rooted through the cabinets for tea, then pulled out cups, the sugar bowl, and a box of cookies.

As she waited for the water to boil, she looked into the living room to see why Sandor was being so quiet. He'd fallen asleep with his head tipped back, and he was snoring softly. When the kettle started to whistle she hurriedly took it off the heat, not wanting to wake him.

She picked an afghan off the back of her rocker and gently tucked it around him. Then she set her tea on her desk and booted up her computer.

Before she could settle in, something stirred outside. She stared at the door, trying to decide what had caught her attention. It hadn't been a noise as much as a feeling that someone was there. Yet she wasn't afraid. Why was that?

Ranulf.

He was close by, though she had no idea how she knew that. Curious, she peeked out the window beside the door. It took her a minute to spot him in a cluster of trees across the street, his body looking only slightly more solid than the surrounding shadows. A light drizzle had started falling, and the combination of being chilly and wet had to be miserable.

What was he doing out there?

Then it hit her: he was standing guard, protecting her. But couldn't he do that better from inside the apartment? Rather than think too hard about why she wanted him closer, she threw open the door and motioned for him to join her. He hung back, apparently reluctant to come inside.

She started down the stairs, prepared to drag him into the apartment if necessary. Before she reached the bottom step he was moving toward her, so she stopped and waited for him.

He wasn't happy. "What are you doing out here? Haven't you got a lick of sense?"

"I'm not the one who doesn't want to come in out of the rain." She gave him an impudent smile. "Come inside before we're both soaked to the bone."

He glared down at her, considering his options, then followed her up the steps. "Where's Sandor?"

She put her finger in front of her mouth and pointed toward the couch. "Shhh. He's asleep."

Ranulf shook his head. "Fine guard dog he turned out to be."

"Leave him alone. He must be exhausted to fall asleep like that, although I suspect he didn't really want to talk, anyway." She led the way into the kitchen and motioned for Ranulf to sit at the table. She fixed him a cup of tea and pushed a plate of cookies toward him.

He immediately picked up a handful. "What were you going to talk about?"

Kerry lifted her cup of tea and blew on it. After risking a sip, she set it back down. "I don't really know, but it sounded important. Maybe he's going to tell me all about the two of you."

If she'd expected to get a reaction out of him, she was disappointed. He simply shrugged and ate another cookie. Interesting. She sensed that on some level the two men were rivals, but Ranulf showed no interest in being the one to fill her in on the details. She changed tactics.

"So why were you hanging around outside my apartment?"

"Don't act coy, Kerry. You might not want a bodyguard, but you've got one. I've already told you that the arsonist isn't done playing his vicious little games. He's already killed that arson investigator. You're likely next on his list."

His matter-of-fact statement sent shivers straight through her. "Was there anyone else watching my apartment?"

"If he'd been here, the rain erased any trace of his . . . presence."

"You could tell that in the dark?" she asked, letting her disbelief show.

"How did you know I was outside?"

The abrupt change of subject confused her. "I must have heard something," she responded. "Maybe your footsteps when you got here." That didn't really ring true, but she couldn't think of any other explanation.

"That would make sense, except for one thing. I was already in place when you got home, so you couldn't have heard me arrive."

Then he got up and walked out of the kitchen, leaving her staring at his back.

The whole night had left Ranulf feeling on edge. If he didn't put some distance between them, he was likely to do something they'd both regret. Like rail at her for opening the door and waving at him without considering who else might be watching. Or rant at her for tucking Sandor in like a baby on her couch, when the stupid bastard was supposed to be protecting her.

Worse yet, he might give in to the temptation to yank her back into his arms and kiss her senseless. That would complicate an already difficult assignment—not to mention the fact that she'd likely tear a strip off his hide. Unexpectedly, the thought lightened his mood considerably. Kerry Logan was certainly no hothouse flower.

In fact, she reminded him of Judith back in the day. His Dame was a small woman, too, yet a force to be reckoned with from the day he'd met her. Neither of them had seen their twentieth birthday when they'd first crossed paths, but that hadn't meant much back then.

He'd been taken prisoner on a raid, along with the few other survivors from his village. The pain of seeing his family dead had turned him into a berserker. During the ensuing battle, his enemies had seen him fighting barehanded, using his energy to hold them at bay. They'd immediately attacked him en masse, overwhelming him with sheer numbers. In minutes they'd had him trussed up, ready to provide the evening's entertainment. His back still carried the scars from the fiery brands they'd used to get the ball rolling.

He'd been praying for a chance to fight his way into Valhalla when a little slip of a woman had arrived with a single warrior at her side. With sheer force of will, she'd ordered his captors to free him into her custody. In return for saving his life, she'd demanded his allegiance, glaring up at him with the regal bearing of her birthright.

He had a feeling that Kerry and Judith would get along famously, but he wasn't sure that the world was ready for the two of them to join forces.

What should he be doing now? After considering his options, he settled for the one that brought him the most pleasure. Crossing over to the couch, he kicked Sandor's feet off the coffee table with enough force to jar the idiot awake. The Talion came up sputtering and ready to fight.

Ranulf stepped back, giving Sandor time to wake up completely. It didn't take long for him to get back to glaring at Ranulf.

"You could have just said my name." He stretched his arms over his head.

"I could have, but I doubt Bradan would have been so polite before he killed you and then Kerry." Ranulf kept his angry voice low. Until Sandor explained everything to her, Ranulf didn't want Kerry to know that they had inside information about the arsonist.

Sandor looked chagrined. "You're right, I shouldn't have fallen asleep." Then he frowned. "What are you doing here? I thought you were going to keep watch outside."

"That's exactly what I was doing—until Kerry

opened the front door, looked straight at me, and waved me in. I would have ignored her, but she was coming down the steps. Besides, I needed to know what happened to you."

He reached for his coat. "It will be dawn soon, so Judith will be expecting a report. Do you want to do it, or shall I? She'll want to know how—" He shut up when he felt Kerry walk up beside him.

"Who's Judith?" Kerry watched them both as she sipped tea out of a big red cup covered with cats.

"Have fun." Ranulf met Sandor's gaze and shrugged. "I'm out of here."

Kerry caught his arm. "Oh, no you don't, big boy. Sandor already admitted that you two knew each other long before you showed up on my doorstep. He promised me details, and I might want some answers from you, too."

No way he'd stick around for *this* little session. Kerry's whole world was about to come crashing down. Either she would accept what Sandor had to say or she wouldn't. Most newly discovered Kyths were relieved to find answers for why they weren't like other humans. Once they learned how to handle their energy needs safely—and a surprising number of them had already made some pretty creative adaptations—they went on to live fairly normal lives.

A small number had a hard time adjusting.

Being other than purely human came as a shock, especially to those who weren't open to new ideas or alternative life choices. Neither of those would be problems for Kerry Logan.

The real reason Ranulf wanted to leave was that he didn't want to be there when Sandor explained what Ranulf was. And he would, because Sandor would feel it was his duty to warn her. Right now Kerry trusted Ranulf on some level, but how would she react when she found out that his job was to kill his own kind? If she ever had occasion to see him in action, she might run in terror. The idea of that hurt far more than he expected.

He gently pried her hand off his arm. "Sorry, but I'm out of here. I'll be back to relieve Sandor after I've gotten some rest."

She followed him to the door. "Promise you'll be back?"

He nodded. "Expect me around sundown. Sooner if you need me."

"All right." She stepped out onto the porch after him. Since he stood two steps down, they were almost eye to eye. "What would you like for dinner?"

Anything, as long as you're dessert. A surge of energy burned along his fingertips. "You don't have to cook for me."

"But I do have to eat, and it's just as easy to cook for two," she replied, tipping her head to one side with a teasing smile.

He needed to get away while he could still make himself leave. "You choose and I'll eat it."

"Okay, liver with creamed canned spinach—my favorite." She ruined the threat by giggling.

"I said I would eat it, but I didn't promise to like it." When was the last time an attractive woman had dared to tease him? Maybe never? He could have spent the rest of the day staring into the sweet heat of her dark eyes.

Was she actually leaning toward him? Was she crazy? Even though they'd shared a couple of beers and slow dances, she didn't know him well enough to think about kissing him again.

And if she didn't know better, he definitely did. She had enough of a shock waiting for her once Sandor explained things, without finding out that she'd kissed the one Kyth that the rest of their kind loathed or feared.

Yet all of his good intentions didn't keep him from swaying toward her, watching her eyes drift shut as she waited for him to get on with kissing her. They both wanted it, they were both adults, and at least one of them was an absolute fool.

Then the apartment door swung open with a shade too much force as Kerry's white knight came charging out onto the porch to rescue her from the evil barbarian. Ranulf managed to back down another couple of steps in time to keep Sandor from seeing how close they'd come to kissing. Though it was for the best, that didn't keep him from wanting to strangle the interfering Talion.

"She shouldn't be out here. It's too exposed," Sandor said.

He was right. Ranulf continued down the stairs, saying, "Take her inside. I'll relieve you later."

Then he walked away, wondering if he'd still be welcome when he returned.

Chapter 7

*B*radan couldn't wait to watch the tape he'd recorded of his latest fire. This one had been much smaller than the dance club, but it took time to plan one of that magnitude. It still rankled that Kerry Logan had screwed up all those weeks of planning.

This time his efforts had been satisfyingly successful. The small bookstore was now little more than wet ashes and charred timbers. With all those books, there'd been no lack of raw material for the hungry flames. He'd taped the whole thing from the motel room he'd rented across the street using a false identity.

He had regrets about a few of the books that had been destroyed, but the owner shouldn't have jacked up the price on the first edition Bradan had been trying to buy. They might have eventually reached a compromise, but it was the principle of the thing. Once you gave ground on one issue, it would be far too easy to do so the next time. He had his standards, and it was up to everyone else to live up to them—or go up in flames.

He turned on the VCR and settled back with a big bowl of popcorn and a glass of wine. This was better than the movies; the scrambling firemen and billowing black smoke were both real. He could almost feel the heat and smell the pungent scent of burned paper and wood.

The spectacle put him in a good mood. Once the tape was done, he'd get a couple of hours of sleep and then firm up his plans for the evening. Kerry Logan had to stay home sometime.

He hadn't decided on punishment yet; he needed to see her again to get a better feel for her. If she *was* a Kyth, he wouldn't want to take her until she was fully charged. He smiled at the image of living batteries who stole their current from the humans around them.

Most Kyth were ordinary batteries, but a few could hold a stronger charge, like the Talions—and especially the rarest ones like that Viking barbarian. If Bradan had Ranulf's talents, he would have reveled in his ability to kill. But the fool had foolish notions of honor and a pathetic loyalty to the Dame. What a waste!

Bradan always performed best when sated with

the sweet taste of pain and suffering. With luck, Kerry Logan would serve his needs quite well. The chains were ready and waiting for her. He had a few more surgical instruments to purchase—then it would be time to invite her to their private party.

Until then, he had a front-row seat to watch the bookstore burn to the ground over and over again. Unfortunately the owner, who lived over the store, had managed to escape. Feeling the money-grubbing bastard die would have been wonderful.

Braden picked up his wineglass and toasted the spectacle on his plasma television. Life was sweet.

Ranulf dragged himself inside Judith's front door, hoping that she wouldn't be waiting up for him. Right now, he needed a bed more than he needed to be interrogated over the progress he'd made in tracking down Bradan—or more accurately, his complete lack of it.

His bones ached with exhaustion, to the point where his control was slipping. It wouldn't take much provocation for his darker side to take over. And the last thing any of them needed to deal with was the wrong side of his temper.

Josiah was in the dining room setting the table, and looked up when Ranulf staggered into the room. He rushed to Ranulf's side and tried to help him into the nearest chair.

"Are you ill, sir?"

Ranulf shook his head, which only made him more dizzy. He tried to string together a coherent answer. "Tired. Hungry. Empty."

"I'll let Dame Judith know that you've returned and then bring you something to eat."

"Just the food. Let her sleep." Ranulf slumped back in the chair, wishing like hell he was horizontal, but he'd only feel worse if he didn't take care of his body's needs first.

"She's been up since Sandor called."

Ranulf looked up at the elderly retainer, seeing the disapproval there. He didn't know why he felt compelled to defend Sandor, but he did. "The call was necessary."

The elderly man's face was drawn with worry. "I didn't mean to imply otherwise, sir, but she so rarely sleeps through the night anymore."

"We all worry about her, Josiah." By Thor's hammer, when had he started worrying about other people's feelings? Wouldn't Sandor howl with laughter over that. "Now, about that breakfast?"

"Yes, sir, right away."

Josiah scurried from the room, leaving Ranulf alone in blessed quiet. His head was pounding, and his body ached from head to toe. And despite it all, his wayward dick was still at attention from that near kiss with Kerry. A thousand years ago, he could have just tossed her over his shoulder and carried her off as a prize of war. A cold shower was a piss-poor substitute for the good old days.

He suddenly noticed that Judith stood next to him, immaculately groomed as always in slacks and a pink sweater.

"Good morning." He struggled to get up. He managed to sit up straighter, not having the strength to stand in respect.

"You look like hell." Her comment was laced equally with humor and concern.

"It's been a long time since I've slept."

"And fed, I would guess."

She reached out and her gentle fingers settled over his neck to replenish his store of energy. The sensation held none of the sweet heat he'd experienced with Kerry when they'd been dancing, but the familiar taste of Judith's touch healed the ragged tears in his control.

He caught her hand in his. "That's enough."

"I can spare it."

"No, you can't."

She stepped away when Josiah carried in a tray and set it down in front of Ranulf.

"Go ahead and eat," Judith said. "Your report can wait until you're feeling better. Bring me a pot of Earl Grey, Josiah, and then leave us alone for a bit."

The energy she'd given Ranulf gave him the strength to lift his fork.

Allowing him time to eat without interruption, Judith thumbed through a magazine. After Josiah came in with her tea, she closed the magazine and set it aside.

Ranulf pushed his plate away, his stomach full and his energy partly replenished. He still needed some serious sack time. He stretched, definitely feeling better.

Time to get serious. "There's no question about Kerry Logan being one of us. She has all the symptoms," he began.

Judith bristled. "I don't ever want to hear that word again. Being Kyth is not a disease."

"Sorry. Let me rephrase it. Kerry Logan shares numerous characteristics in common with the humanoid species who call themselves the Kyth." He smiled; finding another of their kind was a cause for celebration. "She's definitely one of us, Judith. In fact, she reminds me a lot of you. She's feisty and takes no prisoners, even though a stiff breeze would blow her over."

"Do you find her attractive?" Judith sipped her tea as she waited for him to answer.

What the hell difference did it make if Kerry Logan had huge eyes the color of dark chocolate, or if she was the only person besides Judith who dared to tease him?

He pinched the bridge of his nose as he considered his reply. "She's pretty, but she's also fiercely intelligent and independent. She's giving the two of us a run for our money."

"How so?"

"When I refused to let Sandor cut in on the dance floor, she ripped into us good and then left us standing there like fools." He grinned at the memory.

Judith set her teacup down hard on the table. "You actually danced with her? In all the years I've known you, I've seen you dance maybe a handful of times. And then only when I ordered you to."

"I told you she reminded me of you." It would be a long time before he forgot how it had felt to hold Kerry in his arms, but he wasn't about to admit that to Judith. It was hard enough to admit it to himself.

"Well. Interesting as that is, we have other things to discuss. There was another fire last night."

Son of a bitch. It looked like Bradan's love for flames was escalating.

"Are you sure it was Bradan?"

"No, but something about the fire feels the same even though the target was a small used bookstore. Bradan used to collect first editions. He was always bragging about the deal he got or cursing when someone outbid him."

"I'll see if I can talk to one of the investigators or the bookstore owner." Ranulf frowned. "Was anyone hurt?"

"No, but judging from the newspaper report, that was nothing short of a miracle. The owner, who lives over the store, happened to be up getting a drink of water and smelled the smoke. He called the fire department from his cell as he ran outside. The building was completely destroyed."

Another life damaged by Bradan's murderous nature. "I'll find him, Judith."

"I know you will, Ranulf. Between you and Sandor, you'll keep Kerry Logan safe and take care of the renegade." Her shoulders slumped.

"Bradan is not your fault, Judith. None of us saw this coming."

"I know, but I have to wonder what else I've missed these past few years. There was a time he wouldn't have been able to hide from me this long."

Ranulf suspected that was true, but he wouldn't add to her guilt. "I'm going to get some sleep, but I'll be up at four. I want to do some scouting before I relieve Sandor at Kerry's." He paused. "He was going to tell her everything after I left."

"And that worries you?" As usual, she saw too much. "If she's as intelligent as you say she is, she'll understand the necessity for how you have served me and our people."

"Right—especially with Sandor explaining things. She can think whatever the hell she wants of me, as long as she jumps when I tell her to. Her life may depend on it." He stood to end the conversation. Worrying about one small brunette's opinion of him did *not* fit his image of a total badass killer.

He stayed vertical long enough to strip down and shower, then he crawled into bed, enjoying the feel of Egyptian cotton against his naked skin. Only a few more hours until he would be back with Kerry—but this time she'd know who and what he was. With that cheery thought, he fell asleep.

Kerry sat down on the coffee table, effectively trapping Sandor on the couch, and crossed her arms across her chest. He'd promised her answers and she wasn't going to let him tap-dance around it. How could she sleep, wondering what he had to say that had made Ranulf look so grim when he left? "All right, Sandor. I want the truth, and nothing but the truth, or God help you."

Sandor blinked. "Don't you mean 'So help me, God'?"

"No. Talk, or else."

"Fine. But first I'm going to get something to drink. Talking is dry work."

She made herself comfortable in her favorite chair. When Sandor came back he downed half a bottle of water, then set it down. "Normally I prefer to have this discussion over some good food and wine. Since you want it straight up, though, I'll give it to you that way."

"Stop stalling and tell me what's going on!"

There was a flash of temper in Sandor's eyes. "Fine. Kerry Logan, you're not human."

Silence hung between them for several seconds, and then Kerry laughed.

"Damn it, Kerry, hear me out!" Sandor's handsome face was set in rigid lines. Then he let out a slow breath. "Normally I'm the diplomat of our people, but you're not making this easy for either of us."

Kerry rolled her eyes. What was his game? "Okay, so I'm not human. What planet am I from?"

Sandor leaned forward, resting his elbows on his knees, and stared into her eyes.

"You're a Kyth, spelled K-y-t-h, just like me and like Ranulf. Our people originated in northern Europe, especially Scandinavia. Due to a genetic mutation, we developed the ability to absorb energy from other humans. It meant we could survive without food if necessary, but now we need that energy, as well as food, to thrive. Humans give that energy off all the time, but especially in crowds. A very few of us can also share energy with one another, like our Grand Dame and the warrior class we call the Talions."

"Oh, brother." She crossed her arms over her chest.

"Give me a fair hearing, and then tell me how much of what I say rings a bell. If none of it does, then we're wrong about you being one of us and I'll apologize. But either way, Ranulf and I will protect you until the arsonist is brought down. Deal?"

What choice did she have? The cops hadn't been exactly knocking on her door offering to keep her safe. "Fine, give it your best shot."

"When you were growing up, you had a reputation for being brilliant but not a team player. You had a hard time sitting still for long, yet you managed to ace your classes without much effort."

"So maybe I was ADHD. It's common enough."

"Yeah, but the first time they tried meds for it, you got sick enough to require immediate medical intervention." There was a note of sympathy in his voice by now.

So he'd hacked into her medical files. Big deal. Lots of people had drug reactions.

"Other than that, you've never been sick a day in your life. No colds, no flu, no fever, not even the usual childhood maladies."

He was freaking her out here. "Okay, so how would you know that?" The allergic reaction would have been documented, but doctors didn't keep records of people too healthy to need medical care.

He ignored the question. "You prefer to work alone and find it hard to put up with most people crowding your space. On the other hand, you feel a compulsion to spend time at places like dance clubs or sporting events." He looked past her to where she had a collection of bobblehead dolls wearing her beloved Seattle Mariners uniforms.

Another good guess. Anyone who followed sports would recognize the home game giveaways.

"And the only time you feel completely relaxed is after you spend hours on a crowded dance floor or you've been surrounded by a bunch of rabid sports fans." He sat back.

Some of his guesses were just common sense, but the rest hit too close to home for comfort. Who had been following her around, watching her live out her life?

"When you're around me or Ranulf, though, it's different. The edginess is missing."

He was right. Normally, having someone in her home this long would have had her climbing the walls or shoving them out the door. Instead, she'd covered Sandor up with an afghan, content to let him sleep on her couch. And she'd been reluctant to see Ranulf walk away, despite his promise to return.

Something of her thoughts must have shown on her face, because Sandor asked, "Didn't you wonder how you knew he was outside?"

He didn't have to say who "he" was, because the answer was obvious. "That was the second time he watched my apartment, wasn't it?"

Sandor's mouth dropped open in shock. "Yes, but you couldn't have known he was there the first time."

"Why not? Maybe I have spidy senses that detect tall redheads at a hundred paces."

Sandor didn't take it as a joke. He got right up in her face. "Listen to me carefully. If you don't believe anything else I tell you, believe this: Ranulf is dangerous."

Like she couldn't see that for herself! The man had some kind of military commando training. In fact, she'd bet both men did.

"If he's dangerous, so are you. I'd bet you're both part of that warrior class you mentioned. Think I didn't notice how much the two of you have in common? Computer geeks don't usually have all those muscles or constantly scan their surroundings looking for danger. Besides, Ranulf would never hurt me."

Sandor's eyebrows snapped down in a frown. "He might not mean to, but he's not to be trusted. Not completely, anyway."

She saw red. "Are you still sulking because he wouldn't let you cut in on the dance floor? Because if that's what all of this is about, I don't want to hear another word!" She started to get up, but Sandor blocked her.

"Look, Kerry, you have to understand that Ranulf is a killer—every bit as dangerous as Bradan Owen, the bastard who set the fire."

From the look in his eyes, Sandor obviously believed every word he said, enough that he was bruising her arm to force her to listen. She jerked her arm free, surprising both of them by how easily she did so.

"You know the killer by name?"

Sandor reluctantly nodded. "He's one of us, too, but he's gone renegade. That's what we call a Kyth who's developed an addiction for the darker energy from human pain and death."

Fury burned straight through her. "If you know who he is, why haven't you called the police or the fire department with that information?"

"Because Bradan would eat them alive. The only one who stands a chance against him is Ranulf— and that's only because he's only a fraction of an inch away from being just like him."

Kerry snapped, "That's it! Don't say another thing, Sandor, especially about Ranulf. I'm seriously weirded out by everything you've said, and I'm going to bed. Deal with it." She stood up.

Sandor's temper snapped. "If you think the arsonist is scary, why do you think Ranulf is the one who has been ordered to take him out? That Viking bastard isn't even close to civilized. He's a weapon that our Dame only drags out to do jobs that none of the rest of us can stomach. He strips renegades of all their darkness. You cannot imagine how many he has killed in his lifetime."

She didn't want to hear it. She wouldn't believe it. The picture he'd painted of Ranulf simply didn't jive with the man who'd held her so close in his arms and kissed her so sweetly. But right now, none of it mattered. If she didn't crawl into bed in the next five minutes, she was going to explode.

"Good night, Sandor. Crash on the couch if you want to, but don't say another word to me right now."

Then she walked away, leaving one very angry man—or whatever he was—staring at her back.

Stubborn woman, why wouldn't she listen to reason?

Despite his best efforts, she wasn't buying what he was selling, not by a long shot. It didn't help to have the Viking looking over his shoulder. If Ranulf had stayed in the background as planned, Sandor wouldn't have had to compete with the bastard for Kerry's trust.

For a smart woman, she had a streak of stupid when it came to the Viking. How could she not see him for the monster he was? She had even defended Ranulf!

He'd have to tread carefully or risk alienating her completely. If only Dame Judith would order her pet killer to concentrate on his real job and leave Kerry to Sandor's care.

But that wasn't going to happen. In fact, the Dame seemed to be pushing both Sandor and Ranulf right in Kerry's path. Something about that bothered him. If Judith insisted that Ranulf help protect Kerry, she needed to order him to stay outside, where he belonged.

The Dame probably thought Sandor was just being petty, but she only saw what she wanted to when it came to Ranulf. The two of them had known each other for centuries before Sandor had come along, which made it harder for her to see how Ranulf had changed over the years.

All the dark energy Ranulf had consumed had to have had a negative effect on him. Renegades had all developed an addiction for the stuff, to the point where they killed for it. When Ranulf was sent to take them out, he executed them by stripping them of every scrap of ill-gotten energy. Over the years, he'd consumed far more negative human energy than any renegade ever thought about.

How could he not be renegade himself? Maybe that was it: maybe Judith knew that if she didn't provide him with a lawful source for his energy needs, he'd be out there killing with the worst of them.

Sandor stopped at the front window and stared out at the early sunrise. It was long past time to get some rest. Maybe things would look brighter after some sleep.

He retreated to the couch, but it took considerable effort for the night's tensions to drain away enough so that he could sleep. He had a nasty suspicion that he'd need all the strength he could muster to deal with what the day would bring.

Chapter 8

$\mathcal{K}$erry Logan was home.

Bradan smiled, pleased that his patience had finally paid off. He hoped she didn't have plans for the coming weekend, because whatever she had in mind wouldn't be nearly as much fun as what he had in store for the two of them.

Right now he needed a new place to hide—one with a better view of her windows. He studied the road and saw a clump of trees that should hide him well. He walked down the sidewalk, then knelt down on the pretense of retying his shoes, looking to see that the coast was clear before easing into the shadows of the trees.

He wasn't there to abduct her yet, but if the perfect opportunity presented itself, he wouldn't hesitate. The few instruments he was still waiting for should arrive in the next couple of days. How much fun it would be to keep Kerry caged in his special place and tell her that the party would begin as soon as the mail carrier delivered one more box.

Besides, she could serve him in other ways before the real fun started. Had she ever slept with a Kyth? He rather liked the idea of being her first—and last. It was highly unlikely that she'd cooperate, so he'd have to chain her to the bed. That would limit the possibilities more than he'd like, but sacrifices had to be made. Especially by her. Oh, yeah, that idea worked for him.

The sound of a powerful engine coming down the street made him move farther back beneath the heavy branches. But the spicy tang of cedar wasn't the only scent there. No, he knew this particular scent far too well, and it made his blood boil.

Ranulf had been under those very trees recently. There was no use in wondering how the bastard had found out about Kerry Logan. That interfering old witch, Dame Judith, must have had one of those spooky moments of intuition during which she'd seen a truth that no one else would have guessed based on the few facts she'd been able to gather from the newspaper.

The only question was whether she and her Viking assassin also knew about him. It would be safer to assume that they did, but what had made them suspect a Kyth was involved? Probably the fact that he'd set the fire in the Dame's home city—but he'd done that deliberately to show that the old bitch wasn't infallible.

The Kyth were stronger than the humans who surrounded them. Why shouldn't the weak serve them? And more importantly, why should the Kyth make do with the benign human energy of everyday life when they could soar with the crisp, sharp taste of human pain and fear? Even in nature, predators ruled, not the prey they fed on. If Dame Judith was too old or too squeamish for reality, she deserved to die.

Her death was item number five on his to-do list, right after destroying the heart and strength of her Talions: Ranulf Thorsen and that goody-goody Sandor. Their sense of honor alone made him want to hurl. Both would rather die than betray their people. Bradan smiled. Well, that could be arranged.

The car he'd heard had slowed to a stop close by. He saw a glimpse of a big white fender and recognized it immediately. Ranulf was still driving that behemoth of a Packard. The car was a real beauty, and deserved a better owner. He'd have to add that to his list of things to do when he got back home.

Bradan froze at the sound of the car door opening. It was unlikely that Ranulf would sense Bradan's presence, but he was a cold-blooded killer. Eventually Bradan would have to fight the red-headed Talion; however, when that time came it would be on Bradan's chosen turf and on his terms. Only one of them would live through the experience, and he wanted to make damn sure he was the one who walked away the victor.

Once Ranulf was safely on the other side of the road, Bradan peeked out through the trees. Kerry opened her front door and greeted Ranulf like a long-lost friend, and Bradan grabbed onto a tree branch for support. The carnal heat shimmering between the woman and the Talion made his stomach roil and his hands ache with the need to kill.

How dare his mate look at the barbarian in that way!

Was she planning on spreading her legs for Ranulf? The thought made him ill. If that happened, Kerry's short life would end without her ever knowing the pleasure he'd planned on sharing with her. Instead, she would watch Bradan carve her lover up into little bitty pieces. Then it would be Kerry's turn.

The apartment door opened and closed again. Was Ranulf leaving so soon? His mood vastly improved, Bradan checked to see how Ranulf was taking being thrown out so quickly. But it was Sandor stomping down the stairs, temper showing in each step. Judging from the look he shot back toward Kerry's apartment, he wasn't happy about Ranulf being alone with Kerry, either.

For the moment he and Sandor were on the

same side, so although Sandor had to die, Bradan would ease his passing.

It was the least he could do.

Ranulf didn't understand how it was possible, but Kerry's apartment shrank considerably the second Sandor walked out the door. With the other Talion glaring across the room, there had been plenty of space between him and Kerry. Now, even though she hadn't moved since plopping into the over-stuffed chair by the couch, Ranulf felt crowded. The air in the room had the same thin feel as it did high up on his mountainside, and with every breath, he breathed in the sweet scent that was unique to her.

But it wasn't the lack of oxygen that had him panting. No, it was that swishy red dress that clung to Kerry's lithe form, outlining every curve in exquisite detail. From the moment she'd sashayed across the room after inviting him in, all the blood in his head had plummeted to pool painfully much lower down. He crossed his right leg to rest on top of his left to disguise his erection.

If Dame Judith hadn't called Sandor back to her house, Ranulf would have had to physically heave the other Talion out the front door.

The strange thing was that Ranulf had half expected Kerry to refuse him entry because of Sandor's little talk earlier. Instead, she'd greeted him with the same dark heat in her eyes as when they'd almost kissed the night before.

Right now, he'd give anything to do a whole lot more than just kiss her, but that wasn't going to happen. Neither of them could afford to get tangled up in something that couldn't go any further than her bedroom. Once he'd eliminated Bradan Owen, he'd return to the peace of his mountain home, and Kerry would get on with her life as a Kyth.

No doubt Dame Judith planned to introduce Kerry to a whole bunch of nice, eligible Kyth men. He pictured Kerry dancing with her own harem of men, and deep blue flashes of power flickered under the skin of his hands as he ached to teach the bastards a lesson about messing with Kerry. His eyes flashed hot and bright, burning with the urge to do battle.

"Ranulf, what just happened?" Kerry was staring at his eyes and then his hands as if she'd just seen a ghost—or, more likely, a monster.

Her reaction made him angry. "Figure it out for yourself. Or didn't you listen to any of that explanation Sandor gave you last night?"

His abrupt answer clearly startled her. "I listened, but I didn't buy what he was selling." She chewed at her lower lip as she stared at Ranulf's hands, where energy sparked and flew from their tips. "Until now."

Great. So now she knew he was the bogeyman. Which hurt a surprising amount. "Look, I can guard you from outside as easily as I can from in here. Better, actually." He was halfway to the door when Kerry caught up with him.

She managed to get between him and the door. "Don't go, Ranulf. Please."

He noticed that she made no move to touch him. "Look, we'll both be happier if you don't have me around," he growled.

"But dinner is almost ready." She kept her dark eyes focused on his face, making him want to wave his fingers in front of her face.

Denying the truth didn't make him any less of the monster she feared him to be, but he shoved his hands in his jeans pockets, out of sight. If she was willing to ignore what she'd seen, he was willing to let her. "Are you sure you really want me at your table?"

"Maybe not, but if it's any comfort, I definitely didn't want Sandor as a dinner companion." She gave him a small smile with a twinkle in her eyes. "He's a little too full of himself for my taste."

"Why? Did he give you the whole 'you're lucky to be one of us' speech?"

"We didn't get to that part. And I'm not sure how much I'm willing to believe of what he did tell me." In a surprise move, she looped her hand through Ranulf's arm and led him back toward the kitchen. "Come sit at the table while I put the final touches on dinner."

This scenario wasn't going down at all as he'd envisioned it. He'd expected to be back under those trees across the street and staring up at Kerry's window from the outside. Instead, he was sitting at her kitchen table with a mug of hot coffee and an even hotter woman for company.

How weird was that?

Kerry could feel Ranulf's eyes following her every movement. It made her glad she'd given in to the impulse to wear a dress instead of her customary jeans and T-shirt. She was on the slender side, but the soft drape of this dress emphasized the positive and hid the negatives. A few weeks ago, she'd blown one whole paycheck on it. Judging by the way Ranulf was looking at her, it had been worth every dime.

She took a small taste of her homemade marinara sauce, enjoying the rich bloom of the spices on her tongue. After adding a pinch more salt to the pot, she turned her attention to making the salad and preparing the garlic bread for the oven.

"Hope you like Italian."

"I do. But I was really looking forward to that liver and creamed spinach you promised me."

He hid a smile behind his coffee cup, but she

saw it in his eyes anyway. "It's not too late. I could always freeze the sauce and make a quick run to the store for liver. And I think canned spinach has that same slimy texture we all love so much."

Ranulf actually chuckled. "That's real tempting, but I wouldn't want to be any trouble."

"Somehow, I think you've been trouble your whole life," she teased, wiping her hands on a dish towel.

Kerry raised up on her toes to reach for her good dishes on the top shelf, but the plates were just out of her reach. Before she could grab her step stool, the warmth of Ranulf's body surrounded her as he reached around her to lift the plates down.

She froze as his scent and heat bathed her entire body with the sensation of a gentle massage, and she couldn't help moaning at the pleasure. Arching back, she pressed against him, which strengthened the exchange of . . . energy? No, that was too weak a word. It felt more like heat lightning arcing back and forth between them. Was this what Sandor had wanted to explain? If so, she doubted she would have understood, because the words hadn't been invented yet to describe this wondrous sensation.

But as soon as she came into contact with Ranulf's broad chest, he sucked in his breath and took a quick couple of steps away from her. She turned to face him, not knowing what to expect. Had she breached some Kyth rule of etiquette?

Ranulf all but shoved the plates into her hands as he backed away to resume his seat at the table.

She set the dishes down and eyed him narrowly. "So are you going to explain why every time we touch, I feel like I've just been hooked up to a battery charger?"

"No, I'm not. That was Sandor's job."

She put her hands on her hips. "But Sandor's not here, is he? Besides, big guy, I want to hear it from you, not him."

Ranulf rose to his feet, clearly trying to use his height to intimidate her. But just because she was petite didn't mean she was easily frightened. If she had been, those spooky eyes of his, which were flickering with what looked like blue flames, would have sent her running for cover earlier. Instead, she wanted to get lost in them.

She stepped closer, glaring straight up into his angry blue eyes. "I'm waiting, Ranulf. And don't think you scare me! Sandor tried to make me afraid of you, and I didn't buy it. You would never hurt me, especially not with those," she said, pointing at his fingertips. "Now tell me the truth. Who or what are you?"

Ranulf's face turned to stone. "Whatever he told you about me, the truth is a hundred times worse, Kerry." He held up one hand as his fingers curled like claws and energy made their tips glow.

She couldn't tear her eyes away from his hand.

"I need the truth, Ranulf. *Your* truth, not Sandor's." She raised her free hand up and twined her fingers with his.

Ranulf stared at their joined hands with pain-filled eyes. "I kill my own kind because someone has to, and because I'm damn good at it. I ought to be. I've had centuries to perfect the skill."

Kerry blinked, not believing his age. He continued on, the words pouring out as if he needed to share his truth with her even if she threw it all back in his face.

"Whenever one of our people goes on a rampage, I hunt the bastard down and bring him to Kyth justice. The word *Talion* means 'punishment meted out in kind,' 'an eye for an eye.' That defines the justice of our people. If a Kyth turns renegade and kills for energy, he dies the same way he lived. When I track the bastard down, I strip away every bit of energy he ripped away from innocent humans and then every scrap of his own life force. There is no middle ground."

There were still a lot of pieces missing in this puzzle, but Kerry's heart knew Ranulf was speaking the truth, even if her head was having a hard time accepting his words. Maybe she should have been repulsed by what he was. At the very least, she should have ordered him out of her house and out of her life. But how could she stand and listen to the pain in his voice and not know how much he hurt? Maybe Sandor was right that their Dame had used Ranulf as a weapon for the good of their people, but at such a horrific cost to him.

The price he'd paid for his service to his people was written there in his face, and in those broad shoulders built strong enough to bear a terrible burden for the good of others. Instead of seeing a monster, she saw a warrior who was weary of battle but still fought on because his sense of duty and honor would not allow him to do otherwise. Common sense told her that there was nothing she could do to ease his soul. She had her own life to live, and it didn't include a man whose eyes burned with blue fire and skin flickered with darkness.

She grabbed Ranulf by the collar to haul his angry mouth down to where she could kiss him.

Kerry's kiss tasted of oregano, basil, and the sweet hot flavor of a woman's passion. Ranulf wrapped his arms around her slender body, holding her closer but careful not to crush her. His last coherent thought as their lips touched was that Judith would have his head for this. But he'd happily pay the price to share these few seconds of heaven with Kerry in his arms.

He lifted her high against his chest, teasing her lips apart with his tongue. He felt her mouth smile against his as she wrapped her legs around his waist and tangled her hands in his hair. Their tongues took turns advancing and retreating until he wasn't sure where Kerry began and he left off.

He splayed his fingers across the curve of her bottom, squeezing slightly. The pressure settled the core of her body directly against his erection, making him feel that he was about to go up in flames.

He eased Kerry onto the counter and kissed his way from her mouth, down her throat, to where the neckline of the dress plunged over the gentle swell of her breasts. The scent of her silken skin made him want to howl. He tugged the stretchy fabric down to reveal her lacy bra. Using his tongue and teeth, he teased her nipple into a tight bud.

"Ranulf!" She briefly pulled away, then pulled her dress down off her arms. With a quick flick of the front clasp of her bra, she freed her breasts and offered them up to him.

He couldn't remember ever receiving a more perfect gift. "Gods in heaven, you're beautiful, Kerry."

She leaned back on the counter, trying to pull him down on top of her, but he resisted long enough to cup her breasts and pay them homage. His self-control crumbled to pieces as she pressed him firmly against her soft flesh, demanding more from him.

"I want to feel your skin against mine, Ranulf."

It took all of his remaining willpower to step

away long enough to peel off his shirt. When he came back to her, she gave him her siren's smile in approval. The skin-to-skin contact increased the strength of the energy connection between them. The high voltage made her hair float in a halo around her gamine face as the sweet innocence of her energy mingled and mixed with the darkness of his to form a flavor that he'd never tasted before.

He burned to toss her over his shoulder and head for the bedroom, where he'd take her hard and fast, claiming her body and her soul for his own. And from the way she was digging her nails into his back as he kissed her, he doubted she would object. He muscled the two of them back upright, supporting her supple weight with his arms, loving the press of her sweet breasts against his skin.

"Which way to your bedroom?"

Kerry pointed, and as he carried her down the hall, she did her best to distract him with her roaming hands and a series of small kisses along his cheek. Somehow she'd figured out that the back of the neck was especially erotic for their kind, and kept fluttering her fingers up to his hairline and then back down almost to his shoulder blades. The ripples of pleasure threatened to overwhelm him, but damned if their first time was going to be a desperate coupling up against a wall.

How long *was* this damn hall?

Finally they reached her bedroom. He was too focused on Kerry to notice many details, but the impression he got of the room was bright colors, clean lines, and a great big bed that dominated the room. Perfect.

He set her feet on the floor and pulled the zipper of her dress down her back. The dress slid to the ground in a pool of crimson, leaving her wearing nothing but a heated smile and lacy panties, and leaving him speechless. He towered over her, yet she radiated feminine strength.

"You have too many clothes on," she pointed out. He swiftly stripped, leaving on only his boxers as she watched appreciatively. When he straightened back up, her gaze slowly traveled from the top of his head down to his feet and then back up to his face. Her cheeks flushed hot, and the minx licked her lips as if he'd been tonight's blue plate special.

That was fine with him.

He swooped her up in his arms and laid her out on top of the quilt, then knelt beside her, the possibilities overwhelming.

She reached up to cup his cheek with a gentle hand. "Don't think so hard, Ranulf. I'm not going anywhere."

But *he* would. She needed to know that before this went any further. No matter how willing she was to welcome him into her bed and into her body, they would only have tonight and maybe a few more days.

"I'm not a happily-ever-after kind of guy, Kerry. And I'm more often cast as the villain, not the hero."

"Kiss me, Ranulf."

"But—"

She placed her fingers across his lips. "I heard you the first time. Maybe what you're saying is true, but I don't care how others see you. I'm my own woman, and right now, I'm yours for the taking."

Damned if he was going to listen to his conscience a second longer. He wanted Kerry more than he'd wanted anything for a hundred lifetimes. He laid beside her and cupped her breast as he kissed her. The tingle of energy flowing between them slowly built in intensity until his skin burned with the need to melt into hers.

He'd been cold for so long that her warmth drew him like fire after a long winter's freeze. He lost all restraint and settled in the cradle of her body, pressing his erection right against her damp core. Instinct outweighed reason and he began surging against her despite her underwear, kissing her passionately. Her flavor made him feel drunk on life, as her lithe body made him feel as if all of his life had led to this one moment. There was a distant roaring in his head that wouldn't quit.

He rolled to one side far enough to slide his hand under the elastic of her panties. Energy thrummed through his fingertips, the slight buzz causing Kerry to moan softly. Her passage was tight as he gently caressed her, craving her the way his body needed air to breathe. Kerry clamped her legs demandingly around his hand, holding it captive as he stroked her slick folds.

He tugged her panties down over the curve of her hips, and his boxers and her panties soon joined the rest of their clothes scattered across the floor.

He snagged his jeans back to remove a condom, hoping he'd brought enough to last the night. When he'd sheathed himself, he returned to Kerry's arms.

She pushed him over on his back to straddle him, centering her body directly over his. Then with a wicked smile, she gave as good as she got, her hands kneading his chest muscles as she kissed him. Although he was used to being in charge, he liked letting Kerry take control. Her obvious pleasure in him was like stepping out of the darkness and into the warmth of a summer day.

In a quick move, he rolled to the side, taking Kerry with him and surprising a laugh out of her.

"I want you." He rocked against her, showing her exactly what he meant.

"I want you, too," she whispered, toying with the back of his neck and driving them both crazy.

He was about to enter her when he heard an odd sound. His blood ran cold. Raising up, he asked, "Do you hear that?"

"What?" she whispered, lifting her head to hear better.

"That ringing sound . . . son of a bitch! That's your smoke alarm! Wait here while I check out the situation."

He lurched up off the bed and grabbed his clothes. Hopping on one foot and then the other, he pulled on his jeans as he headed for the living room. Although the air in Kerry's apartment was still fresh, he could see smoke billowing up outside her front window. He put his hand on the front door and felt the heat.

On his way back to the bedroom, he yanked out his cell phone and dialed 9-1-1 to report the fire. When he got back to the bedroom, Kerry was pulling her dress back over her head. He tried to ignore the fact that she didn't bother with her bra.

"There's a fire out front and I can't tell how bad it is. The fire department is on the way, but we need to get out. Grab your shoes while I check the back door. We can't go out the front."

He wanted to kick himself six ways from Sunday for letting himself get distracted. He'd known full well that it had been only a matter of time before Bradan struck out at Kerry.

As if she'd heard his thoughts, Kerry asked, "It's him, isn't it? The arsonist."

"Probably. It would be hard to believe a fire at

your apartment so soon after the other night was just a coincidence."

He could hear the sirens screaming outside. "The fire trucks are almost here. We need to get out and get someplace safe." Judith's home was the only place he could think of.

Telling Kerry to wait for him, he went from window to window, looking for some sign of Bradan. He wasn't about to step outside into a trap. Luckily, the firemen started pounding on the back door, and Kerry came running down the hallway. Ranulf yanked open the door and all but shoved Kerry outside.

When they reached the safety of the sidewalk, she asked the closest fireman, "How bad is it?"

"Someone set the bushes out front on fire. We should have it out in a few minutes. There might be some cosmetic damage to the building, but nothing serious."

The firefighter looked grim. "It was probably some teenagers, ma'am. We'll canvass the area to see if any of your neighbors saw anything. Do you know who lives in the apartment below yours?"

"It's vacant right now, because the owners only live here part of the time. They're at their other home in Arizona, but I expect them back in the next couple of weeks. If you need to talk to them sooner, I've got their address and phone number inside."

"Good. That'll help." He turned weary eyes on her. "The smoky smell will linger for a while. Will you be all right here tonight, or do you want a ride to a friend's house?"

"It's kind of you to offer, but I'll be fine. My friend can give me a ride."

The fireman looked over to where Ranulf watched the fire crew in front of the building. He looked so alone as the firemen swirled and eddied around him. It was hard to see any sign of her gentle would-be lover in his fierce expression. For the first time, she could see Ranulf as the barbarian killer that Sandor had claimed him to be. The shiver flitting up and down her spine had little to do with the late evening chill.

But before she talked to him about leaving, she needed to tell the fire department that she knew who had most likely set the fire. As if he knew what she was about to do, Ranulf abruptly turned in her direction and shook his head. He held a single finger over his lips, and the words reluctantly died on her tongue.

Why? Wouldn't it make sense to let the authorities know the arsonist's name? Surely they stood a better chance of tracking him down than Ranulf and Sandor did. When she had Ranulf alone, she'd demand to know why the gag order. And if his answer didn't make sense, she'd call the fire department and tell them everything she knew.

Chapter 9

*W*ell, on second thought, not *quite* everything—especially the whole "not being human" thing. That brought her up short. When had she accepted what Sandor and Ranulf had told her as the truth?

Probably about the time she'd welcomed Ranulf into her bed. Bradan's timing was another black mark against him. Another few seconds, and it would have taken a direct nuclear hit to distract them from finishing the horizontal dance they'd started. Ranulf had stopped so abruptly that she was surprised he hadn't sprained something important.

And now, when she needed his warmth and support, he stood too far away. The distance separating them was an invisible wall that he'd erected the minute he'd pushed her out the back door into the waiting fireman's hands. She huddled in the darkness and waited to see how long it would take for Ranulf to let her close again.

Every so often, he'd turn his eyes in her direction. Each time, she could feel the strength of his power simmering at the boiling point with the desire to kill his enemy. Her lover had disappeared, and a stone-cold warrior had taken his place. Temper pushed her fear aside. Ranulf had a mission to accomplish—fine. But he was the first man she'd allowed so close in a very long time, and the distance he'd put between them hurt.

Finally, he stalked toward her, saying, "The fire is out. We can go back inside."

"I can. You're going home." She crossed her arms over her chest and waited for him to contradict her. It didn't take long.

Ranulf silently glared at the firefighter who had stayed with her, causing the poor man to stumble back, then hurriedly rejoin his crew.

"Nice trick, but I'm not impressed," she smirked. Although she was. Was mind control another one of his talents?

"You should be. Now—we're going to go inside, you're going to pack enough clothing to last a few days, and then we're leaving—together." He stared down at her, his eyes like shards of indigo ice.

"And if I don't want to leave with you?" It was a childish question, especially when he was big enough to make her do anything he wanted her to. But despite his temper and size, she knew he wouldn't hurt her.

"We don't have time to play games, Kerry. My job is to keep you alive. Right now, that means taking you someplace safe until Bradan has been eliminated."

His words hurt. "So I'm just a job? Was getting naked with me part of your benefit package?"

He glared down at her from his superior height. "Woman, your tongue's so sharp, I'm surprised you don't cut yourself!"

She glared right back up at him. "You weren't complaining about how I used my tongue a little while ago."

"Um, excuse me, ma'am."

Oh, Lord, neither of them had noticed the firefighter's return. Her cheeks burned with embarrassment. "Yes?"

Ranulf immediately positioned himself between the fireman and Kerry. She rolled her eyes and shoved Ranulf to the side. Although he let her, the fireman kept his eyes focused somewhere over her left shoulder, looking uncomfortable.

"Is there something you needed?" she asked.

"Just to tell you we're leaving now, and not to hesitate to call us or the police if you need to." He glanced past her to where Ranulf stood. "That offer of a ride still stands."

She smiled. "That's all right; I'll be fine. Thank everyone for me. I appreciate everything you did."

"Yes, ma'am, I will." He backed away, clearly relieved to escape without a major confrontation.

She headed for her back door with Ranulf right on her heels. She would have preferred to have the solid weight of a locked door between them, but maybe it was better to take their fight back inside. No use in entertaining the neighborhood.

"Start packing, Kerry. I don't know how long you'll have to be gone. We'll spend tonight at a friend's house and then play it by ear." His expression unexpectedly softened. "I want you to know that I am sorry you got sucked into all of this."

"I'll bet you are."

Then she retreated to the sanctuary of her bedroom, except she carried the memory of Ranulf in her bed with her. It was impossible to ignore the twisted jumble of her blankets and sheets or the empty foil package on the floor. Her traitorous body remembered the delicious weight of Ranulf's body covering hers, his heat burning her up.

She resolutely turned her back on the bed and yanked her suitcase out of the closet. She stripped off her pretty dress and tossed it toward the hamper, then pulled on her oldest, most comfortable sweats.

It didn't take long to fill the suitcase with jeans, T-shirts, and the necessary basics. Then she hesitated. It was too warm for her flannel nightgown, but it was her least sexy sleepwear. Her normal taste in clothing ran to casual and comfortable, but she had a secret weakness for sexy underwear and nighties.

She wasn't planning on Ranulf seeing any of them—not after the way he'd acted since the smoke alarm had gone off. But if he *did* get a peek at her sleepwear, she wanted to remind him of exactly what he'd missed out on. She shoved the flannel back in the drawer and reached for the satin and lace.

After grabbing a few toiletries from the bathroom, she looked around the room to see if she'd forgotten anything. Her laptop ensured that she'd be able to work wherever they ended up, but that still left a lot of hours in the day. She grabbed the stack of books she'd left on the bedside table and tossed them in.

Ranulf appeared in the doorway. "Do you need help with anything?"

She picked up her suitcase. "Nope, I've got it. I need to pack up the computer and then I'm ready to roll."

She dropped her flashdrive in her purse, then took one last walk through her apartment, as if on some level she was saying good-bye. She shook off the creepy feeling and turned out the lights. There was no reason to think she wouldn't be back in a day or two.

Ranulf took her computer and suitcase to the back door. "Stay put while I take a quick look around outside," he announced.

She let the fact that he was back to issuing orders slide this time. "Do you think he's out there?"

"I'll know more in a minute, but I suspect he's gone. He's had his fun for the night."

"I'm glad someone did," she muttered under her breath, although she suspected Ranulf heard her anyway.

Her pulse sped up as soon as he was out of sight, making her glad that he hadn't listened when she'd told him to leave earlier. Bradan might be gone, but that didn't mean he wouldn't come back, especially if he knew she was alone.

Minutes ticked by with excruciating slowness. How long had Ranulf been gone? She checked the clock on the stove, but that was pointless since she didn't know when he'd left. Surely he should be back by now. What if he was injured? Or worse? She'd give him another thirty seconds and then go after him.

But what good would she do him unarmed if Bradan had managed to get the drop on him? She needed a weapon. The kitchen offered several possibilities. She wasn't sure she'd have the nerve to use a butcher knife, but hitting someone over the head with a cast-iron skillet was a possibility.

She dug out the small one that had belonged to

her grandmother, and she tested its weight. Perfect. Drawing a deep breath, she opened the door and stepped outside. She listened for any sound that seemed out of place, but other than the muted rumble of distant traffic, all was quiet.

Which way should she go? She hadn't thought of asking Ranulf where he'd parked or even what kind of car he drove. Keeping the skillet raised and ready, she sidled along the shadows by the building, scanning for some sign of Ranulf. At the front of the building, she edged up to the corner and leaned out to scope out the front yard.

Nothing. She drew back, planning on trying the other direction when a hand clamped down on her shoulder and another covered her mouth, stifling her scream.

"Looking for me?" a familiar voice whispered near her ear.

Her knees collapsed as relief washed over her. He was safe. When he abruptly released her, she had to grab onto him to keep her balance. It was like leaning against a brick wall, an angry brick wall.

"I told you to wait inside," he growled.

"I did, but you were gone so long, I got worried." Ingrate—see if she ever came to his rescue again! She headed back to retrieve her luggage.

His big hand stopped her, catching her hand in a death grip. He tugged the skillet free of her grasp. "You were going to use this to rescue me?"

Her first impulse was to say *"Duh,"* but something in his voice made her hold back. He was staring at the skillet with an odd look on his face, his eyes glowing in the darkness.

"What's the matter?"

"I'm just trying to remember the last time anyone thought I might need rescuing." As if realizing how much he'd revealed about himself, he briskly handed back her makeshift weapon. "We need to go."

She followed him up the steps, fighting the need to hug him, knowing he wouldn't accept it.

"I'll get my things."

Stubborn little thing that she was, Kerry had insisted on lugging her own suitcase, only grudgingly allowing him to carry her computer case. He still hadn't gotten over her decision to fight Bradan, armed only with an eight-inch cast-iron skillet.

He wanted to yell at her for taking such a foolish risk, then kiss her senseless for caring enough to try. But right now, Bradan might still be lurking nearby. He wasn't among the trees where Ranulf had hidden before, but he'd definitely been there earlier. And of course, with the Packard parked there, Ranulf might as well have rented a billboard announcing his whereabouts.

Speaking of the car, though, he wondered what

Kerry's reaction would be to the old girl. When they reached the sidewalk out front, he said, "I'm parked across the street," then waited to see which one she'd choose as the most likely candidate. She ignored the SUV and the white sedan. Her gaze lingered a bit longer on a slow-slung sports car before moving on to the Packard. Her face immediately lit up with a huge smile.

"She's beautiful!" Kerry scampered across the empty street, straight for his prized possession. Setting her suitcase on the curb, she circled the car, trailing her fingers along the elegant long fenders and smiling at the hood ornament.

She grinned up at him. "They sure knew how to make cars back then. Is this how she originally looked?"

His chest swelled with pride. "Yep. Everything is original except for the tires, the stereo, and necessary maintenance and repairs."

Kerry's dark eyes looked at him in disbelief. "She's not been restored?"

"No need. I've taken good care of her since the day she rolled off the lot in 1940."

That comment slowed Kerry down. "Now I know you're yanking my chain. If you were old enough to drive in 1940, you'd have to be in your eighties."

"I told you earlier that I'd been around for centuries. I can't help it if you didn't believe me."

She put her hands on her hips, her whole attitude pure, stubborn disbelief. "All right, big guy. Just how old are you?"

He gave her the truth. "I don't know exactly, but a thousand years, give or take half a century."

He half expected her to either laugh or run to the nearest neighbor for sanctuary. Instead, she looked back at the Packard and then back at him with a smile teasing at the corners of her mouth.

"Then I guess it's good that I've always had a thing for older men."

That did it. He laughed, loud and long, as he set her suitcase and computer in the trunk before opening the passenger door with a flourish. She slid into the leather seat and sighed with pleasure.

When he joined her inside, she looked up at him with a hopeful expression. "We don't have to go straight to your friend's house, do we? Can we go for a ride first?"

For the first time in what seemed like hours, her eyes were alight with happiness. He would have given her anything within his power to hold the ugly reality of Bradan at bay. "We can take the long way."

"With the top down?"

"Sure. It'll be chilly, but I'm up for it if you are." He reached around for a blanket and tossed it to her.

By the time they hit the highway, Kerry had the

stereo cranked up and was singing at the top of her lungs. Ranulf headed for the mountains to the east, determined to keep Kerry to himself for as long as possible. As long as they kept moving, she was safe, and that was all that mattered.

Sandor looked up from his laptop. "Judging by these two entries, Bradan's staying close by. Or maybe that's just what he wants us to think."

"Well done, Sandor. This is the first real lead we've had on him." Dame Judith moved closer to read over his shoulder. "How old are those withdrawals?"

Sandor pointed at a column on the screen. "Three days ago for the first one. The second was from yesterday." He turned to face her. "Just as we guessed, he's paying cash rather than risking us tracking him down by his charge cards."

"No one ever accused Bradan of being stupid."

Sandor's expression turned harsh, reminding her that the two men had been close friends. This had to be tearing him up inside. She gently touched his shoulder, sending him a small burst of energy meant to soothe, but he shrugged off her hand. Well, she couldn't force him to accept comfort.

"Speaking of walking on the dark side, has Ranulf reported in?"

She drew a sharp breath at the barbed question.

"No, he hasn't, and you *will* refrain from such remarks in the future."

Sandor's dark eyes narrowed, his frustration plain to see. But after a few seconds, he nodded. "I apologize, Judith. I know I'm being a bastard, but this whole situation has me worried. Nothing is as it should be."

"How so?" Although she could guess, she'd listen if it would help Sandor to talk it out. She returned to her chair and settled in, making it clear that she was in no hurry.

Sandor moved away to stand by the window and stare out into the night.

"I feel disconnected from everything. My honor demands that we track down and destroy a man I thought I knew as well as I know myself, but it will be like killing a brother. Only a few days ago, I would have fought anyone who had questioned Bradan's honor. He was a Talion and one of the best."

He was silent for a few seconds. "And then there's Kerry Logan. I failed miserably when it came to explaining to her what it means to be Kyth. I've dealt with tough resistance in the past, but she beats them all, hands down."

He looked back at Judith with a half smile. "She's much stronger than you'd think at first glance. There's no moving her once she digs in her heels."

"What? A pretty woman didn't fall for Sandor Kearn's legendary charm?" Judith held the back of her hand to her forehead, pretending to swoon. "Has the world come to an end?"

He accepted her teasing with good humor. "Very funny, Judith. But if Kerry refuses to believe the truth, it will be that much harder to keep her safe."

"How does she react to Ranulf?"

Sandor's smile faded. "I tried to warn her about his true nature, but she wouldn't listen."

"Sandor . . ."

Sandor staved off her defense of Ranulf. "I know what you think of him, Judith. I know what he's done for our people, and I honor that. But there's a reason he hides up there on the mountain: he's not stable, and he knows it—even if you won't admit it. So far, we've been lucky that he's been able to absorb all that dark energy from his targets without going renegade himself. But one of these days he's going to cross that line—and when that happens, who will die because we failed to stop him in time? Me? Kerry Logan? You?" He walked out of the room.

Each word felt like a physical blow to Judith. Yes, she had faith in Ranulf, but she'd also trusted Bradan. Had her judgment become that faulty? If so, she was a danger to their people, too. Would one more execution be more than Ranulf could handle? Could he still walk away intact?

Gods above, she grew so weary of the burden of ruling their people. If Kerry Logan was as strong as Sandor said she was, she might be the first real hope for the Kyth in a very long time. The ability to rule rested not in the royal blood that ran in Judith's veins but in the genetically rare ability to manipulate energy to heal and control other Kyths.

If the reports of the dance club fire were true, Kerry Logan probably had that ability, even if she wielded it subconsciously and with no training. A simple touch, a brief invasion of Kerry's thoughts, and Judith could confirm what she very strongly suspected.

How many times over the centuries had she seen a hero appear at the very moment he was most needed? Perhaps it was the gods' way of protecting the lesser beings they cared for. If they had chosen this moment to send Kerry to the Kyth, Judith would gladly teach the younger woman the history of their people, share her wisdom and advice, and pray that when it came time to step aside, Kerry would be ready.

She reached for the telephone. It was time to meet Kerry face-to-face.

"Shut up, bitch, and quit whining. I know the ropes hurt, but they're supposed to, aren't they?"

The woman stirred again, her eyes glazed and

confused as she tried to figure out how she'd come to be naked and tied to Bradan's bed. She tried to speak, but the words were muffled by the duct tape over her mouth.

Bradan set out his scalpels in a neat row alongside a box of surgical gloves. After pouring himself a glass of wine, he studied his test subject. She wasn't Kyth, of course, but with her athletic build, he'd had high hopes for her ability to withstand his games. But she should have shaken off the drug he'd slipped into her dinner by now. So far, this woman he'd dragged into his lair was a disappointment.

He'd planned on inviting Kerry Logan to this particular party, but she'd chosen to defile herself with that damned Viking. The fire he'd set outside her apartment might have been a mistake, though. Up until that point, the Talion warrior had only suspected that Kerry would be the next target. Now he knew it for certain and had driven Bradan's mate off into the night.

But it was only a matter of time before she returned to her apartment, or perhaps to Dame Judith's ostentatious home—one reason Bradan hadn't yet made a move against the Dame herself. He studied the pieces of paper taped to the wall, each with a name at the top: Kerry Logan, Ranulf Thorsen, Dame Judith, Sandor Kearn.

With a smile, he lifted his glass in a toast to the neatly printed lists. "To each in their own time."

The woman tied to his bed struggled to break free of her bonds. Did she really think he wouldn't notice? But he did admire the sleek lines of her muscles and the delicious scent of pain mixed with sweat and blood. His body stirred in response.

He sat down on the side of the bed and studied her perfect breasts and the sweet curve of her waist as it flared out to her hips. Ah, yes, she knew what was coming. She flinched when he laid his hand on her ankle and slowly, so slowly, stroked the length of her leg, just to flirt with the blond curls at the top. He let his fingers hover there briefly before starting a slow downward journey back to her ankle. Oh, yes, this was going to be fun.

Panic had her straining against all four bedposts at once, but all she was doing was wearing herself out and stoking his fire. At least her fear had burned away the last haze of the drugs. Perfect. He pointed the remote at the stereo across the room, and soft music filled the air.

Then he reached for the first button on his shirt and smiled. "Shall we begin, my dear?"

Ranulf's cell phone vibrated for the third time in thirty minutes. As much as he wanted to ignore it, he knew he couldn't. Whether it was Sandor or Judith, he needed to report in.

He flipped the phone open and saw Sandor's

number. Keeping his voice low, he said, "I'm on my way in," before hitting the disconnect button to avoid any questions. After accelerating around a slower car, he looked at Kerry, who was curled up asleep under the blanket.

He could taste her scent on the night air, teasing his senses with memories of how sweet it had been to hold her in his arms, skin to skin, hearts racing as their bodies had strained to be one.

He hated to be grateful to Bradan for anything, but the firebug had kept Ranulf from making one of the worst mistakes in his life. He'd learned to live alone, safe within the wards he set to guard his home and content with his own company. Even now, he was fighting a powerful compulsion to turn around at the next exit and drive straight back up the Cascade Mountains where he belonged.

Once he had Kerry there, he could coax her into his bed and spend the next few days burning up this craving he had for her. Or weeks, if that's what it took. He jerked his eye back to the highway again. Over the centuries, he'd watched too many people he'd cared about age and die, and he didn't want to leave himself open to that kind of pain again.

The average Kyth lived only slightly longer than their human neighbors. Only those with the strength to manipulate energy, like the Talions and the Dame, were gifted—or burdened—with longevity. The dark energy he'd consumed over the centuries had kept his exterior youthful, but it did nothing to alleviate the weight of all those years. It was his hope that once he retired from serving his people, he would begin to age, living out his life as normally as possible.

Now even Judith was fading away, because she'd started dying the minute Rolf's heart had stopped beating. Once she was gone no one else would have a claim on his soul, and he'd be free of the burden of his office as Talion. Kerry stirred slightly, drawing his attention back to her. *No one*, he repeated more firmly to himself; even he recognized the lie. This waif of a woman had already burrowed under the wall he'd built around his heart and taken up residence there.

As if feeling his attention, she stretched and yawned before sitting up with a sleepy smile. "Have I been asleep for long?"

"A couple of hours," he answered a bit gruffly.

She adjusted the blanket and looked out the window. "Where are we?"

"Coming down off Snoqualmie Pass. We'll be back in town soon. Are you hungry? We never had a chance to eat that dinner."

"I'd love breakfast, but anything will do."

"There should be something in the next town."

He let the silence settle between them, but he figured it wouldn't last long. He was right.

Kerry finger-combed her hair, only to have the

wind muss it up again. "So who's the friend you're taking me to? Sandor?"

"He'll be there."

"But he's not your biggest fan, and you said we'd stay with a friend. The only other name you two have mentioned is Judith."

Ranulf considered how to describe the Dame. "Did Sandor mention that the Kyth are a matriarchal society?"

"No, but I didn't give him much of a chance to explain anything." Kerry's smile made her look like a cat who'd swallowed a canary. "As I said before, I didn't particularly like what he had to say."

"And why was that?"

She shot him a narrow-eyed look. "Stop avoiding the subject and tell me what's going on. Start at the beginning and pretend Sandor and I have never met."

Kerry settled back in the seat and pulled the blanket higher as she waited for Ranulf to gather his thoughts. What was he thinking that had his mouth set in such a grim line? She slipped a hand free and gently laid it on his arm. A zing of warmth immediately shot up her arm; Ranulf's eyes gave her hand a quick look before turning back to the road again. He'd definitely felt it, too.

"Why don't you go first? I know you're a graphics designer, but you haven't mentioned any family or friends."

She frowned and looked away. "I have this sneaking suspicion that our good buddy Sandor has already ferreted out every bit of information that he could on me. Are you telling me that he didn't share?"

"He shared, but that's all facts and figures, not the truth of who you are. I want to hear that from you."

For some reason, that pleased her enough to make her want to answer. "I don't know much about my family background. My birth parents gave me up for adoption, and the records were lost in a fire. My adoptive parents did their best by me, but raising me was no picnic. Sandor was right about me not fitting in at school, even though I got high enough grades to get into a good art school."

She stared out at the Douglass firs that lined the highway. "Losing myself in my art brought me some peace. I've always been happier in one extreme or the other—either working by myself or lost in a crowd. Not much in between. I occasionally hang out with some friends, but mostly I work out of my apartment. I buy a pair of season tickets for several of the local sports teams, but always go by myself." She dragged her gaze back around to the silent man next to her. "Pretty pathetic, don't you think?"

Blue flames flared briefly in his eyes. "No, I

think you're a Kyth who had no one to teach you how to cope. From everything I've seen, you've done a damn fine job on your own. Besides, at least you have coworkers and neighbors. I live by myself up on a mountainside. If Judith doesn't need me, I go months, even years, without talking to another person."

Her heart hurt for the loneliness she heard in his voice, but she knew he wouldn't appreciate any show of sympathy. "So we're kindred spirits. Now it's your turn. Start talking."

He let out a long breath. "Once upon a time, there was a small community of people living in the far north end of Scandinavia. Somewhere along the line, they developed a genetically based talent that none of their neighbors had: the ability to share energy with those around them." He looked at her again. "Let me know when I get to the part you haven't heard before."

"Keep going, big guy. I'm listening." She scooted closer and rested her head against his arm, not sure if the comfort of touch was for him or for her. Most likely both.

"Fine. These people not only survived, they thrived in areas that other, more normal, humans couldn't. On a good day, one successful hunter with the right genes could absorb enough energy to 'feed' his tribe, but that ability was far rarer than the ability to steal energy from other humans. That little talent worked like a charm, as long as there were enough humans around to feed off of."

Though Ranulf's story was even more outlandish than Sandor's, she found it much easier to believe. Or maybe it was because it was Ranulf doing the explaining.

"Then the Kyth began to outnumber the normal homo sapiens, to the point that both groups were suffering. Since the Kyth were stronger, they took to the seas in search of new homes." He smiled. "Ever wonder why the Vikings and their kin traveled so far afield? Well, now you know. It takes a certain number of humans to support each Kyth's energy needs."

"And they figured that out way back then?"

"Not in so many words, we didn't. All I knew was that I felt better when I went out on raids with my chieftain than I did hanging around my village."

"When you said earlier that you'd had centuries to perfect the ability to take care of renegades, you were serious, weren't you?"

He jerked his head in a quick nod. "We returned from one of our raids to find that our village had been destroyed. After caring for the few survivors, we went after the attackers. That went badly, and I was captured. Before they had a chance to do permanent damage, Judith showed up with only Rolf, her Consort, at her side."

Ranulf's mouth quirked up in a smile. "I can still

see her standing before all of us big hulking brutes. Judith is on the small side, like you, but no one could mistake her for anything but royalty."

"So she's a queen?"

"She's actually called a Grand Dame, but the meaning is the same. There wasn't one of us who dared defy her, especially when Rolf was backing her up with both his energy and his sword. She's ruled all of our kind for longer than I've been alive."

"And now I'm going to meet her?" She sat up to whack Ranulf on the arm. "You're taking me to meet royalty, and I'm wearing my oldest sweats!" Did the man not have a lick of sense?

"So? Judith won't care."

"When's the last time you saw her in sweats? Or even jeans, for that matter?"

His only answer was another of those laughs that made her smile. But that didn't mean she was going to forgive him soon for not warning her about where they were headed.

"I'm sorry, Kerry. It's been a long, long time since I last brought a woman to meet Judith, and even then it wasn't someone I—" He stopped talking abruptly.

"You what?" she prompted.

"It's nothing." He immediately changed the subject. "If I remember right, there's an all-night restaurant at this next exit."

She knew he'd been about to say something important, and so did he. She'd wait until his guard was down and then pounce.

"Will there be anything else?"

The waitress set a plate heaped high with bacon, eggs, and fried potatoes in front of each of them. Kerry didn't waste a second before digging in.

"I'd like another cup of coffee." Ranulf picked up his fork and fought the urge to shovel the food in as fast as he could. His energy levels had dropped to a dangerous level. Protein would help, but it wouldn't hold him for long.

When the waitress returned to top off his coffee, he considered taking a hit of her energy, but she could ill afford the loss. Skinny as a rail and with hair bleached to a brassy yellow color, she looked like the poster child for famine relief.

Kerry looked up from her plate and smiled at the woman. "That's a pretty watch." She reached over and touched the crystal on the cheap timepiece.

The waitress looked surprised but pleased by the comment. When she walked away, she had a little more zip in her step. Ranulf yanked his eyes back to his companion, not believing what he'd just seen. Kerry had used the brief encounter to feed the woman energy. He'd seen Judith do the same thing countless times, sharing energy with humans and Kyth alike, replenishing their supply with her own.

Kerry noticed he was staring at her. "What? Do I have jelly on my chin or something?"

Was *this* what Judith had been hiding from him and Sandor? That Kerry carried the prized gene for healing?

He needed to talk to Judith before saying anything to Kerry, especially if he was wrong. But if he was right, it was more imperative than ever to get Kerry someplace safe until Bradan was brought to justice.

"Are you about finished?"

She gave him one of those looks women use when men say something particularly stupid. "No, I'm not, and after we eat, I want to stop back by my apartment to pick up something more suitable to wear."

"That's not going to happen." Rather than continue the argument, he concentrated on finishing his own food. Judging from the dark looks Kerry was giving him, he was going to need all the strength he could muster.

Bradan watched the body bounce down the side of the gully, landing with a soft thud at the bottom. He'd been wrong about the blonde. She'd proven to have an impressive amount of stamina and will to live, especially considering everything he'd put her through. With a sharp salute to honor her contribution to his cause, he walked away, feeling as if he'd been able to fly.

Right up until she'd breathed her last, the woman had fed him with the sweetest energy he'd ever encountered. His skin tingled and felt tight, as if he'd absorbed more than his body could contain. Gods above, what a rush! The sex-blood-and-death combo had everything else beat, hands down.

Would Kerry Logan live up to the high standards set by her unfortunate predecessor? He hoped so. He really did. Dame Judith had definite possibilities, too. Considering the Dame's advanced age, he had no interest in having sex with her, but blood and death had definite possibilities. He'd have to be careful, though. If she was at full strength, she could immobilize him before he had time to strike. Maybe it would be better to kill her from a distance, although that seemed cowardly.

He needed to get back to the remote house he'd used as a base of operations. There were a few things he needed to retrieve before going after Kerry Logan. If traffic was with him, he'd be done in time to greet the dawn with his latest victim—a very good start to the day.

As he drove back toward town, though, he passed a young man standing on the shoulder of the road with his thumb out. Hadn't he heard how dangerous hitchhiking was? Well, well. It was almost Bradan's civic duty to remind him. Easing his car over to the shoulder, he waited. The gods were definitely smiling on him today.

Ranulf nosed the Packard into the private driveway and punched in the code that would swing the heavy wrought-iron gates out of his way.

As the house came into sight, Kerry's dark eyes widened slightly, and she seemed to shrink back into her seat. Then just as quickly, her chin came up and she straightened her shoulders.

"Thanks again for the warning, Ranulf. I should have known that royalty went hand-in-hand with being rich. Does she wear a crown and carry a scepter?"

"She used to, but she gave it up when people started staring at the mall." He barely managed to keep a straight face.

Kerry's eyebrows shot straight up. "Why, Ranulf Thorsen, I do believe that was a joke! Gosh, you've laughed at least twice and told an actual joke." She fanned herself with her hand. "I think I might be overcome from the shock. Imagine—a big, bad thousand-year-old Viking with a sense of humor."

He liked making her laugh—which was not good. The sooner he put some distance between them, the sooner he could go about making the world a safer place for her.

As he pulled up in front of the house, the front door swung open and Sandor walked out. He stood with his arms crossed over his chest, his expression grim.

After Ranulf parked, Sandor opened the car door for Kerry. "Glad to see you're alive and well."

As she climbed out of the car, Ranulf popped the trunk to retrieve her luggage.

Sandor turned his bad mood in Ranulf's direction. "We thought you'd be here hours ago. Kerry needs protection, not a midnight ride all over creation with you," he snapped, glaring at him over Kerry's head.

She stomped up the stairs and turned to face him down. "Listen here, Sandor Kearn! I do *not* need or appreciate your caveman tactics. I appreciate the fact that you're worried because of Bradan, and that you take your orders to keep me safe seriously. But it was Ranulf who protected me when Bradan set fire to my building."

Sandor's face went ashen. "He what?" he stammered, looking to Ranulf for confirmation.

Kerry explained, "After Bradan set fire to the bushes outside my front door, Ranulf was going to bring me straight here, but I wanted to go for a ride. We missed dinner because of the fire, so we stopped at a restaurant to eat before coming here.

Ranulf's been a perfect gentleman. If you want to yell at somebody about us being late, yell at me."

Ranulf soaked up the warmth of the smile Kerry shot in his direction. "Let's get inside. I feel like we've got targets on our backs standing out here like this. Is Judith waiting for us?"

"Yeah, and Josiah is having a fit."

Kerry looked like she was being led to her execution. "Is Josiah another member of the royal family?"

Judith stepped into the foyer. "No, he's supposed to be my butler, but he believes his job description says 'mother hen.'" She smiled and held out her hand. "I'm Judith, my dear. I am delighted to meet you in person at last."

Ranulf noticed that Kerry surreptitiously wiped her hand on her sweatpants before taking Judith's hand in hers. The two women held on to each other seconds longer than a normal handshake would take, but if Kerry noticed, she gave no indication of it.

Judith's eyes widened as she nodded at Kerry. "So have you come to believe that you are indeed one of us?" She linked her arm through Kerry's and led her into the living room, leaving the two Talions to follow.

Kerry frowned slightly as she considered her answer. "I'd have to say yes, although I'm not particularly happy about it."

Judith gave her a wry smile. "There are many days that I feel that way myself. Why don't you have a seat while I have Josiah fetch us some tea. Sandor, would you ask him, please? Once you've delivered the message, you can retire for the night."

Sandor frowned at the dismissal and stalked past Ranulf, who had stopped just shy of entering the room, waiting for . . . what? For Kerry to pat the couch next to her, inviting him to remain close by her? He shifted Kerry's bag to his other hand, drawing Judith's attention.

"I'm sorry, Ranulf, did you need something?"

He fought to keep his eyes on Judith. "When do you want my report?"

Judith's smile was a little too knowing. "I'm sure Miss Logan can fill me in on everything that happened."

Now *there* was a thought that could make certain parts of his anatomy shrivel up. Judith could read a lot from a touch, but she'd always been closemouthed about what form that information took. If she was able to pick up glimpses of what had gone on at Kerry's, he was in big trouble. Right now, he'd give anything to know how much she had sensed in that handshake.

He needed to get out of there, and fast. "Which bedroom do you want Kerry to use?"

"I'll let you be the judge of the best place for her to sleep. Pick one on your wing of the house."

He walked out, wondering about that odd glint in Judith's eyes. The room next to his was empty, but so was the one next to Sandor's—a much safer choice. Before he even realized what he was doing, he'd opened the door to the room that shared a bathroom with his. He couldn't stand the thought of her toothbrush hanging next to the other Talion's, much less the chance that Sandor would see that bit of lavender lace and satin Ranulf had seen Kerry tuck into her bag.

At her apartment, he'd been about to walk into her room to hurry her along when she'd held up the skimpy nightgown with a determined look on her face. He'd silently walked away, knowing that if he'd gotten any closer to her at that moment, they would have ended up right back in her bed.

And now she was going to be sleeping only a few feet away from him, wearing that skimpy gown. He stared at the king-sized bed, his mind filling with all manner of ideas on how fast the two of them could mess it up.

The talisman at his throat burned with the intense reaction of his body to the mental image of Kerry welcoming him into her bed. He hurried his steps to put some distance between them before his resolve to walk away disappeared. Rather than risk running into Sandor or Josiah out in the hallway, he cut through the bathroom. Once he reached the safety of his bedroom, he firmly closed the door and locked it, putting its solid weight between him and the possibilities he'd just turned his back on.

It was the smart thing to do. The moral thing to do. And it was the hardest thing he'd had to do in a very long time.

Chapter 10

Kerry liked Dame Judith, even though the formidable woman scared her. First of all, there was the whole royalty thing. Then there was the suspicion that the older woman knew everything there was to know about her.

Judith's sharp gaze reminded Kerry of the raptors at the zoo, seeing her in far more detail than she was comfortable with. She felt like a very little mouse with an elegant eagle soaring overhead. Any second now, the woman would swoop down, claws extended, and expose every thought that Kerry had ever had.

"So tell me, my dear, how are you getting along with my Talions?"

Yep, she'd guessed right.

The tea and cookies and polite conversation had been designed to lull her into feeling safe. The gloves were off now.

"Which one do you want me to start with?"
Kerry topped off her cup and held the teapot up in
an unspoken offer to do the same for Judith.

"Why don't you begin with Sandor?" Judith gave
her an encouraging smile.

"Okay." Kerry sipped the tea, buying herself a
few seconds. "We had a good time dancing at the
club, and we had fun at dinner."

"But?"

Frowning, Kerry tried to find a diplomatic way
to tell Judith what it was about Sandor that bothered her. She didn't know if Judith played favorites
and didn't want to offend her.

"Don't pull your punches, Kerry. I'd rather have
the truth."

"He's obviously strong and probably a good . . .
warrior, I guess is the right word, but he's a little
too perfect for my tastes." Setting her cup aside,
she struggled to find the words. "He's handsome
and quite the charmer when he wants to be—until
the subject of Ranulf comes up."

"And that bothered you?"

"It made me furious, actually. Although he's
the one who first told me about my being Kyth and
what that means, that doesn't make him my Yoda.
I don't need him telling me who I can and can't
trust."

Feeling agitated, she stood up. "To be fair,
I think part of my anger was hearing that I'm not

completely human. It gave me the willies to hear him describe what it had been like for me growing up, as if a stalker had been watching me."

"That's understandable, Kerry. You've been through a lot in the past few days, what with the fire and finding out that you're Kyth. As strong as you are, it was still a lot to absorb."

The woman acted as if it were perfectly natural to have a guest power-walking laps around her elegant living room while carrying on a conversation. Maybe it was rude to stay on the move, but ever since Ranulf had walked away, it was all Kerry could do not to go hunt him down.

"And how about Ranulf?"

Kerry smiled. "He's as blunt as Sandor is slick, which I find easier to deal with. It was much easier to accept his explanations of how things are for us, but that might be because I'd already heard some of it from Sandor and just needed confirmation."

She stopped in front of Judith's chair. "Did you know that Ranulf planned on standing out in the rain to watch my apartment, instead of coming inside?"

Judith didn't look at all surprised. "I assume Sandor told you he was out there?"

"No, actually he didn't—mainly because he'd fallen asleep on my couch." Frowning, she tried to recall the exact moment she'd known he'd been there. "Somehow I just knew that Ranulf was nearby. It's happened twice now. Before the first time, we'd only met briefly during the fire, so I had no way to know he was there. It was more a feeling of being safe inside my apartment. The second time, I walked outside and looked right at him."

"How did he react to that?"

Kerry chuckled. "As you'd expect, he was mad because I didn't stay tucked safe inside my apartment. But then, so was Sandor. Maybe this mother hen problem you have with your butler is catching."

The remark startled Judith into laughing. "I'd never thought of that. Perhaps I should order all three of them into isolation while we launch an immediate investigation."

"If you do, give me enough warning to take cover when you break the news to Ranulf. I doubt he'd take it well."

"Sounds like you know my Viking warrior pretty well for such a short acquaintance."

She would have known him even better if that damned arsonist had waited a few minutes longer to start the fire.

"I've never known anyone exactly like him before."

"How so?"

"He makes me feel calm. You know, in better control of myself. I don't feel all edgy around him, like I'm being crowded all the time. I've always been rather uncomfortable around most people, but he's different." Especially when he had his arms around her or his skin next to hers. Even with his full weight on top of her, she'd felt cherished, not crushed.

The clock in the hall chimed twice. Good grief, where had the night gone?

"I'm sorry, Dame Judith. I didn't mean to keep you up all this time."

"That's not a problem, my dear. I often roam the house at night, unless Josiah catches me," she added with a wink. "But you should get some rest. We'll talk more tomorrow."

"Can I ask you one more question? Well, two really."

"Please do."

"Are you sure that Sandor and Ranulf have to be the ones to hunt down this Bradan fellow? Wouldn't it be better if the police were involved?"

"Bradan has special abilities that would make him extremely dangerous for even well-trained police officers to handle. It takes one of our kind to bring down a renegade—especially one as strong as Bradan." Her voice cracked on his name. "And your second question?"

"This one is easier. Where am I sleeping?"

"I left that up to Ranulf, but I suspect you'll find your things in the first room on your left in the guest wing."

"And if they aren't there?"

"Try the last room on the right. I'm sorry that you won't have a private bathroom. I rarely have this many guests at one time, so it's not usually a problem."

"It's not a problem at all, and I want to thank you for your hospitality. I hope this isn't too much of an inconvenience." Kerry walked to the end of the hallway with Judith, where their paths separated.

"I am most happy that we've found you, young lady. I will see you at breakfast, but don't feel like you have to get up at any certain time. My schedule is always flexible." Judith took several steps, then stopped. "And don't worry about upsetting Sandor and Ranulf. They could both use a good shaking up."

Then Judith walked away. Kerry grinned when she spotted a man lurking just out of sight in a doorway a short distance away. She assumed it was the elusive Josiah, ready to pounce if Judith wanted him for anything. She smiled, acknowledging his nod.

Following the directions Judith had given her, she quickly found the hall with the four doors Judith had described to her. Now to figure out which room was hers. She got it right on the first try, spotting her bag where Ranulf had tossed it. She closed the door and looked around at the room furnished with a king-sized bed and expensive antiques. Of course, if Judith was as old as Ranulf had said, she'd probably bought them all when they'd been the latest fashion.

She opened her suitcase. As comfortable as her sweats were, it felt good to slip on her nightgown and its matching cover-up. Not that it covered up very much.

Too bad a certain someone wasn't there to see it. Picking up her toiletry kit, she peeked out in the hallway, trying to guess which door led to the bathroom. There were only four doors, all of which were supposed to lead to four bedrooms, and she hadn't passed any bathrooms on the way.

That's when she realized that there were three doors in her room. She had to be running on fumes not to have noticed that sooner. Besides the door to the hallway, there was one that opened to a large walk-in closet. Crossing the room, she gasped in delight when the third door revealed a huge bathroom with a raised tub big enough for a pool party, a counter with two matching sinks, and a glassed-in shower with a tiled bench and multiple shower-heads. The room was done in pastel green and rose, giving it the feel of a spring garden. Directly across from her door was another one just like it.

When Judith mentioned that Kerry would have to share a bathroom, she hadn't realized that it would be with only one person. Suddenly she knew that at that very moment, Ranulf was only a few feet away, separated from her by the thickness of one door. She looked around for other signs that he'd been there. Sure enough, there was a single toothbrush in the holder, an old-fashioned straight-edged razor on a hand towel, and a well-worn leather shaving kit tucked in the corner of the counter.

She put her bag next to his, but then moved it to the other side. He wouldn't like being crowded, even in such a small way. She quickly brushed her teeth and then returned to her room to crawl into the big bed, feeling more alone in this house full of strangers than she did all by herself in her apartment.

Would she be too much of a coward if she left the lamp on all night? Even if it would help her sleep, she'd be embarrassed if anyone noticed the light under her door and came to investigate. It would be just like Sandor to come poking his nose in where it didn't belong. She wouldn't mind Ranulf checking on her, but he needed his rest more than he needed to babysit her.

She gradually drifted off to sleep, hoping that if she dreamed, it would be of a blue-eyed Viking and not a crazed killer with a scary smile.

Ranulf flopped over onto his back. He'd been restless ever since he'd heard Kerry enter the room next door. He should have insisted on Judith giving Kerry a room in her wing. Instead, he'd had the choice of keeping her too close to him or too close to Sandor, which had been the same as no choice at all.

The water ran in the bathroom as she got ready for bed. Was she wearing that nightgown? Damn, he wished he hadn't thought about that again. He couldn't remember the last time he'd taken a lover. Now that his body had rediscovered the pleasures of a woman's body, it wasn't going to let him forget the sweet touch of skin on skin—although he suspected that it wouldn't settle for just any woman.

Kerry had finished whatever she was doing, but she was still in there. He could feel her presence, like a heady cologne that drew all of his senses. His fingers clenched the sheet that covered his body. She was temptation itself, but he knew better than to entangle his life with another woman who could lay claim to his loyalty and his heart. His soul was too tired, his control too fragile to bear that burden again.

Finally, the far bathroom door opened and closed again, followed by the muffled sounds of Kerry moving around in her room. For the moment, he was safe from her dark eyes and soft touches.

A heavy silence settled over the darkness. He was alone, and he wanted it that way. He really did.

And if anyone believed that, he had some swampland in Death Valley to sell them.

• • •

A whimper invaded Ranulf's dream, making him frown. He'd been sailing the coast of what was to become Ireland, tasting the salt-laden mist of the sea, feeling the solid weight of his sword at his side. The sun felt warm on his face as the sails billowed overhead.

A second whimper slowed the breeze, causing the sails to hang loosely with only the current moving the ship forward. His dream self looked around, trying to find the source of the problem. To the east, he could see a human form struggling to reach the shore and safety. He shouted orders, and the ship immediately tacked in that direction as strong Viking arms pulled long oars through the water.

The third whimper, louder this time, shattered the dream completely. Ranulf charged out of his bed and across the room. Flipping on the bathroom light, he stopped in the doorway to Kerry's room. She'd kicked off her blankets and lay sprawled down the center of the bed, her head rolling from side to side.

It didn't take a genius to realize that she was trapped inside a nightmare. Not wanting to scare her more than she already was, he approached the bed cautiously.

"Kerry?" He pitched his voice low. "Kerry, wake up."

She turned away, her legs twitching, as if she'd

been running. Her silky gown had ridden high up near her waist, but at the moment all he could think was that she looked chilled to the bone. He reached for the sheet, intending to cover her, when the hall door slammed open with no warning.

His first instinct was to jump back, but that would have made him look guilty in Sandor's eyes even when he'd been doing nothing wrong. Rather than acknowledge the other Talion, he pulled the covers back up over Kerry, but she immediately tried to fight free of them again.

"What are you doing in here?" Sandor glared at him from the foot of the bed.

"Same thing you are. Trying to figure out why she's making all this racket." Although since he'd entered the room, she'd quit moaning.

"She's having a nightmare."

As if Ranulf couldn't figure that out for himself. "I know." He knelt by the head of the bed. "Kerry, wake up."

"Let me try." Sandor moved around to the other side. "Kerry, it's me, Sandor. You're safe here."

Sandor shot a look in Ranulf's direction, saying without words that *he* was the reason she was in no danger. She still didn't wake up, but she scooted closer to Ranulf, an action that Sandor clearly did not appreciate.

Ranulf could feel the jagged edges of her emotions. "Her control is slipping." He automatically sent a small burst of energy toward her, only to have it blocked by Sandor. When he pushed harder, shoving it past the barrier Sandor tried to throw between Ranulf and Kerry, Sandor muttered a curse and clenched his fists. It didn't help when the expression on Kerry's face immediately smoothed out as she snuggled into the pillow with a sigh.

"She shouldn't be tainted with that vile brew of energy that you put out," Sandor snarled in a harsh whisper. "If she needs to be fed, it should come from me."

Thor's thunder, he got tired of Sandor's insults, but common sense said this time he might have the right of it. He'd already sent small bursts to Kerry over the past couple of days. So far she seemed to be handling it fine, but who knew what prolonged exposure would do to her?

He started to back away from the bed, then stopped when Kerry immediately started inching closer toward him. If she went much farther, she'd fall off the bed.

Ignoring the waves of disapproval coming from Sandor, Ranulf knelt at the side of the bed and repeated Kerry's name, each time with a little more emphasis. When that didn't work, he gently shook her shoulder. She fought against his touch, trying to burrow deeper into the pillow. The small display of stubbornness made him smile. She definitely had a warrior's soul.

"Kerry, just open your eyes. Once we know you're out of the nightmare, we'll let you go back to sleep." He shook her again; this time she batted at his hand with hers.

"Leave her alone. She's sleeping better now." Sandor crossed his arms over his chest.

Ranulf rose to his full height. "And you think your standing over her will keep the dark dreams at bay?"

"Better than you will. Don't forget, I've seen what you're capable of, Viking. It's one thing to protect those who need it. It's another to enjoy killing."

He wasn't about to defend himself to the younger Talion. Yes, he had killed. Yes, he was good at it. But only monsters and madmen took pleasure in ending another's life, even if that person deserved to die. "Go back to bed, Sandor, while you're still in good enough shape to get there on your own."

Bristling, Sandor snarled, "Like hell I will. Not until you go back to your room and promise to stay there."

Ranulf's bark of laughter sounded ugly even to his own ears. "That's rich, pup. You call me a monster and a killer, yet you would accept my word?"

Sandor ran his fingers through his hair in frustration. "She deserves better."

Ranulf stared down at the woman in the bed, a

little surprised she'd been able to sleep through the anger burning between the two men in the room. "Yes, she does. But right now, we're all she has standing between her and Bradan."

He met Sandor's gaze. "After this is over, you and I will settle this between us once and for all. Now, we both leave and let Kerry sleep."

"You leave first."

"We both go," Ranulf repeated, stalking toward Sandor, smiling when the younger man backed up two steps before he caught himself.

"Her door stays shut."

"No, Sandor. If she needs me, I will come." Ranulf started for the bathroom door, hesitating long enough to make sure Sandor was leaving at the same time. Then he stepped through.

He knew he wasn't hero material, at least not the kind Kerry needed. But if his presence eased her, he would stay near.

The dream was back. Bradan stood before her with death in his eyes—her death. She tried to run, but her feet were mired in thick sludge and she exhausted herself after only a few steps. The renegade smiled and held up his hands, which lit up like a pair of torches, burning bright and hot. Her throat ached with the need to scream, but even breathing was an effort.

Her skin burned with cold fear, seeing the inevitability of her death, which he was offering with those flames. She wanted to escape, she wanted to live, she wanted . . . Ranulf. Suddenly he was there, surrounding her with his warmth and holding the darkness at bay.

His scent filled her senses . . . but wait. Since when did dreams have smells? Her eyes fluttered open to realize her room was no longer dark, and she was no longer lying on the pillow. Instead, she was cradled in a pair of strong arms with her head against Ranulf's bare chest.

"You were having nightmares." His voice rumbled near her ear.

Her face flushed hot with embarrassment. "Loud enough to wake you in the next room?"

His fingers toyed with her hair. "I'm a light sleeper."

"Liar," she said. "But thank you. I guess that fire earlier brought back memories of the dance club."

"That's understandable, but you're safe for now. Go back to sleep."

He started to slide away, but she caught his arm. "Don't go." She hated sounding needy, but she felt better with him close.

His blue eyes darkened. "I'll sit in the chair."

She pressed him back against the headboard, even knowing he could shake her off in an instant. "You won't get any rest sitting up all night,"

He traced her lips with the pad of his thumb. "And if I stay in this bed much longer, neither of us will get any sleep." Then he gave her a little smile. "I've already had to throw Sandor out of here once tonight. If he comes to check on you again . . ."

"Don't the doors have locks on them?" She ran her hand up his chest to caress the side of his face, liking the whiskery feel of his skin against hers.

He focused his attention on the lock across the room and frowned. "Yes, they do."

Two audible clicks followed hard upon his answer. "However, if Sandor or Judith wants in badly enough, they can unlock the doors just as easily."

"I don't care." If they were rude enough to barge in uninvited, that was their problem. Right now, cocooned in the strength of Ranulf's arms, her skin tingled with warmth and a growing desire for more than a quiet snuggle. She slid her leg over his, slowly turning to sprawl across his chest.

"Kerry . . ."

"Please, not another lecture on how wrong we are for each other, or that you're not a stick-around kind of guy. I already know all that." She shifted so that the core of her body was centered directly over the impressive evidence that he wasn't immune to her efforts.

He caught her wandering hand in his. "Correction. You've heard what I've been telling you and what Sandor tried to tell you before that. That doesn't mean you believe it. If you did, you'd be across the hall with Sandor instead of with me."

That did it. She sat up, aware of the delicious feel of his erection pressed against her bottom. "We've already had this discussion. Maybe Sandor is the perfect Kyth, but that doesn't mean he's perfect for me. Maybe I've always had a thing for tall redheads who drive Packards."

Ranulf rolled his eyes. "Yeah, right. And how many of those have you met?"

"One, and that's enough for me." Maybe more than enough, judging by the size of his erection.

His expression settled into its usual grim lines. "Tomorrow I go on the hunt for Bradan. When I find him, I'll kill him." He lifted her chin to look straight into her eyes. "Then I'll go home. Alone."

His brutal honesty hurt, but she preferred that to empty promises. "Then let's not waste another minute."

When Ranulf didn't immediately shove her off his lap, she knew she'd won. It was just taking him a bit longer to reach the conclusion she had: something that burned this bright and hot shouldn't be wasted. Maybe she could hurry him along. Slowly, slowly, she rocked forward and then back, creating a lovely bit of friction between them. Her eyes drifted shut as heat burned through the thin fabric that separated them. She couldn't wait until he was on her, in her.

"Kiss me." His big hand caught the back of her head.

She'd kiss him, all right. Giving him an impudent smile, she slid down his body, planting small kisses and tasting his skin as she made her way down to her intended target.

The low growl in his throat pleased her greatly as she nuzzled his erection. Before she could release the drawstring of his flannel pajama bottoms, though, he reached down to haul her up for a kiss as he flipped her onto her back. Anchoring her there with one heavy leg, he showed her what a man with a thousand years' experience knew about kissing.

The tingling burn of energy between them increased with each second, flickering up and down her back, making her arch off the bed even as he pressed her down. His hand slid down to peel her nightgown off, pausing long enough to rub the soft fabric against his face.

"Like it?"

"Very much, but I like you naked even more." He tossed the gown over his shoulder and she giggled.

Then he caught her hands and anchored them over her head as he kissed her, starting off with small flutters across her lips before moving on. The slick swirl of his tongue across the sensitive tips of her nipples had her going up in flames.

She usually closed her eyes on the rare occasion she kissed someone, not liking having someone that up close and personal. With this man, though, it was as if he short-circuited all of her misgivings about intimacy. With her eyes wide open, she savored watching the changing shades of blue in his gaze. In a matter of seconds, his irises ran the full gamut from pale blue to indigo and back again, the colors swirling and mixing in heated desire.

She lost herself in the skyrocketing passion as he directed his intense focus on her breasts. She moaned with a deep hunger as he suckled first one nipple and then the other, tugging at them with his teeth and tongue. What the man could do with his mouth should have been outlawed. She was burning up, inside and out, with the need to get closer to Ranulf.

She tried to separate her legs to coax him inside her, but he was having none of it as he nuzzled and licked her nipple before recapturing the sensitive tip with his lips. At the same time, he let go of her hands.

Her fingers immediately dug into his shoulders, holding on to the solid comfort of his strength as he made her world spin out of control. When he moved farther down her body, she held her breath, waiting and wanting.

Ranulf breathed deeply, loving the fact that this woman was so aroused by his touch. She was a generous lover, giving as well as taking as the two of them learned by touch and taste and sound how to please each other. Right now, he was going to send her rocketing over the edge. He looked up the curved planes of her body to see the anticipation in her smile.

The lady knew what she wanted, and he was eager to indulge them both. With firm pressure, he spread her legs wide apart, lifting them over his shoulders. "Hold on, honey. This is going to be a fast ride."

At the first touch of his lips and tongue, she arched back, her head rolling from side to side. He was a warrior, trained from birth to never lose sight of the target. Using that same intense focus, he learned what Kerry merely liked and what drove her crazy, and he used that knowledge mercilessly.

As soon as she started to shatter, he surged forward, claiming her mouth to absorb her keening release. When the tension drained away from her body, he briefly left her to fetch a condom from the bathroom.

Kerry was waiting for him with open arms. His feet stuttered to a stop at the sight. Her smile was a siren's call, drawing him back. Although his body had cooled in the few steps to the bathroom and back, hot blood came rushing in as he returned to the bed, covering Kerry with the full weight of his body.

Aware of the differences in their size, he promised, "I'll go slow."

Her smile brightened as she wrapped her legs around his. "Not too slowly."

The flow of energy between them burned hot as he eased into her tight passage, pausing every little bit to kiss her sweet lips and to give her body a chance to adjust. Damn, she fit him like a glove, the warm slide of her inner muscles caressing each inch of him. With one last push, he completed the union of their bodies.

"Ranulf!" Kerry's hips thrust up, seating him even deeper.

The urge to ride her hard burned up the last bit of his hard-fought control. Withdrawing almost to the tip, he rocked forward again and again, each time faster and harder. The world narrowed down to the confines of the bed and this woman. In all his life, there was no moment more perfect than this one.

He drove them on and on, claiming her with his body and his energy. His instincts burned hot and primitive, a celebration of life in an existence that had been too full of death for centuries.

"Come for me, Kerry!" His breath came in shallow pants as he strained toward completion for them both. "Let go and fly. I'll catch you."

"Yes! Yes!" she chanted as her nails dug into his ass to drive him even deeper. When her body seized his in a pulsing grip, he poured out his climax in a hot, pulsing surge as she careened right over the edge with him. Together they soared with the gods, then slowly settled back to earth, mortal again.

For an eternity, the only sound in the room was ragged breathing and racing heartbeats. The world had been remade in bolder, brighter colors, and the energy still pulsing between them was honey sweet and sizzling hot.

When Ranulf could string words together, he rested his forehead on hers. "Are you all right?"

She ran her hands up his back to his shoulders before pushing his hair back out of his face. "If I was any better, I'd explode."

"I'm pretty sure you already did."

Kerry laughed and kissed him. "I think we both did."

Reluctantly, he withdrew from her body. "I'll be right back."

On his way to the bathroom, he retrieved her nightgown and tossed it to her. "You might want this. It's getting close to dawn, and Sandor might decide to check on you again."

"He'd better knock first."

When Ranulf returned to the room a minute later, he noticed that Kerry had followed his advice. His first thought was how much he would enjoy taking the gown right back off her again, but then he realized they weren't alone.

Sandor was in the doorway, staring at the thoroughly trashed bed and looking thunderous.

"Go away, Sandor. I've already said you can't come in."

Kerry tried to close the door, reminding Ranulf of his first meeting with her. She didn't have any better luck keeping Sandor out. The Talion pushed his way in, careful not to hurt her, and headed straight for Ranulf.

"You son of a bitch! You just couldn't keep your filthy hands to yourself!" As soon as he was in range, he started swinging his fists.

Ranulf blocked two punches before Sandor got lucky and managed to connect with Ranulf's jaw. From the way Sandor winced and started cursing, the blow had done more damage to his hand than it had to Ranulf's face. That didn't mean he was going to let the idiot use him for a punching bag. When Ranulf let fly with a punch of his own, he didn't hold anything back. It was bad enough the bastard was always insulting him, but he'd just spoiled the most perfect moment Ranulf had experienced in centuries.

Kerry was railing at both of them as they took the fight to the floor, finally giving vent to all their pent-up hostility toward each other. She had the good sense to stay back, but she clearly didn't appreciate a brawl breaking out in her room. Suddenly the two men froze in place, unable to move.

Damnation, that meant Judith had joined the festivities. They'd be lucky if she didn't plaster them both on the ceiling for pulling such a stupid stunt. Her control was shaky, though, because he was gradually able to push himself off of Sandor.

He looked around for the Dame, but she was nowhere in sight. Which meant . . . His gaze snapped back to Kerry, who was glaring at him and Sandor equally, her hands outstretched. Sparks of energy flashed in her dark eyes as she held two of Judith's strongest warriors pinned to the floor. Son of a bitch. She wasn't just a Kyth but the rarest of their kind: a healer with the talents to become a Dame like Judith.

Chapter 11

*B*efore he could say anything, Judith entered the room, assessing the situation in one glance.

"Kerry, my dear, I'll take over now." She stepped between Kerry and the two men, breaking the energy connection. Kerry collapsed in a nearby chair, looking a little green.

Ranulf finished pushing himself up from the floor, trying to make sense of what he'd just seen. Without thinking, he offered Sandor a hand up. The two of them stared first at Kerry and then at Judith. Slowly, Ranulf began adding up a few things that had bothered him about Judith's behavior since she'd found out about Kerry's existence. The answer he got did *not* make him happy.

He turned his temper on Judith. "She's like you, isn't she?"

Judith gave him a distracted nod as she stood

next to Kerry, stroking her shoulder. He knew from personal experience that Judith was both soothing and energizing Kerry, helping the younger woman stabilize.

He took a step closer. "How long have you known?"

"I suspected from your first report and from the condition of the people she saved. It was obvious she's a healer and a strong one. I had to think she and I might have other qualities in common."

He had other questions, but rather than risk saying something that might hurt Kerry, he stalked over to the bathroom door and slammed it behind him.

A hot shower would clear out the cobwebs and wash Kerry's scent off his skin. He cranked the dial all the way, figuring being boiled alive would be better than letting himself get tangled up with another Dame for the next millennium. He couldn't face another year of killing for the good of their people, much less a thousand of them.

Sandor wasn't the only one who worried about the long-term effects of absorbing the twisted, dark energy of bastards like Bradan. Ranulf had only been down off the mountain for a few days, and except for the time spent with Kerry, his skin hurt with the need to break free of the confines of civilization.

As the water pelted his body, he closed his eyes and leaned against the cool tile wall. Was Kerry all right? He shouldn't have left her alone, even though Sandor and Judith would see that she was taken care of. But he couldn't face her—not now that he understood why he felt this powerful attraction to her.

He was the strongest of the Talions and had special talents that most of the others lacked. The only Kyth who was stronger than he was in some ways was Dame Judith herself. It was one reason he'd willingly served her for so long.

And now Judith had finally found someone with the right gifts to serve their people as the new Dame when she herself stepped down. He now knew why she'd been so adamant about sending both Sandor and Ranulf to protect Kerry.

If Kerry assumed the throne of their people, she'd need a Consort. Who would be more perfect than Sandor, the diplomat among the Talion? And who would get to spend a hundred lifetimes watching the two of them whenever they dragged him down off the mountain to kill? No way in hell he was going to let that happen.

Even if he was willing to serve the new Dame, he sure as hell wasn't going to dance to any tune Sandor played. Nor was he about to watch that smarmy son of a bitch following Kerry around, sharing her life and her bed. Especially now that he knew that their shared passion was as close to Valhalla as he'd likely ever know.

He shut the water off. The sooner he dressed and ate, the sooner he could hit the streets and track down Bradan. The hours spent in Kerry's bed had been the best in his life, but he had a job to do. Reaching for a towel, he made his plans.

Sandor hated—HATED—being shooed out of Kerry's room like a child, even though he knew Kerry had questions that only Judith could answer. But as long as Ranulf was lurking in the next room, he would stay close, too.

It didn't take a genius to figure out that the Viking had used Kerry's nightmare to worm his way into her bed. And judging by the tangled blankets and sheets, he'd done a helluva lot more than just wake her up from the dark dream that had ensnared her.

Damn it, they had been ordered to protect Kerry, not seduce her! Sandor stared at his image in the mirror and frowned. Was he jealous that Ranulf and Kerry had spent the night in each other's arms? Maybe a little. He suspected making love to a woman with such strength and power would be like getting hit with a bolt of lightning.

Brutal honesty forced him to admit that she had never looked at him with the slightest hint of interest. Normally he would've taken her rejection with good humor; he didn't expect every woman he met to fall at his feet.

But what did she see in Ranulf? Was it that big a thrill to take a barbarian to bed? Or was Kerry drawn to the darkness in Ranulf? The idea sent fear for their race coursing through his veins. Judith wasn't the only one who had suspected that Kerry was most likely a healer after reading the reports about her reaction to the dance club fire.

But if Kerry's affinity was for the dark end of the energy spectrum, what would that mean to the Kyth as a whole? Had they found her too late, when she'd already been tainted?

Clearly Ranulf couldn't be trusted now. So if Dame Judith decided that Kerry was beyond redemption, he himself would likely get the execution order—a first for him. Although he'd brought other Kyth to face justice, he'd never been given an execution order to carry out. Judith had always said it had been because his talent as a diplomat had kept him busy enough. He'd always wondered if perhaps she'd doubted his ability to kill.

It would be hard enough to take out a fellow Talion, but to execute a woman, especially this woman? A part of his soul would die. He stared again at his reflection in the mirror. The Kyth culture sprang from a warrior culture where a man's worth was tied to his ability to wield weapons in the defense of their people. Underneath the veneer of civilized behavior, they still held on to those values.

As much as Sandor despised the choices Ranulf

had made in his life, the man deserved respect as a proven warrior.

A sharp rap on the door disturbed the silence in his room. Banishing his dark thoughts, he opened the door. The Viking filled the doorway.

"What do you want?"

"We've got work to do."

Ranulf had showered and shaved, but the deep indigo blue of his eyes warned that his mood was still volatile. Diplomat that he was, Sandor knew how to talk his way around moody Kyths.

"There's no 'we.' I've been doing my job. You're the one who's been screwing . . . around."

Who knew indigo could go black so quickly? Ranulf's hand snaked out to grab a fistful of Sandor's shirt for the second time in as many days, yanking him up close.

"Never insult her, Sandor. Watch your mouth or I'll close it permanently." Ranulf's words rang with cold death.

If they really went at it, there would be no rules, no quarter given. And right now, the only two people with the strength to stop them were too busy to do so. Sandor braced himself to do battle, but Ranulf abruptly released him and stayed in the hall, giving Sandor enough space to calm down.

"I know you want a piece of me, but now isn't the time. Bradan's out there stocking up on death energy. We need to take him out while we still can."

The arrogant bastard was right. Even if they hated each other's guts, it was imperative that they find some way to work together. Once Bradan was permanently out of the picture, there would be a reckoning.

The Viking nodded, as if he'd read Sandor's thoughts. Hell, maybe he had. There was no telling what secret talents he had honed over the years.

"Where do you want to start?" Sandor asked calmly.

The crisis over, Ranulf's eyes faded to a lighter blue. "With breakfast."

Sandor acknowledged the peace offering with a quick nod. "Tell Josiah that I'll be there in a minute. I need to change my shirt."

Ranulf glanced at the button hanging by a thread. "Put it on my tab." Then he was gone.

Drying his hands, Bradan studied his studio. An artist had to have a place to practice his craft, and this was his. The smell of bleach would fade as the cement floor dried, but otherwise the room met with his approval.

The boy had put up quite a fight. His efforts had been futile, of course, but quite remarkable for all that. His death had topped off Bradan's tank, so to speak, leaving him buzzed and ready for more.

It was time to go after his real targets: Dame

Judith, the Viking, Sandor, and the delicious Kerry Logan. The order didn't matter, although he leaned toward keeping Kerry for the last. Maybe if she saw how the others died, she'd be more willing to cooperate. Fat lot of good it would do her. In the end, he would bed her, either breaking her or killing her in the process.

The stage was set. His instruments were all lined up neatly on the counter. The chains were reinforced, designed to stand up to the strongest of guests. He could see Ranulf straining against them, blood dripping from his wrists and ankles. The Dame probably thought Ranulf would prove to be Bradan's most worthy opponent, but she would be wrong.

All Bradan had to do was take either Kerry or Judith prisoner, and stupid, noble Ranulf would offer himself up in exchange for the woman's life. Not that he'd trust Bradan to honor the agreement, but neither would he stand by and let a woman die without trying every possible way to save her.

Bradan would keep him alive long enough to watch Judith breathe her last. The Viking had served her for God knew how long; it was only right that they die together.

He left the house, locking the door and setting the alarm. He'd chosen the wooded lot for its remote location. When a man had unusual tastes in entertainment, it didn't do to live too close to neighbors.

He should reach Seattle by midafternoon. It was time to give Sandor another few hits to track down: a charge here, an ATM withdrawal there, all geared to keep the Talions spinning their wheels like hamsters in a cage, running like crazy and getting nowhere.

Climbing in his rental car, he started the engine and drove down to the highway, careful to observe the speed limit. A state trooper had a nasty habit of setting up a speed trap along the ramp that led back down to Interstate 90. Only a fool would risk years of planning for the fleeting pleasure of exceeding the speed limit.

Delayed gratification was always the sweetest.

"For the last time, NO!"

Kerry paced back and forth, wishing she'd been anywhere else except trapped in this room with an unnerving old lady watching her every move. "I'm sorry, but I don't want to hear any more about my so-called heritage. I don't want to explore these newfound secret superpowers, and I don't want a lecture on accepting the burden of my gifts. What I do want to do is shower, grab breakfast at a fast-food drive-up window, and get back to my life. My *real* life."

She turned to face Dame Judith, who had listened to Kerry's tirade for the past half hour with the patience of a saint—and the stubbornness of a bulldog. Once the two men had retreated, Judith had done her best to reassure Kerry that it was perfectly normal to control two pissed-off males with the flick of a wrist. Oh, yeah, that made all the sense in the world.

It made just as much sense to Kerry as finding out that she and Dame Judith must have had a common ancestor—or maybe that Dame Judith *was* the ancestor. If she accepted the fact that Ranulf really was a thousand years old, could Dame Judith be any younger? It was a sign of how far gone Kerry was that she actually believed what they'd been telling her.

Praise be, the shower in the next room finally stopped running. How could she concentrate when her mind insisted on picturing Ranulf standing naked under that hot spray? His body was that of a warrior, and she'd reveled in being the sole focus of all that power and strength. Just thinking about it had her feeling restless and achy. A shadow of the sweet heat she'd experienced making love with him washed over her, leaving her staring at the bathroom door. If the Dame hadn't taken up residence in her room, Kerry would have joined him.

The man definitely had a body built for hard driving sex, the likes of which she'd never known and might never know again. Ranulf found the solitude of his mountaintop home necessary to cope with what life had thrown at him, and if the scars he carried on the inside matched the ones on his back and chest, maybe he was right. But the thought of never seeing those startling blue eyes staring down into hers as he relentlessly drove them both toward climax made her unutterably sad.

The other woman brought her back to the moment. "You have strong feelings for Ranulf, don't you?"

Kerry jumped when Dame Judith laid a hand on her shoulder. A small surge of warmth spread out from the old woman's touch, a feeling Kerry was learning to associate with being in physical contact with another Kyth. Not that Judith's touch made her feel anything like Ranulf's or even Sandor's did.

She avoided answering Judith's question by asking one of her own. "Does each Kyth have his or her own"—she struggled for the right word— "taste? Or maybe feel is a better way to put it?"

Judith glanced at the bathroom door one last time before turning away. "Yes, they do. Why don't you get dressed, while I do the same? After breakfast I'll answer all your questions."

"All right. Give me about twenty minutes to get showered, and I'll meet you in the dining room."

Judith patted her shoulder again. "Make it thirty minutes. I'm afraid I don't move quite as quickly as I used to."

"Thirty, then." Kerry surprised them both by planting a quick kiss on Judith's cheek. "That's for coming to my rescue."

"It was my pleasure, young lady. It's been a while since I've had men fighting over me, but I haven't forgotten what it was like. Flattering, of course, but hell on the furniture."

Kerry looked around the room, only now noting the broken lamp on the floor. She bent down to pick up a piece of the shattered pottery. "Good grief, I can't believe they did that. I'm so sorry."

"Don't be. It's hardly your fault that two of the best men I know are smart enough to appreciate a beautiful woman—especially one with brains to match."

Kerry gave Judith a wry smile. "Thank you for saying that, but we both know that I was just the excuse. I suspect those two have been at each other's throats for far longer than they've known me."

Judith sighed and shook her head. "Unfortunately, that's true. Normally I try to keep them apart as much as possible."

"Maybe pounding on each other will finally knock some sense into both of them." But she doubted it.

"So do I, Kerry. So do I," Judith agreed as she left.

Kerry stared at the closed door. Had she said that last part aloud? If not, that was one spooky woman. Kerry headed for the bathroom, convinced she'd ended up in the Twilight Zone.

"One of us will be his next target."

Kerry looked up from buttering her toast. She didn't have to ask who Ranulf was talking about, and his pronouncement cast a pall over what was already a pretty grim meal. She set down her knife and pushed back her plate.

Judith looked up from her newspaper. "Did you find new information already this morning?"

Ranulf kept his eyes pinned somewhere between Judith and Sandor, effectively cutting Kerry out of the conversation. She hadn't had a moment alone with him since he'd stormed out of her bedroom after asking Judith how long she'd known something about Kerry. She didn't much appreciate the cold shoulder after the night they'd spent together.

"A little. We'll be following up on a couple of leads after breakfast."

He obviously wasn't in the mood to share, but it had definitely put him in a foul mood. Heavy lines bracketed his mouth. Sandor was making more of an effort to hide his thoughts behind a façade of good humor, but she could practically see the tension thrumming in his veins.

"Will one of you have time to drive me to my

apartment this morning? I need to pick up some papers and then go into the office." She didn't really want to go to either place, but darned if she'd let him talk around her as if she'd just been another piece of furniture.

"Hell, no!" Ranulf's eyes flashed dark and furious. "If you set foot outside of this house, we might as well stand you on the street corner with a target on your chest. You're staying put."

She met him glare for glare. "And just who died and made you king?"

Ranulf leaned forward and planted his elbows on the table, all business and temper. "I promised Dame Judith I would keep you alive. If I have to tie you to the bed to do so, I will."

"Ooh! Sounds kinky, big guy." She gave him a sweet smile designed to tick him off. "But sorry, not interested."

Judith held her napkin to her mouth, hiding a smile, clearly delighted at seeing her fiercest warrior tangled up in knots. Even Sandor looked amused.

Ranulf's big fist came down hard on the table. "Kerry, I am not about to—"

His tirade was cut off by the sound of a cell phone ringing. It wasn't hers. She'd turned it off and left it back in the bedroom. Sandor checked his and shook his head. Ranulf frowned and stepped out into the foyer. A second later he was back with a phone, glaring at the screen as it continued to ring.

Kerry asked the question that all of them were wondering about. "Aren't you going to answer it?"

Ranulf looked around the table. "The caller's ID is blocked."

"Then the best way to find out who's calling is to ask. Unless you'd rather I did." Kerry held out her hand, knowing full well he'd never surrender that much control to her.

The look he shot in her direction as he punched the button and held the tiny device up to his ear warned her that retribution would be forthcoming. "Yeah?"

His eyes turned glacial and the temperature in the room plummeted. "Bradan. How nice of you to call, you murdering son of a bitch. I hope you've been putting your affairs in order."

Although she couldn't hear the other's response, she knew it had to do with her because Ranulf's gaze immediately went to her and stayed there. As he continued to listen, her heart fluttered in her throat and her breakfast turned into a queasy lump in her stomach. Whatever Bradan was saying had Ranulf holding the phone in a white-knuckled grip.

Ranulf had clearly had enough. "You forget whom you're talking to. I don't take orders, especially from weaklings like you."

He listened for another few seconds, and when

he laughed, it had nothing to do with humor. "You go right on believing that if you want to, boy. But your hours are numbered. You've seen renegades die before, so you know there's only one way this is going to end for you—badly. Come in now, and I'll ease your passing."

When Bradan replied, Ranulf fell silent, his face chiseled out of granite. "You touch one hair on her head, and I'll rip away every ounce of the energy you've stolen while your skin burns and you beg for mercy. Then I'll dance on your grave."

His voice dropped to a scary whisper. "And while you turn blue and choke on your own spit, I'll be smiling."

He slammed the phone shut, his breath coming in jerks, as if he'd run a marathon. Knowing he wouldn't like being stared at, Kerry turned her gaze toward the others. The Dame looked pale, but resolute. Sandor muttered, "Gods above," and shook his head as if to clear it, looking like his worst fears had just been confirmed.

Which irritated the hell out of Kerry. How dare he pass judgment on Ranulf? He wasn't the one who'd been forced to listen to Bradan's filth. And it had to have been horrific to have affected Ranulf so strongly.

She got up and went to stand by Ranulf, hating that he looked so alone. "What did he threaten to do to me?"

Ranulf stared down at the phone in his hand. "He said that he's been practicing, and now that he's got it right, he's ready for the real thing."

"Practicing what? More fires?"

Ranulf didn't want to answer, because repeating Bradan's horrendous promises would only give him more power. But knowing Judith and Kerry, they wouldn't settle for a watered-down answer. He met Sandor's eyes briefly, reading the usual disapproval and maybe a hint of fear in them.

"He said he's killed a woman and a young man to get the hang of how it's done. That's all I'm going to tell you, except that we're dealing with one sick bastard."

He shoved the phone into his pants pocket, resisting the urge to smash it with his fist. "He knows Kerry is here, and thanked me for herding all of his intended victims into a convenient spot. He called it 'one-stop shopping.'"

"Dear God." Judith went ashen.

As Kerry scooted closer, Ranulf gathered her into his side, knowing she needed the comfort that touch would provide. They needed to make plans, ones that included getting Kerry safely out of harm's way until he and Sandor could corner their prey.

He let Kerry's scent seep into his bones, aware that the comfort being offered was a two-way street. The press of her body along his warmed him from the inside out, her acceptance of who and what he was, a balm to his raw nerves.

The truth of what he did for the Kyth didn't seem to repel Kerry. She even accepted the necessity of Bradan's death without hesitation. He met Judith's gaze across the table. The older woman gave him a nod of approval, which reminded him that the two of them were long overdue for a talk.

"We need to get out of here today, and that includes Josiah. We can't leave anyone behind who could be used as a pawn in Bradan's game." It took all of his strength to ease away from Kerry. "Go get packed up, Kerry. Sandor, you'll take the women and Josiah someplace safe while I wait here for our friend. I'll call when it's over."

"Won't he be expecting us to do exactly that?" Kerry wrapped her arms across her waist. "Then all he'd have to do is follow us from one place to the next."

"Maybe, but we won't be leaving by the front door. Will we, Judith?"

The color had returned to her face. "No, you won't. Kerry, dear, would you go to the kitchen and ask Josiah to put on a fresh pot of coffee for me? I need to talk to these gentlemen for a minute, privately."

"Have I told you how much I hate secrets?" Kerry asked as she stalked out of the room.

Ranulf stared after her, unable to tear his eyes

away. He wanted nothing more than to chase her down and drag her back to her bedroom for a repeat of last night's performance, maybe adding a few things they hadn't had time to try out yet. But this definitely wasn't the time for such thoughts.

"All right, out with it, Judith. What else do you know about Kerry that you haven't been telling us?" He sat down, determined to get a straight answer out of his leader.

Chapter 12

Sandor bristled. "What are you talking about?"

"Earlier, when we were fighting. Maybe you didn't notice, but it wasn't Judith who stopped us. It was Kerry." Ranulf turned back to Judith for confirmation.

She saw no use in denying it. "Yes, it was Kerry."

Her younger warrior was shocked. "How can that be? You're the only one we know of who has the capability to control Talion warriors like that."

Judith shrugged. "That may have been true before, but it's obvious that our Miss Logan is a powerful young woman. We also have solid evidence that she can use energy to heal. I would guess Ranulf has more direct experience with her other abilities."

Ranulf sat in stubborn silence, dark energy flickering across the tips of his fingers. Events were rapidly coming to a head, and she needed to know if Kerry was the one she'd been waiting for.

"Ranulf, Sandor." She struggled to find the right words. "I'm getting weaker all the time. Although I can still perform my duties, it takes me much too long to recover. The Consort to the Dame is more than an ordinary spouse; his energy both balances and amplifies hers. The two of you and Josiah have tried very hard to fill in the gap Rolf's death left in my life, and I appreciate all you have done. But without Rolf as my Consort to keep me stable, I cannot serve as the Dame of the Kyth for much longer."

Sandor started to protest, but she stopped him. "It does no good to argue. The truth is simply the truth, Sandor, even if it is not what we want to hear. I am dying, and sooner rather than later. If I die before someone else can assume my duties, our people will suffer. The Kyth bloodlines have already become too dilute. I do not want to see our heritage disappear altogether."

She stared out the window. How many different homes had she lived in? How many gardens had bloomed and died in front of her eyes? She was ready for this to be the last one, even if her people weren't.

"Kerry is the first candidate I have found who has all of the necessary abilities to take my place, and my purpose in assigning both of you to watch over her is twofold. Obviously, I need someone to handle the problem of Bradan. He will be difficult to bring to justice, but I have faith that you two will be able to carry out your duties. However, it is because of the other reason that I ordered both of you to keep our Miss Logan safe."

She braced herself for the explosion she knew was coming. "Should we be able to convince her to take on the job, which is by no means certain, she cannot serve alone. Even though she is young and powerful, the job will take a toll on her unless she has the right help."

Ranulf figured it out first. "You don't mean help, Judith. You mean stud service," he sneered.

"There's no need to be crude, Ranulf." She resisted the urge to pin him to the wall to remind him of his manners. She couldn't spare the energy, and he wasn't totally wrong.

"You have every right to be angry, but I most certainly did *not* order you into Kerry's bed. You managed that all on your own. It was my duty to introduce her to the strongest possible candidates for her Consort, which meant the two of you. You each have different gifts, but either of you would serve her well."

Her Viking warrior rose slowly to his feet. She couldn't decipher the expression on his face, but it frightened her. "Ranulf?"

His hand went to the talisman he wore around

his neck, wrapping his fingers around it as if to rip it off. Made in the image of Thor's hammer, it was the symbol of his fealty to her. Had she offended Ranulf to the point that he would consider renouncing his duty? It didn't bear thinking about, not when she needed him the most. The seconds stretched to the breaking point as she waited. Slowly his stance relaxed, his decision made.

"Share your thoughts, Ranulf." It wasn't a request, but an order.

"Dame Judith, I have served you faithfully for ten centuries. My honor has been yours to command, but you have gone too far this time. Maybe Kerry is everything you think she is, but you're playing fast and loose with her life. Hear my words and know that I mean them: This is my last mission for our people."

He walked to the window, turning his back on her. His words lashed out like a whip. "Damn it, Judith, I've killed for you and bled for you long enough. I want some peace in my life. I've earned that with my life's blood, and I won't spend what time I have left playing stud for you or the Kyth."

Ranulf's cold fury beat against her senses until he managed to contain his emotions. One minute his eyes were ablaze with blue fire and the next they were the color of ice.

"I am truly sorry that I have offended you. However, as your liege lord, Ranulf Thorsen, I will command you as I see fit. I am too old and too tired to go on the run. I will not leave my home. My wards are strong enough to keep Bradan at bay. Your duty—your only duty—right now is to take Kerry from here and keep her safe. Whether you do that from a distance or from her bed is up to you."

Ranulf nodded once and stalked from the room without looking back. As soon as he was out of sight, Sandor stood.

"Do you have something you'd like to add?" Gods above, if she lost Sandor, too, how would she go on? The same way she always did: one day at a time, one tough decision after another.

"You should have told us your suspicions about Kerry from the beginning, Judith. She deserved better from you, not to mention me. And God knows Ranulf did. He has served you far too long to deserve such disrespect."

Had she heard right? Sandor was defending Ranulf?

Angry at his rebuke, she snapped, "I am your ruler, Talion! I don't have to explain myself to you or Ranulf. Your loyalty is mine to command. Do not dare to question my decisions!"

He jerked back a step, as though she'd slapped him. "Very well, Grand Dame. If you'll excuse me, I have work to do."

Then he walked away, leaving her feeling alone and so very old.

• • •

Bradan shifted in his seat, his body objecting to the long hours wasted sitting in the car. If there wasn't any action in the next few minutes, he'd call it a day and try again tomorrow. He'd been sure that his phone call to Ranulf would have sent those fools scurrying for cover. Then it would have only been a matter of tracking them down one at a time for fun and games.

The images in his head were so clear that it felt as if he really could have tasted their blood and smelled their sweat. He was so lost in the promise of his plans that he almost missed seeing the gate to the Dame's home rolling open. Ranulf pulled out onto the street and turned in the opposite direction from where Bradan was parked.

The Viking was alone. Turning the key, Bradan decided to follow long enough to see where Ranulf was headed. Once he knew for certain, he'd decide whether to go after Ranulf—although he could have an army in the trunk of that land yacht.

Yet Ranulf's departure might be a ploy to lead him away so the rest could escape. Should he go after Ranulf, no easy target, or wait to see what the wily old bitch was up to?

He put the car back in park. He'd stirred the pot; it was only a matter of time before it came to a boil.

• • •

"Where's Ranulf?" Kerry set down her suitcase and computer case. "Aren't we leaving?"

Sandor was standing near the front door, watching the street outside. "He already left."

Her breath caught. "Why? I thought we were all going to leave together."

He still wasn't looking at her. "Ranulf is going to circle around the area for a few minutes. Once he's sure he's not being followed, he'll pick us up down the street. Evidently there's a tunnel that leads out of this house that Dame Judith never told us about." He turned away from the door. "Seems there are a lot of things she hasn't bothered to tell us."

Something about the Talion warrior was off. His voice had a flat quality that hadn't been there before. "What hadn't she told you?" Kerry asked.

He ignored the question. "We need to go now if we're going to meet Ranulf. Since the two of you are so close, why don't you ask him any questions you might have?"

He'd only known her a few days, so why should her relationship with Ranulf bother him so much? And how could she explain it to him when she didn't understand it herself?

Either way, she wasn't going to play his game. "Fine. I'll do that. Lead the way."

He did as she asked without speaking another word. His suitcase was sitting beside the pantry in the kitchen. After he felt around the bottom of the shelf, she heard the sound of metal gears turning, and the back wall opened up to reveal a hidden staircase. Sandor started down the steps, leaving Kerry to follow.

"Is Dame Judith already waiting down there?"

Her question was met with silence, except the echo of their footsteps in the narrow passage.

"Sandor, quit being an ass. Where are Judith and Josiah? Are they coming?"

Her companion shook his head. "No, they're not. She won't leave her home, and Josiah insists on staying with her."

"But isn't that dangerous?"

His steps faltered. "Hell, yes, but try telling that to Judith. She seems to think that since you're Bradan's real target, they'll be safe as soon as you're out of here."

Kerry caught him by the shoulder. "And you believe that?"

He turned, his dark eyes blazing with frustration. "Frankly, I don't know what to believe anymore. As she pointed out to me, her job is to issue orders. Mine is to carry them out."

"Maybe I could talk to her." How could they drive away leaving the older woman alone with only her butler for protection?

"You could talk till you're blue in the face, and it won't change a thing." He started back down the stairs. "Once we're sure you're safe, I'll check on her and Josiah."

At the bottom of the stairs, he finally turned to face her. "Seriously, we need to get you to safety. I'm sorry you ever got sucked into our business."

"That was hardly your fault, Sandor. And if you and the others are to be believed, I'm part of you anyway. That makes it my business, too."

He set down his bag and took hers as well. After setting it out of the way, he stepped closer to her. She backed away, not sure she liked the odd expression in his eyes.

The Talion was close enough for her to feel the heat of his body and the soft brush of his breath on her skin. He reached out to place his hands on her shoulders. Was he trying to scare her? She didn't think so, but whatever he had in mind, she wanted none of it.

"Come on, Sandor, we need to keep moving. Ranulf's not the most patient of men, you know." She knew she'd made a mistake in mentioning his name as soon as she said it. Sandor's eyebrows snapped down as his eyes locked onto hers.

"You have no idea what you're messing with by getting involved with him, Kerry. The kind of energy Ranulf's been living on for centuries is poison, plain and simple. It's the same stuff Bradan is harvesting from his victims. Keep that in mind the next time you decide to invite Ranulf into your bed. The man is a killer. It may not be his fault, but that doesn't make it any less true."

"Sandor, whatever happens between me and Ranulf is none of your business. No matter what you think, he's a good man, and nothing you say will convince me otherwise." Despite the differences in their heights, she felt like an adult dealing with a child's disappointing behavior.

Sandor stepped back and ran his hand through his hair, clearly frustrated with her refusal to listen. "Look, Kerry, I'm sorry about how all of this has been thrown at you at once. All I ask is that you give yourself some time to adjust. When we've taken care of Bradan, I'm sure Judith will see to it that you have the opportunity to meet other suitable Kyth men."

"Suitable? Meaning more like you, Sandor?"

"I never said that, but you need someone who is—"

She finished the sentence for him. "Handsome and charming and judgmental?" She put her hand on his chest and shoved him back a step. "Well, you know what? I'll take Ranulf, rough edges and all, over your backstabbing any day."

It was all she could do not to smack him upside the head. She might not find him attractive, but she had *liked* him.

"Look, I know you mean well," Kerry continued. "We're all tired and worried, and that makes for short tempers. But if you try interfering again, I'll—"

A door down the hall slammed open to reveal Ranulf. He clearly picked up on the tension, because his hands closed into hard fists.

"What the hell's going on, Kerry?"

He asked her the question, but his eyes burned holes through Sandor.

"Nothing. I was just asking about Judith."

He didn't believe her for a minute, but she wasn't going to give him the chance to tangle with Sandor again. "Come on, both of you. We need to get going."

She picked up her bags and walked toward Ranulf, giving him no choice but to back out the door so she could get past. He shot Sandor one last dirty look before finally giving ground. He already had the trunk open, so she hefted her bags into the car herself.

When she walked around to the passenger door to get in the car, she realized that there was no way that someone as tall as Sandor could fit his long legs in the rear seat. When she started to climb in back, Ranulf stopped her.

"You ride up front with me. Sandor can have the back."

"There's not enough room for him back there."

"Too bad. He can sit sideways if he needs to."

Sandor just couldn't stay out of it. "Why don't you just stick me in the trunk?"

Ranulf's smile was not friendly. "Fine with me."

Lord save her from the male of the species—whatever species that might be.

"I'm riding in back. You two figure out what you're going to do so we can get moving." Then she plopped down on the leather seat and settled in.

Ranulf gave her a disgusted look that matched the expression on Sandor's face almost perfectly. Neither of them appreciated her laughing, especially when they didn't know what they'd done that she found so amusing.

The Packard's engine roared to life, and Ranulf gunned it out onto the street.

After a couple of blocks, Sandor broke the heavy silence. "Take me to the closest hotel. I can keep working from there."

Ranulf jerked his head in acknowledgment. A few seconds later he cranked up the stereo, preventing any further conversation. That was fine with her. She had enough to think about without trying to negotiate a peace settlement between the two men.

From the vantage point of the backseat, she studied her Kyth companions. Both were strong men, powerful, assertive, so clearly warriors. With Bradan on a killing spree, they were exactly the kind of men she needed to keep her safe. But their tendency to be domineering was a whole different ball of wax; that had to stop.

If she was honest with herself, she was even more irritated with Ranulf than with Sandor. Ever since Ranulf had climbed out of her bed that morning, he'd been acting like a bear with a thorn in his big glow-in-the-dark paw. Before they'd even gotten started, he'd warned her that he wasn't going to stick around. She could accept that and had made no demands on him. So what was he so angry about?

She planned on having it out with him once they were somewhere private. She wasn't about to tiptoe around, trying not to say or do anything that would set him off.

She shifted around until she found a comfortable position and closed her eyes. She hadn't gotten much sleep in days, and before the next song ended, she was asleep.

The highway stretched out in front of the car with only trees and mountains for company. Ranulf adjusted the rearview mirror to study the woman sleeping in the backseat. He didn't know when he'd made the decision to take Kerry to his mountain home for safekeeping, but it felt right.

Other than the occasional messenger from

Judith, he'd never allowed a single person across his threshold. But now he found himself wondering whether Kerry would like his sanctuary. And why did that matter, since their relationship wouldn't extend more than a few days?

A few miles farther east, he moved into the exit lane. By the time he reached the stop sign at the top of the ramp, Kerry was stirring, probably due to the change in speed. After a few seconds she sat up straighter and looked around, blinking to clear her eyes and her thoughts.

Finally, she smiled. "I seem to spend a lot of time sleeping in your car. Sorry, that doesn't make me very good company."

"No need to apologize. You obviously needed it. While we're stopped, do you want to come up here with me?" He tried to keep the question casual, as if her answer didn't matter one way or the other.

But it did matter, because when she immediately climbed into the front seat, that meant he hadn't totally screwed up whatever time they had left together. Judith's high-handed behavior still rankled, but she was right in thinking that Kerry would need a suitable Consort if she was to rule the Kyth. That didn't mean he had to like it.

"Ranulf, are we going to sit at this stop sign all day?" Kerry softened her remark with a smile. "Where are we, anyway?"

He put the car in gear and followed the narrow

road to the north and east. "We're headed to my home."

His answer clearly shocked her, and he wasn't sure how he felt about that. "I need a safe place to stash you while I hunt for Bradan."

"Won't that be the first place he'd look?"

"Maybe, if he knew where it was. Only the Dame and Josiah know where I live, and she'd die before she'd give that information to Bradan."

"Why would she do that for a total stranger? Even if I am a long-lost relative, she hasn't known me long enough to care that much."

"She cares more than you know." He didn't want to be the one to tell Kerry why, but he had a feeling that decision had already been made for him. Kerry confirmed that suspicion with her next breath.

She shook her finger at him. "Once we're not moving *and* we've had something to eat *and* you've had a chance to rest *and* we've exhausted whatever other excuses you can come up with, we're going to talk."

She said it with a bit of a smile, but that didn't lessen the determination behind her words. And she was right. It was long past time that they quit playing games with her life. She deserved better, especially from him.

"I promise, and no more excuses," he told her, clasping his talisman in his hand. She didn't yet know the power that gesture had among their people, but that didn't make it any less binding. "You can tie me to a chair if you want to make sure I don't try to escape."

As he'd hoped, she laughed.

"First you were going to tie me to the bed, and now this. Tell me, have you always been into bondage, or is this a new development?" She waggled her eyebrows, looking more ridiculous than flirtatious, but it was good to see her enjoying herself.

"I'm willing to give it a shot if you are." And then he held his breath, waiting to see if she'd slammed the door on that part of their relationship.

She turned those dark eyes in his direction, looking at him so intently that it felt as if she'd been able to see straight through to the heart of him. When she looked away again, he resumed breathing and concentrated on doing the least possible damage to his car as he turned off the blacktop onto the almost invisible gravel road that led back to his property. The silence dragged on as the trees swallowed them up, cutting off the rest of the world.

Kerry reached over and turned off the radio. "I hope you don't mind, but heavy metal doesn't belong out here."

"Fine with me. We'll be at the house in about five minutes."

"Good. When we get there, we can flip a coin to decide whether we need that rope or not." She put her hand on his thigh and squeezed.

His prick immediately sat up and took notice, and he had to fight the urge to floor it. If he hit a chuckhole and bottomed out the car, it would be that much longer before he got Kerry behind closed doors and in his arms.

Bradan's watch beeped, reminding him that time was up. He'd decided to wait outside the Dame's house for two more hours before giving up. There hadn't been any more activity since Ranulf had left.

Maybe it was time to stage a frontal assault on Judith's home. With Ranulf gone, he'd be facing his old buddy Sandor, two women, and an old man. How hard could it be to bypass the security on that gate? Sandor was computer literate, but Judith's ability with electronics was limited.

This time of year, it would stay light until almost ten o'clock. When the sun set, he'd come back prepared for every eventuality.

And the games would begin.

Sandor paced the floor of his hotel room. He'd been spending too many hours in front of a computer, hours that would be put to better use protecting his Dame. Not that she'd allowed him to return to her house, stubborn woman that she was.

How would all of this play out? It would take both Ranulf and him working in tandem to bring Bradan to bay. Someone had to protect Kerry while the other went one-on-one with the renegade. *He* should be with Kerry since the Viking warrior was the logical choice when it came to down-and-dirty fighting: He would strip Bradan down to dust.

The thought made Sandor sick, since Bradan had been his friend. Had he ever known the other Talion at all? Probably not. It was time to report in again. He picked up his cell and hit her number on speed dial.

"Judith, I finally found a paper trail. Bradan has rented a place we didn't know about. He did a thorough job hiding it from us, but I've made progress digging through the layers."

After they talked for another few minutes, Judith said, "Sandor, never doubt that I appreciate all you've done." Judith's voice sounded tired through the phone. "Keep me posted."

"Of course. I'll tell Ranulf when I hear from him. He didn't tell me where he was taking Kerry, but it will be someplace secure."

He'd like to think that if Ranulf *was* worthy of a woman of Kerry's strengths and abilities, he'd be man enough to wish the two of them well. But right now, the best he could hope for was that Kerry was taking a short walk on the wild side. Once she accepted her new role as future Grand

Dame of their people, surely she'd understand that Ranulf would be the worst possible choice for her Consort.

His phone rang again. He closed his eyes and wondered how much trouble he'd be in with Judith if he let her call go to voice mail. He reached for the phone and was surprised to see that the number on the screen wasn't one he recognized.

His hand went for the knife he carried strapped to his waist, the urge to protect himself against even a verbal threat riding him hard. He flipped open the phone.

"Bradan, I was just thinking about you." And wishing he was already dead and buried.

"Funny, Sandor, you've been on my mind as well. Are you and your good buddy Ranulf plotting up a storm? I know how much you love working with him."

"What do you think?"

Bradan's laugh rang out over the phone line. "I think Judith is forcing the two of you to play pretty together, and you're about to break your jaw from gritting your teeth over it."

The man knew him too well.

"You've given up all claim to knowing what's going on among the Talion warriors, Bradan." He let silence hang between them for a few seconds. "There's only one bit of business left between us, old friend, and we both know what that is. You can die fast or you can die slow, but the bottom line is that you die."

He disconnected and ignored the phone when it began to ring again a few seconds later.

Ranulf watched in amazement as Kerry walked through his wards of protection without hesitation. If she sensed them, she gave no sign of it. As soon as he'd stopped the car, she'd jumped out with a huge smile on her face.

"This whole place is beautiful, Ranulf!" She followed the wraparound porch around to the back, where it looked out over a small stream tumbling down off the mountainside.

While she listened to the music of the water rushing over the rocks to the valley below, he tested the wards he'd set before leaving for the city. Nothing had damaged or weakened them, so his defenses had simply recognized her as a friend and let her pass. Amazing.

She started toward him. Despite the shadows of the late afternoon, she brought the warmth of the summer sun with her. "I can see why you live here."

So she sensed the ancient peace of the glen, too, where the sparkling stream sang to him when he woke up in the morning and murmured a lullaby when he turned out the lights at night. The short summer and long winter of the mountain suited his Viking soul, but it was the sheer natural beauty that kept him sane. When he was down among the jumble of humans and Kyth in the lower lands, he swiftly burned up his store of energy just by holding the constant crush of their frantic lives at bay.

Here on his mountain he could simply breathe. This was his home, his refuge, his cell in what he'd meant to be a life sentence of solitary confinement. But now that he knew what Kerry looked like smiling at the rainbow in the spray from the creek, how could he stand to watch it alone?

He watched her close the distance between them, her too-clever eyes seeing more truth than he would have her know about him.

"I'd ask how many friends you've brought here over the years, but I already know the answer. None."

He glowered down at her. "What makes you think that?"

"I'm not sure, but I know it's true." She frowned as she tried to puzzle it out. "You don't live perched up here on the mountain because you like it—or at least, that's not the only reason. You live here alone because you need the quiet."

She cocked her head to the side and studied his face. "You could have taken me to a hotel like you did Sandor. Instead you brought me here, and now you're having second thoughts."

He turned away, not liking the way those big eyes of hers saw too much. "Let's get inside."

With a whisper of power he banished the protection wards on the door before Kerry reached it, not wanting to know if they'd recognize her like the others had despite being stronger. When the door swung open of its own accord, she jumped.

"Nice one, big guy. Can you teach me that trick? It would come in handy when I'm loaded down with groceries." She stepped across the threshold gingerly, as if wondering what would happen next.

Rather than spook her any more, he hit the light switch, casting the interior in the glow of electric lights. Normally he depended on oil lamps, which he could light with a flicker of energy from across the room, preferring their softer glow.

When she didn't immediately say anything, he moved past her on the pretense of setting their bags down. When he turned to face her, he stopped at the look of utter awe on her face. She clasped her hands as if in prayer as she looked about the room, her eyes lighting in one spot for a brief time before moving on.

"Your house is simply amazing. You built this yourself, didn't you?"

How did she know that? "I designed it. And I did as much of the work as I could by myself."

This was his tribute to a Viking hall, built as accurately as money and a long memory could make it. There were concessions to modern technology: electricity, indoor plumbing, comfortable furniture, and a stereo system that he updated every chance he got. But the rest came from the culture that had given birth to him so long ago.

She walked over to run her fingers over the carvings and inlays he'd done on the wooden beams, then gave him a reproachful look. "Why didn't you tell me you were an artist? When did you learn how to do this?"

"Winters were long where I was born. Most everyone had some kind of craft they worked on. I learned mostly from watching them."

Kerry wandered over to the glass case where the torque and matching bracelets were displayed, along with an ancient sword and handful of beads. She gave him a puzzled look. "I know this sounds crazy, but I swear I've seen jewelry just like these somewhere. Maybe on the History Channel?"

He waited in silence to see if she succeeded in teasing the memory free.

Then her face lit up. "I remember. It was all over the news late last year. An international team of archaeologists were excavating a burial dig and uncovered what they thought was the grave of a female warrior. They found her weapons and a set of jewelry very similar to this, but it disappeared between the site and the museum. The thieves were never caught."

When he didn't immediately reply, the dominoes started falling, leading her to one conclusion. "Oh my God, it was you. *You* stole them."

"They had no right to these." He opened the case and lifted out the torque. Tracing the pattern with his fingers, he remembered how it had looked on the woman in the grave.

"But how are we supposed to learn about the past if we don't study the artifacts we find in a cairn?" There was sympathy mixed with simple curiosity in her voice.

He forced his hand to relax enough to avoid crushing the torque, his memories burning his nerves raw. "Those so-called scientists learn nothing real from their studies. No matter how hard they try, how deeply they dig, they'll never know the sound of her laughter or that her eyes were the color of the summer sky. They might know what they see, but they won't know *her*. And for the sake of their stupid fairy tales, they desecrated the dead."

His pain washed over Kerry in waves and the truth finally hit her hard. "Oh, dear God, Ranulf! You knew her, the woman that necklace belonged to."

He closed his eyes against the memories. "She was my wife. The jewelry was my present to her on our wedding day. The sword was her gift to me."

Kerry stepped away from the case, wishing there

was some way to ease the pain Ranulf had endured seeing his wife's grave ripped open and put on display.

"Tell me about her." She tugged Ranulf toward the sofa. "What was her name?"

"Berta."

Although he stared down at the polished silver piece in his hand, Kerry had the feeling that he wasn't seeing it at all. He'd obviously loved the woman, and at that moment he was back in his past.

"How did you meet her?"

There, that was better. His mouth softened at the memory playing out in his head.

"Berta was a chieftain's daughter, used to every eligible warrior vying for her hand in marriage. She ran them all in circles, trying to curry her favor."

She could just imagine his response to seeing other men hovering around the woman he wanted. "Somehow I can't see you putting up with that."

His chuckle sounded wicked. "I didn't want to stand in line on the chance she'd finally take notice of me. Instead, I ignored her. Her father approved of my suit, so he helped make sure that I was around their home enough so she'd notice that I didn't act like those other lovesick fools. My indifference didn't set well with her, not at all."

"Obviously the ploy worked."

"Yeah, it did. We were married as soon as I could make the necessary arrangements."

"Did she ever figure out what you'd done?"

"She was smart, my Berta, and fierce. She forgave me eventually. I think the matching bracelets helped."

Kerry knew better. If his Viking bride had been that strong in her own right, she would have wanted a man whose strength had been a match for her own. Mere trinkets wouldn't have bought the chieftain's daughter's love. Kerry felt an unexpected kinship with the woman who had held Ranulf's heart all those years before.

"What happened to her?" She had to know.

His eyes dimmed to a pale gray as he stared down at the necklace. "She died while I was on a raiding voyage with her father."

He looked up, the blue in his eyes flaring brightly again. "You remind me of her. She was fierce in protecting those she cared about, and didn't tolerate fools well." He startled her when he reached out to fasten the torque around Kerry's neck.

"Ranulf, I can't wear this . . ."

"Not in public, no. There's a chance someone else would recognize it. But here, on my mountain, wear it for me."

Then he kissed her, burning away all thoughts of his past or their future, leaving only the now—and it was enough.

Chapter 13

$\mathcal{H}$is hunger for her was flame hot and spicy sweet. Ranulf's arms closed tight around her as he dragged her up onto his lap. She couldn't draw a full breath, but she'd never felt more alive, more real in her life.

She tangled her fingers in his hair, holding him close as he seduced her with a single kiss. There were so many reasons this shouldn't happen, but at that moment she couldn't think past the frenzied heat washing through her. This was no gentle enticement but an all-out assault on her senses, with the battle being waged with touch and taste and scent.

Skin, she needed her skin on his. Her efforts to rid him of his shirt met with only limited success until he broke off kissing her long enough to peel off the layers that kept them apart. When he pulled her close again, she moaned with the sweet feel of her breasts pressed against the rock-hard muscles of his chest.

It still wasn't enough, and maybe never would be unless she figured out some Kyth mojo that let her sink into his very being.

In a surprise move, he flipped her off his lap and onto her back on the sofa, following her down. The pillows cushioned her against his weight, but she wouldn't have cared. Right then, the need for full body contact between them outweighed small concerns like breathing or a few bumps and bruises.

He tasted desperate as he plundered her mouth. Between kisses he murmured words of desire, of wanting, some in English and some not, but their meaning was clear anyway. Finally, he pushed himself upright long enough to strip her jeans down her legs.

"I can't wait long enough to take you to my bed," he told her, the flames of desire burning bright in his indigo eyes. His wolfish smile might have frightened a lesser woman, but she was feeling pretty primitive herself.

"We'll get there eventually," he promised as he shoved his own pants down far enough for his erection to spring free.

"Take me here, lover. Take me now," she demanded, her body so very ready for his.

He did as she demanded, burying himself deep

inside her in one powerful stroke. The invasion stretched her almost to the edge of pain, but that didn't matter, either. She didn't know where this sense of desperation came from, but they were both feeling it. He rode her hard, bracing his arms on either side of her as he pounded his cock deep inside her again and again.

She loved the sheer power of her warrior lover. With each stroke he drove her higher and harder until the energy flowing between them burned with crystalline clarity. Then he stroked her just the right way to shatter them both.

Kerry screamed and thought maybe he did, too, as his climax pulsed and shuddered hot and deep inside of her. He collapsed beside her, all his tension and strength melting away as he held her close.

Ranulf closed his eyes and cursed himself for a fool. He'd taken Kerry with too much power and too little finesse—not that she was complaining. But he'd also come inside her without protection. They'd have to talk about the possible consequences, but for the moment, he wanted to hold off facing reality as long as possible.

Kerry stayed tucked in the crook of his arm, her head resting over his heart as he toyed with a strand of her hair. He didn't think she'd fallen asleep, but she was awfully quiet. Finally, he couldn't stand the silence any longer.

"Are you all right?"

She lifted her head up high enough to kiss his chin. "I'm more than all right."

"I didn't wear protection. There wasn't time." The words slipped out. But even if he was too blunt, it was the truth. They'd gone from zero to sixty in a heartbeat. All he'd been thinking about had been claiming her.

She brushed his hair back from his face with a gentle touch. "I know, but I think we should be all right. If not, I'll deal with it."

"Alone" was what she meant, as if he'd have no part of any decisions concerning the future of her child—no, their child. He closed his eyes, not wanting her to see the temper burning there. She had no reason to think he'd stick around; he'd told her that from the beginning.

But he was feeling pretty damn possessive, and not sure he liked the sensation. What kind of father could he be, much less a husband? And if Judith was right about Kerry's imminent role as Grand Dame of the Kyth, the idea of him as Consort was laughable. Most of their kind avoided any contact with him at all. Kerry wouldn't be able to function as their leader if no one trusted her choice of Consort.

Which brought him back to Sandor. He could just picture the sneaky bastard standing at Kerry's side with a child at their feet. *His* child. He abruptly rolled off the sofa, tugged his jeans back up, and reached for his shirt.

"Ranulf?"

Kerry sounded puzzled rather than hurt by his sudden departure. When he didn't immediately respond, she covered herself with an old quilt he kept on the back of the sofa. He hated the sudden unease in her eyes, as if she'd been embarrassed being naked while he was dressed.

"I thought I'd fix us something to eat." Piss-poor excuse, but it was the best he could come up with.

"I see." But she clearly didn't. "I'd like to take a shower, if that's all right."

Are you in a hurry to wash my scent off your skin, my seed from your body? His fingers dug into the palms of his hands to keep for reaching out to her. "The bathroom is off my bedroom."

"You don't have a guest room I can use?"

Son of a bitch, he really had offended her. "Nope. You already know I don't like sharing my space."

"Then why am I here?"

She managed to look haughty despite being wrapped up in that old quilt, her hair a mess, and with a good-sized love bite on her neck. But she was like a kitten swatting at a full-grown lion.

"You're here because it's where I wanted you to be."

She marched toward him. "Yeah, right. And that's why you're being so charming right now, you big jerk."

Her display of temper canceled his out, making him grin. Big mistake. She went on the attack.

"Okay, Ranulf, I don't know what your problem is, but *you* brought me here, so deal with it! You kissed me, and that led to what just happened on the sofa. We were careless, and that worries you. Fine—I got that. But you need to lose the attitude."

When she poked her finger at him, she sent a bolt of energy shooting straight at his chest. A lesser being would have found himself flat on his ass on the floor; even he staggered back half a step before he caught himself. The amazing thing was she was totally unaware of what she was doing.

"Judith was right." He reached out to cradle Kerry's hand with both of his.

"About what?" At least she didn't try to pull away.

"You have the same ability she has to use your energy to control Talions."

She hitched the quilt up higher on her shoulders. "If I have all these secret powers, why haven't they shown up before this? It's not like I haven't met other men who made me mad. You're just better at it."

He couldn't hold back a grin. "I'm glad you think I'm good at something."

A wicked gleam sparkled in her eyes as she gave him a slow once-over, pausing for a long time just south of his belt buckle before continuing on. "Oh, I can think of another thing or two you're good for."

If that look had been any hotter, his jeans would have spontaneously combusted! Maybe eating wasn't such a bad idea. He was going to need to keep up his strength.

"Go on and shower while I fix us something to eat. Then we'll have that talk you've been nagging about." He gave her the barest hint of a smile so that she'd know he was teasing.

"All right. Give me half an hour."

"How do you like your steaks?"

"Rare."

"Good choice."

He couldn't let her walk away without holding her again. She read his intent as clearly as if he'd announced his intentions out loud. And gutsy woman that she was, she met him halfway, letting the quilt fall to the floor. As soon as he touched her bare back, his hands slid south to cup her bottom. If he wasn't careful, they were going to end up right back on the couch.

It took all his considerable willpower to keep the kiss slow and easy; the embers were merely waiting to be fanned back into a full burn. When he broke away from her, she grinned up at him.

"Chicken," she teased.

"I need to keep up my strength if you're going to tempt me with your feminine wiles."

"All right, old man," she taunted him. "If you need time to rest up for the next round, I'll give you a break. And next time *I* get to be on top."

She flung the quilt around her shoulders like a cape, and as ridiculous as it looked, still managed to leave him standing there with his tongue hanging out.

Passion, anger, resentment, amusement, and desire all spun through him. He was on a roller-coaster ride that was out of control, but he liked it.

Time to get those steaks defrosting. Then he'd show her just what this old man was capable of.

"Want to go for a walk?"

Kerry looked up from the dish she was drying. "I'd love to."

"As the sun starts to go down it will get chilly. Let me get you something to keep you warm." He grabbed one of his flannel shirts, liking the idea of her wearing something of his.

She was waiting for him out on the porch. "It really is beautiful up here."

And she looked so at home there that it hurt. He held out the shirt and tried not to laugh at the way the sleeves hung down to her knees.

It didn't seem to bother her, though. She rolled them up and then held out her hand, and they walked in peaceful silence until they reached the game trail along the creek. As always, the quiet burble of the water was a balm for the stress of the past few days.

For the second time in five minutes, Kerry looked as if she wanted to say something but then thought better of it.

"I can't answer questions if you don't ask them."

"I don't want to pry."

He chuckled. "Sure you do. You're just not sure how to go about it."

"Okay, you caught me—but you must have questions about me, too. Turnabout will be fair play."

"It's a deal. Ask away."

She watched the water for a few seconds. "What do you do for a living?"

He hadn't been expecting that one. "Besides my duties for the Dame, you mean?"

"Yes. Surely your Talion job doesn't take up all that much of your time."

"The Dame pays all of her Talions enough to live on, but most of us have other sources of income. I'll never make the World's Richest Men list, but I've done all right with my investments. I also make jewelry to sell. Besides, my needs are simple."

"Okay, now ask me something."

"What was your childhood like? I'd like to know more about your family."

She went from relaxed to rigid in a heartbeat. He instinctively moved closer to her, wrapping his arm around her shoulders and pulling her close to his side.

"I already told you that I was adopted. My parents were unable to have children of their own. By the time they adopted me, they were already in their early forties. I know they did their best to love me, but I don't think they realized how much energy raising a child takes. They were so wrapped up in each other, they didn't have a lot left over for me. It didn't help that I wasn't cuddly, like little kids are supposed to be."

That hadn't been her fault. Kyth children raised by normal humans had a hard time because of their energy needs. "I bet you were adorable."

"If you like skinny kids with braces and perpetually skinned knees from doing everything at a dead run, I guess I was."

"So leaping without looking first isn't a new development in your life." He gave her a gentle squeeze. "I'd love to have seen you back then."

His words brought a soft smile to her face. "I've got pictures, if you want to see them sometime. And I bet you drove *your* poor mother crazy with all the mischief you got into."

He stared off into the trees, searching back across the years for a story to share with her. "My father was a bear of a man, probably outweighing my mother by almost double, but there was no doubt which of them was in charge. She was tough, but what I remember is her laugh. She'd play chase games with me but let me win. Then she'd grab me and we'd tumble to the ground in a fit of giggles and watch the stars in the sky. I miss them both still."

"Is losing people the worst part of living so long?"

There were no words to describe it, so he merely nodded.

"And what's the best part about being around this long?" She turned to face him, wrapping her arms around his waist and giving him a quick hug.

It was a time for honesty. "Meeting you."

Feeling a bit crowded by his own admission, without warning he swung her up in his arms, then stepped onto a large rock in the stream. Kerry squealed but then settled trustingly against his chest as he stepped from stone to stone. Once they reached the safety of the other side, he was reluctant to put her down. To delay that as long as possible, he shifted her around so that he could kiss her.

He loved the way she melted into his arms. Her mouth softened and then opened, enticing him to deepen the kiss as she wrapped her legs around his waist.

The scent of the surrounding firs mixed with the perfume that was uniquely Kerry. If the day had been only a few degrees warmer, he would have lain her down in the grass and taken her right there. Instead he did an about-face and headed right back across the stream. In his haste he almost slipped, barely keeping them from landing in the water.

Kerry giggled as he headed straight for his house.

"What's your hurry?"

"I want to get back inside . . . you."

Her eyes widened, then she kissed him long and hard. He moaned and gently pushed her back against a nearby tree to free up his hands to re-mind himself of all his favorite places on her body. "Damn, woman. Keep kissing me like that, and we're not going to make it to the house."

The little tease nipped his ear. "Would that be a bad thing?"

"Sorry, babe, but I'm not into bouncing around on this rocky slope, not even with you. It's hard on the knees, not to mention your sweet little ass. I wouldn't want it all bruised up." He gave her bot-tom a gentle squeeze.

She kissed her way along his jaw. "That wouldn't be a problem since it's my turn to be on top."

"That makes it even more important to use my bed. I spent too many nights sleeping on the cold, hard ground when I was a young man to find it romantic."

"I bet I could make you forget about those nasty rocks." She rocked back and forth, putting pressure right where he'd get the most pleasure out of it.

"Maybe, but we'll save that little adventure for another day." He slowly lowered her to the ground, loving each second their bodies rubbed against each other. "The house is just over the next rise."

"I'll race you!" She broke free and took off running.

He could have easily caught her, but it was more fun to let her win. She stopped on the porch to make sure he was right behind her before she bolted through the door and went straight for his bedroom, shedding her clothing as she ran. He caught a glimpse of a bare breast and a shapely leg before she disappeared around the corner.

She stole his breath away. Not just with her beauty, but with the way she made him laugh and with the warmth of her touch. There was heaven waiting for him in his bed and he didn't know what he'd done for the gods to grant him such a blessing, but he was boundlessly grateful.

"Are you coming?" She sounded a little exasperated.

"Not yet, but we both will be soon enough," he promised and reached for the top button of his shirt.

• • •

When he finally entered the room, he'd stripped off his clothes. She loved the sight of his warrior's body, with all its scars and the jutting arrogance of his thick, powerful arousal making it clear that he was there to claim her in the most elemental way. She wanted it hard and fast and right now.

"I need you over here." Her voice was husky and demanding. She scooted to one side, making room for him to join her.

He prowled over to her side of the bed. With blue heat lighting his eyes, he smiled. "What? No rope?"

She swallowed hard at the image that flashed through her head. "Not this time. Lie down."

"Make me." He braced his feet apart, an unspoken warning that he wouldn't make it easy for her.

Crawling across the king-sized bed, she slipped down onto the floor right in front of him, then ran her hands up the outside of his legs, keeping her eyes firmly on his face. When she repeated the maneuver up the inside of his legs, he closed his eyes and moaned. She cupped his sac in one hand, slowly grasped the hard length of him with the other, then gently squeezed.

He shuddered.

She smiled and did it again, only this time she added her tongue into the mix. Over and over again, she tasted and teased him until she couldn't wait anymore, then parted her lips and took him into her mouth.

She would have thought he'd been in pain if his big hand hadn't come down on the back of her head to encourage her to continue. She didn't have much experience in pleasing a man this way, but Ranulf didn't seem to have any complaints.

Then he abruptly lifted her to her feet. "You keep that up and it will be over before we really get started. Besides, it's my turn to play."

He eased them onto the bed, inflaming her with deep kisses, his tongue raking over hers. She loved the solid feel of him as he lay half sprawled over her, but a promise was a promise.

"On your back, Ranulf."

He obligingly rolled over, taking her with him. She centered herself over his erection, making both of them sigh with the sweet pleasure of it. Then she cupped her hands under her breasts and offered them up to his attention.

He suckled each in turn, using his teeth and his tongue to drive her crazy. She wanted, needed so much more. She rose up, riding his erection, teasing them both with the possibilities. When she'd driven them both to the edge of insanity, she shifted to take him deep inside her body. She slid down slowly, impaling herself with delicious slowness, savoring each long inch of the journey. Ranulf fisted his hands in the sheets, his head arched back on the pillow as flickers of energy danced over his skin and then over hers as their bodies merged into one.

She wasn't sure she'd survive the beauty of it, but she'd die happy.

It took her a few tries to settle into the right rhythm, then she was panting his name as she strove to push them both higher and higher, until she lost all control and coordination.

"Ranulf, please finish it. Finish me."

He didn't hesitate. He withdrew from her body only long enough to flip her over on her stomach. Grasping her waist with his powerful hands, he pulled her hips up to the right angle for him to take her deep and hard. She screamed with pleasure at the power of his thrusts as his belly slapped against her bottom. Over and over and over again, his body pounded into hers, his torso arched over her back, blanketing her with the strength and heat of his body.

This was her Viking lover unleashed, all vestiges of civilization stripped away, leaving behind only the primitive need to mate. Ranulf growled her name, his hand sliding up the center of her back, holding her still when she tried to turn to kiss him. Then he slid his other hand around the curve of her hip to find the damp curls between her legs. He found her small nub and rubbed it in counter rhythm to his thrusts, until the world burst wide open in an explosion of bright colors and the music of her name on her lover's lips.

Another thrust, and he joined her with a shout. An eternity later he withdrew from her body, rolled to his back, and tucked her next to his side.

He kissed the top of her head as she dozed off. "Sleep, Kerry. I have a feeling we're both going to need it."

Josiah walked into the living room, startling Judith. One minute she'd been lost in the past, and the next he was standing in front of her holding a cup of tea and a plate with a sandwich on it.

"One of these days I'm going to put a bell on you, Josiah. You could kill somebody my age, startling them like that."

"Yes, ma'am. But while you're still breathing, perhaps you could eat." He offered her a crisply ironed napkin, then set the plate on the table beside her. "Eat all of that and you might persuade me to offer you a piece of apple pie."

"You are a wicked, wicked man, Josiah."

He backed away a couple of steps. "Do you have everything you need? I could heat some soup to go with the sandwich."

"I'm fine. Why don't you see if the ball game is on and join me?"

"I'd like that."

He turned the game on to find that the Mariners had just scored and were ahead by three runs. The two of them settled into a comfortable silence, broken only occasionally when Judith disagreed with the umpire's call.

The bases were loaded when a pinch hitter belted one with a loud crack. She was cheering as the bases cleared, only to realize that the noise hadn't come from the television. Josiah sat slumped over in his chair, a splash of crimson spreading across the front of his white shirt.

Lurching to her feet, she hoped against hope that her ability to heal wouldn't fail her. She eased her servant, her friend, to the floor, trying to erase his pain.

"Don't waste energy on me!" he rasped. "Call Sandor . . . Ranulf. Too late."

She didn't know if he meant it was too late to help him or if it was too late to call for help. As she heard the front door swing open, she thought he was probably right on both counts.

She fumbled for her cell phone as she held Josiah's hand, shoving all the energy she could muster into him, hoping to staunch the bleeding.

"Hold on, Josiah. Don't leave me, please."

He smiled up at her. "I love you, you know. Always did, even when Rolf was alive."

"I know, Josiah." She'd always known and had

found comfort in his unwavering devotion. What she'd felt for him had been warm and good and essential in her life. And now it was almost too late to tell him. "I love you, too, Josiah. I don't know how I would have survived these past few years without you. I've been a lucky, lucky woman to have such good men in my life."

"Judith . . ." He whispered her name with his dying breath, breaking her heart.

She punched the speed dial on her phone, hitting Sandor's number, since he was the closest. He answered on the first ring. Bradan was already in the foyer, so there was no time for niceties.

"Bradan killed Josiah. I don't know how long I can hold him off. The wards are failing."

Then she hung up and punched Ranulf's landline number on the mountain. He was slower to respond, answering as Bradan stepped into the doorway. In all her long life, she hadn't known that evil could be both handsome and hideous at the same time.

She set the cell phone down, leaving the connection open as she stood to face her enemy. With a flick of her wrist, she sent a surge of power flashing across toward Bradan. He stumbled back, but only a single step. She'd burned up too much of her reserves trying to save Josiah. Under normal circumstances she could have stripped Bradan's energy to replenish her own, but whatever Bradan had been doing to prepare for this attack had made him strong—perhaps even stronger than Ranulf.

When Bradan realized he would be attacking from a position of strength, he started forward.

"Why did you kill Josiah? He never hurt you."

"Neither did the others I've killed. I just enjoy doing it." His eyes were alight with unholy glee.

"I don't want to hurt you, Bradan."

He laughed long and loud. "Don't take up lying for a hobby, because you're lousy at it. If you weren't older than dirt I'd be dead right now, fried to a crisp by one of those blasts of yours."

"Stay back, Bradan."

"Tsk, tsk. Why don't you come along peacefully? Even if you've called for backup, neither of your little pets will make it back here in time to save you."

Ranulf had obviously heard every word, because she could hear him bellowing from the small speaker on the cell.

"Where?" she asked, knowing it was unlikely that Bradan would be foolish enough to reveal his hiding place.

He responded by crushing her phone with the heel of his shoe. "Oh, I'm sure Sandor will be able to figure that out. He's been closing in on my location since yesterday—which has been part of my plan all along."

Retreating was both futile and undignified. Judith stood her ground, wishing she'd had enough left in her for one last blast—but that wasn't going to happen. When Bradan grabbed her arm, she made only a token resistance before allowing him to lead her from the house.

It was a shame her life had to end in such a way, but things didn't always turn out the way you planned. There was so much she could have taught Kerry to ease the young woman's way in the world of the Kyth, but Ranulf would see that she was taken care of. Sandor would help.

Bradan opened the car door for her, acting like the gentleman he'd always pretended to be. She slid into the front seat, glad that he spared her the indignity of tying her up.

When he joined her in the car, she studied his profile, wondering how they'd missed all that anger and viciousness for so long.

"Why, Bradan?" she asked.

"Because I like the taste of death, old woman. Yours won't have much spice, but then, you're just the appetizer. Sandor and Ranulf will be the main course." Then he reached over to squeeze her shoulder hard enough to hurt. "I'm saving the delicious Kerry Logan for dessert."

Judith closed her eyes and began to pray.

Kerry planted herself right in the doorway and prepared to do battle. "I'm coming, and if you don't get control of yourself, Ranulf Thorsen, I'll be the one driving!"

He loomed over her. "Like hell you will! I didn't drag you all the way up here just to have you charging back down the mountain to take on that rat bastard like some kind of tiny avenging angel!"

She ignored the crack about her size. Next to Ranulf, an offensive lineman would look small. "Just because we've had mind-blowing sex doesn't mean you get to make all my decisions for me, Ranulf. I'm going, so deal with it. What if you need my abilities when you face off with Bradan? A fat lot of good I'll do you parked up here in Valhalla West!"

Flames burned in his eyes as he growled, "I need to concentrate when Bradan and I fight. I can't do that and worry about keeping you safe."

"But what if he's stronger than you are? Can you and Sandor combine energies to fight?" She already knew the answer, but she needed him to face it.

He looked offended. "No, but I've never needed anyone's help to do my job. Now get out of my way. Judith won't last long once Bradan gets started."

"He shouldn't be able to hurt her at all, Ranulf. I may not know much about the Kyth, but she hasn't ruled for a thousand years unless she's very strong. If Bradan has her, it's because she couldn't stop him." She hated the pain and grief etched in Ranulf's face, but she had to make him understand.

"What if he's stronger than he used to be because he's been feeding nonstop?"

"Even if he has, so what?"

"So, it might take more than one of you to take him down. Especially if he manages to strip Judith of her energy."

Her arguments were getting through, because he quit trying to intimidate her.

"Damn it, Kerry, I can't fight and protect you at the same time. Don't ask me to try." He stepped through the door, chanting under his breath. When he was done, he turned back to face her one last time. "My duty is to our people—not one person. If you're there, you'll only interfere. Now get out of my way. Judith could be dying."

She marched off the porch, ignoring the strangest sensation of walking through spiderwebs. Skidding to a stop by the passenger door, she jerked it open and climbed in. "You of all people should know I'm stronger than I look. You might need my help. And even if you don't, Judith will need a healer."

He didn't say a word, but the look he gave her spoke volumes. Shoving the car in gear, he tore out, the tires sending up a spray of dirt and gravel behind them.

She let him stew until they reached the narrow forest road they'd taken only hours before. "Maybe I can hold him like I did you and Sandor." If she could figure out exactly how she'd accomplished that.

Ranulf shot her a look. "I guess it's time for the rest of that talk."

"I'm listening."

"Most of this you've heard before. Our people came out of the northern, cold climates. No one knows exactly when or where the gene first showed up that allowed us to use energy differently than other human species, and even among us there were variations."

She turned slightly in the seat to face him.

"Those who were lucky enough to be close together learned how to hide what they were and how to take only what energy they needed to survive. As with any human trait, some were better at it than others and survived to pass the gene along to subsequent generations. A few developed more specialized talents."

"Like you and Judith."

His mouth took on a grim set as he stared down the highway. "Yeah, lucky us." Then he looked straight into Kerry's eyes. "And lucky you."

Even though his calm declaration didn't come as a surprise, she didn't like it. But now wasn't the time to deny reality. "And I'm like Judith. I've got the secret superpowers that she has."

He nodded. "Judith sensed that you were something special, although she didn't warn Sandor or me about . . ." His words trailed off, making her wonder what Judith hadn't told them and why.

"But you didn't know until I stopped you and Sandor from fighting," she said. "That was all it took to convince you all that she was right."

"Hard to argue when the evidence has you immobilized." His mouth twitched as if he'd been fighting a grin. "The look on Sandor's face was pretty damn funny."

She closed her eyes and tried to recall the exact moment when Ranulf had known that the power had been coming from her and not Judith. It had taken Sandor longer to figure it out, but Ranulf had been furious. Not at her, but at Judith. Why?

"Judith was keeping more than just my abilities secret, wasn't she?"

"Like I said, our people have different abilities. Judith is the strongest Kyth to appear in all of the centuries of her life. But the more powerful the gift, the more unstable it can be. Before she met her husband Rolf, her ability to control her gifts was unpredictable to the point of being dangerous. The more you use your gifts, the stronger they become until they reach their full potential."

He turned westbound onto the interstate, falling silent until he cut across to the fast lane.

"When the gift is off-the-chart strong, it can rage out of control without outside help. Luckily, Judith met Rolf before she ran into any real problems. His gift stabilized hers. Judith's mother's gifts had done the same for her father's. Without the right Consort, Judith wouldn't have been able to serve our people as long as she has, and it's why she's fading now. She's literally burning out."

So Judith had sent her strongest Talions to keep Kerry safe. Fine. She could understand the older woman's desire to make sure a potential heir to her position was protected from attack.

But had she ordered them both to protect her for more than the obvious reason? Kerry added up all the facts and did not like the answer she was getting.

"She thinks one of you would make a good Consort for me, doesn't she?" And Kerry had obligingly taken Ranulf to her bed.

Ranulf had lapsed into a dark silence, going somewhere in his mind that she wasn't sure she wanted to follow. "There's more to it than that, isn't there? This has to do with your pledge to serve Judith."

After a few seconds, he slowly nodded. "I owed her my fealty and have served her long and well for a thousand years, never questioning my duty. But I need some peace in my life, and she'd promised that after this one last mission, I could retire for good. I wasn't counting on this . . . this . . . whatever this is between the two of us."

She didn't know what it was, either. She just

knew that it was strong and powerful and good, but Ranulf clearly had different ideas on the subject. Letting go was going to be far harder than she'd imagined. He'd served his Dame and their people in good faith. Although Kerry didn't know what her role with the Kyth was going to be, she did know that she had no right—they had no right—to ask more of this man.

It was time to change the subject.

"Should I call Sandor and see if he's been able to find out anything more on Bradan?"

Ranulf tossed her his cell phone. She scrolled to Sandor's number and pushed the Send button. He answered on the second ring.

"Where the hell are you two? I've been trying to call you for the past half an hour. Bradan took Judith prisoner."

"We know. We were out of cell phone service, but Judith reached us on the landline." She turned to Ranulf. "How long until we reach Sandor?"

"Thirty minutes, maybe a little more. Tell him we'll meet him at Judith's."

"Did you hear that?" she asked, then listened for a few more seconds before disconnecting the call.

"What did he say?"

Kerry felt sick. "He's at her house. Josiah's dead." She'd never been a vindictive person, but right now she prayed that Bradan suffered greatly for the pain he caused.

"Hurt him for me." Her fingers tingled and burned with the need to choke something. "Make him pay for all of this."

Ranulf reached out to cup the side of her face with a soothing touch. "This I will pledge to you: Bradan will die screaming for mercy."

"Good."

His Dame even bled with dignity, making Bradan hate her all the more. Bradan had worked her over pretty well, leaving her bruised and battered, yet Judith remained unbroken by both the pain and the promise of more to come.

"You're going to die."

Her eyes met his, the cold hatred burning in their depths with ferocious power. "I was dying long before you started playing your childish games, Bradan. Nothing you do will change that, except to hasten my final breaths." She coughed and wheezed. "May the gods themselves curse you for what you did to Josiah. He was not your enemy."

Bradan laughed. "He was foolish enough to serve you and your archaic attitudes, Judith. For that alone, he had to die. A new order is coming, and our people will rise up from the thralldom you've ensnared them in to take our real place in the scheme of things. Humans will learn to serve us or die."

"All you will succeed in doing is starting a war,

you fool. Humans will learn to fear our kind, and they destroy that which they fear. It was true a thousand years ago." Her breath came in wheezes. "It is true now."

He shrugged, tired of the discussion. In any war there were casualties, but the strong survived and flourished. "I have some arrangements to make. Save your strength." He patted her on the head. "You'll need it."

Sandor brought a clean sheet into Judith's living room to cover Josiah's body after Ranulf arrived. He'd already been through the room gathering as much information as he could, but the Viking might be able to sense something Sandor had missed.

He paced the hallway. What had the bastard been thinking by taking Kerry so far away? Even if Judith had ordered them out of her house, there had been other places to keep Kerry safe. But Ranulf wasn't thinking with his brain.

Closing his eyes, Sandor concentrated on easing the pounding in his head. It had been days since he'd slept through the night, the need to find Bradan driving him from his bed after only an hour or two of rest. He needed to restore his energy supply and soon, but when was he supposed to fit that in? Sometime between rescuing Judith and killing her kidnapper?

The squeal of tires jerked him out of his thoughts. Drawing his gun, he sidled up to the front window to make sure it was the Viking. Sure enough, that white tank he drove was parked out front, and Kerry was climbing out of the passenger side.

He threw open the front door, ready to rip Ranulf a new one. "Isn't that smart? You drive all the way to hell's half acre to get Kerry out of Bradan's reach and then bring her straight back here."

"Shut the hell up, Sandor. You can—"

"Stop it! Both of you."

Kerry got between the two of them but then instantly took Ranulf's side. "He tried to leave me on the mountain, but I make my own choices, Sandor. Both of you are feeling raw over Judith being kidnapped, and I understand that. But we're not going to do her any good if the two of you keep fighting each other instead of going after the real enemy here."

Though Sandor needed a target for his guilt and his anger, she was right. As tempting as it was to blame Ranulf, he hadn't been the only one who'd gone off, leaving Judith alone to defend herself. He should have argued more, but he hadn't.

Sandor forced his lungs to fill with air and let some of his tension drain away as he exhaled. "Come inside, Ranulf, and look around in case you can pick up anything from the room."

"Good thinking."

Ranulf entered the foyer and closed his eyes, remaining absolutely still for a few seconds before moving on to the living room. His breath came in short jerks, the only sign that Ranulf was disturbed by the sight of Josiah lying in a pool of drying blood.

Kerry started to follow him into the room, but Sandor blocked her with his arm. "Let him work alone."

When she spied Josiah's body, she uttered a soft cry. Feeling her raw pain, Sandor pulled her back against his chest and wrapped a protective arm around her shoulders. He thought she was crying; his time for mourning would come after he'd tasted revenge against Bradan.

The big redhead prowled back and forth across the room, pausing every so often to sniff the air or tilt his head, as if listening to a sound only he could hear. Finally, he returned to Sandor.

"There's not much to learn. Bradan shot Josiah from outside the window. I can feel the afterburn of Judith's attempt to stop the bleeding. Judging from the strength of the residue, she expended a great deal of her reserve energy before Bradan reached her."

Sandor had suspected as much. "Was there a struggle?" Had he hurt her?

Ranulf stared into the room for several seconds

before shaking his head. "No, the only violence I sense surrounds Josiah. I suspect Judith went along peacefully after making sure we knew what was going on."

Kerry pushed away from Sandor's embrace, rubbing the tears from her face. "Why would she do that? Give in to the man without putting up a fight?"

Despite the fury in Ranulf's eyes, he gentled his tone to answer. "It could be that she didn't have any energy left to fight with. Josiah's death would have hit her hard, maybe hard enough to leave her stripped bare. And if she'd resisted, that would likely have triggered more immediate violence from Bradan. She might have been trying to buy herself—and us—some time."

He spotted the sheet Sandor had brought in and picked it up. Stooping next to the dead man, he straightened the body and crossed the man's hands over his chest. After closing the butler's eyes, Ranulf murmured one of the old prayers and then spread the temporary shroud.

It was time to search for Bradan. "If you're done in here, Ranulf, I have some information to show you," Sandor said. "We finally have a lead on where Bradan went to ground."

In the dining room he stood back while Ranulf scanned the computer records. Sandor waited to see if the Viking came to the same conclusion he had. If he was following the paper trail correctly, Bradan had himself a nice little retreat high in the mountains. It didn't take long for Ranulf to finish reading the screen.

Ranulf's smile was a promise of violence to come. "Well, he's got balls, I've got to give him that much."

Something about his reaction seemed odd. "Why do you say that?"

"He's on the property right next door to my place."

Sandor thought he'd heard everything. "Are you sure? Did he know where you live?"

"I don't know, but you pass the turnoff to my place about half a mile before crossing his property line."

Kerry reached out to trace a twisting line on the map. "That state road we take to your home—where does it go?"

Ranulf slammed his fist down on the table. "In Bradan's case, the only place it will lead is straight to hell. Shall we go wish him bon voyage?"

For the first time in days, Sandor felt like smiling. "You bet."

Chapter 14

*T*he drive seemed to take an eternity, giving them plenty of time to worry about Judith. Kerry insisted that they make a short stop at a crowded restaurant at the edge of a town between the highway and the national forest. All of them had gone too long without eating a decent meal, and both men clearly needed to renew their energy levels.

As they waited for a booth and then for their food, Ranulf sat with his eyes closed and drew in deep, slow breaths, taking in energy. By the time the waitress returned with a heavily laden tray, the sickly pallor in Sandor's complexion had disappeared, too.

Neither of them wanted the delay, but they hadn't argued for long. They knew that going against their enemy in a weakened condition was a recipe for disaster. Although Kerry wasn't conscious of tapping into the life force of the humans surrounding them, her own nerves felt soothed. Or perhaps it came from being in such close proximity to the two Talions sitting on either side of her in the circular booth.

She had so much to learn about who and what she was to become. Already her previous life seemed distant and faded; only the immediate present was full of vivid colors and passions. The intensity of her feelings for Ranulf and even Sandor should have frightened her. Now, she wanted to embrace whatever it meant to be Kyth.

She only hoped they lived through the next twenty-four hours. After swirling her last steak fry through the ketchup, she popped it in her mouth and pushed her basket back. Then she swiped one of Ranulf's fries and gulped it down.

"Hey!" He moved the rest of his food out of her reach. "How can a little thing like you pack it away like that and stay so thin?"

She liked the momentary amusement sparkling in his eyes. "I've been burning a lot of extra calories during vigorous exercise lately."

The look she gave him sizzled with heat and made him shift restlessly in his seat. There would be retribution later, she was sure—definitely something to look forward to.

"Ahem." Sandor cleared his throat. "Do I need to remind you two that a) you're in a restaurant, not a motel; and b) we have more important things on our mind than . . . that?"

Kerry couldn't help herself. She giggled. Listening to the sophisticated Talion stumble over the word *sex* hit her as funny, though maybe that was just a release for some of the stress. At first Sandor looked insulted, but then he slowly smiled and shook his head. Ranulf snaked his arm around her shoulders and pulled her into the haven of his warmth.

Ranulf gave her one last squeeze before sliding out of the booth. "I guess it's time we go." He offered her a hand, which she gladly accepted. There was no telling how their mission was going to turn out, and she wanted every second she could with her lover.

Just that quickly, the fear was back. "This is going to be bad, no matter how it turns out, isn't it?" She looked from Sandor and then back to Ranulf, reading the truth in the shuttered looks in their eyes.

Ranulf grasped the talisman at the same time Sandor reached for his. "Bradan will die tonight, Kerry. This we swear."

She believed them, but that didn't mean he would be the only one to die on the mountain. How could she bear to lose Ranulf when she'd only just found him? Her heart ached with the need to hold him, to tell him her truth, and it took her a second to realize that Sandor was talking.

"You two go on out. I want to get some coffee to go." Sandor picked up the check and headed for the register.

Ranulf tugged her toward the door. He leaned down close to whisper, "I think that's Sandor's way of giving us a few minutes alone. Let's not waste them."

Outside, the sky to the west was ablaze with color. Behind them, the mountains were already shrouded in darkness. The natural beauty registered only faintly as Ranulf led her to the shadows under the trees.

There she threw herself at him, unwilling to allow even air to separate them. Then she was in his arms and his tongue was demanding entry to her mouth, the need for touch, for taste, for this burning heat so exquisite and oh, so precious.

"Kerry!"

"Ranulf, please!"

Her name became his mantra, her ragged whisper the amen to his prayer. Tangling her fingers in his hair, she held on as he plundered her mouth. He swept her up in his arms and crossed to a picnic table in a few long strides to set her down on the edge.

Without asking for permission, he nudged her knees apart and stepped in close enough to let her feel how much he wanted her, needed her. There wasn't time for more than a hurried embrace, but if this was their last moment together, he wouldn't waste it worrying about finesse.

She rewarded his audacity by wrapping her legs around his waist as he lowered her back down onto the rough-hewn table. Her hands were everywhere, caressing his arms and then busy digging her fingers into the muscles of his back. He did his own fair share of touching, palming the fullness of her breast, cupping her bottom, lifting her tighter against his erection.

He drove her higher, wanting to feel her coming in his arms, wishing their clothes to perdition so that he could bury his cock in the welcoming heat of her body. Even if he couldn't satisfy himself, he wanted to hear her cry out her release to the heavens.

He thrust against her again and again, until the friction threatened to ignite the cool mountain air. Finally, he yanked down her zipper and slipped his hand between them to settle at the junction of her legs. She was slick and wet and so ready for him. By the gods, this woman was enough to bring a man to his knees.

"Come for me, Kerry." Her body clenched tight around the two fingers he eased inside her, as he was loving the way she whimpered with pleasure as he stroked her, loving the way she clung to his shoulders, loving the way she kissed him as if she could devour him completely, just plain loving her.

He hadn't realized he'd said that last part out loud until her eyes flashed open to meet his. She stilled in his arms and captured his face with the soft touch of her fingers. "I love you, too, Ranulf. I need you to know that."

He closed his eyes to whisper a prayer to his gods that they keep this woman safe from harm. She held his heart in her hands, and if she was to die, he would surely follow her footsteps right to Valhalla. Then he sent her flying over the edge, capturing her cry of release with one last kiss.

When he could again think coherently, he helped her up off the table and waited while she straightened her clothes. He wasn't sure what to say but couldn't regret telling her the truth of his heart.

It wouldn't change anything. Bradan still needed to die. Judith needed to be rescued. And once the dust settled, Kerry would need to find her place among the Kyth.

As for him, he would return to his mountain— but it would no longer be his refuge, but his prison.

If anyone else had been driving, Sandor would have insisted that they have the headlights on as they wound up the mountain on the narrow forest service road. But either Ranulf had superior night vision or he knew the road so well that he didn't need to see more than the few feet ahead of the car. The way he was slamming around the curves, you'd have thought it had been high noon instead of pitch-black outside.

"The turnoff to my place is just ahead. We'll stop there to pick up a few weapons and park Kerry inside my wards. They'll keep Bradan out." He added that last part under his breath, obviously hoping the silence in the backseat meant she was asleep.

No such luck. "We've already had this discussion, Ranulf. Leave me if you want to, but I'll just follow."

The Viking snorted. "And you'll be lost within ten yards of the house."

"No, I won't. I'm betting I can follow your energy signatures right up to Bradan's front door."

Now *that* was a handy talent to have, Sandor thought. Maybe she was bluffing, but he'd bet Ranulf wouldn't take that risk. Better to keep her close than worry about what she'd stumble into alone.

"Fine, but you'll take orders without question. If either of us tells you to duck or run like hell, you'll do it. Got that?"

The soft glow of the dashboard illuminated her face enough that Sandor could see her smile. She laid her head on Ranulf's shoulder briefly, telling him without words that she knew how hard it was for him to let her put herself in danger.

"I'll be the fleetest of the fleet."

The car lurched off the road, following a path that only Ranulf could see. Sandor could feel the grasping fingers of the Viking's wards. They tested him, trying to determine if he was friend or foe. He could understand their confusion, since he wasn't sure which side he belonged on.

The sticky pressure of Ranulf's magic increased as they neared the house, to the point he wasn't sure he could get out of the car.

"Uh, Ranulf?"

"What? Oh, sorry." The other man cursed and returned to the car as soon as he recognized the problem. He murmured under his breath for a few seconds until the threads holding Sandor prisoner gradually faded away.

Kerry had climbed out of the driver's door. "What was that all about?"

Sandor followed Ranulf into the house. "It's his protective wards. They're designed to keep people off his property and out of his house. He forgot to release them before we got this close."

"I never felt anything."

"I suspect he feels differently about you than he does me, and his wards recognize that." He shouldn't have been surprised, considering his own serious doubts about Ranulf.

Ranulf came back into the room. "I know you brought your gun, but do you need knives or explosives?"

"Yes, I'll take these." Sandor reached for the matched set of knives Ranulf offered him. There was no faulting the Viking for his choice of weapons, all first class and lethal.

"I'll lead the way. I've passed by the house a few times in my wanderings. It's a one-story frame house, probably two bedrooms, kitchen, living room and not much else. There's a door on the back side, as well. The house has been vacant for years, but I obviously haven't noticed any activity over there. If he's made modifications, I wouldn't know about it."

"There's no time like the present to find out." Sandor checked his gun, then slipped the knives through his belt.

Ranulf turned the lights off. "Once we get within sight of the house, we can decide how to make our approach."

Out on the porch, he placed Kerry's hand on the back of his belt. "Once we get moving I want you to hold on to me, and no unnecessary talking."

"Okay." She looked at both of them, her dark eyes huge in the night. "Both of you promise to be careful. I don't want to lose either of you to that madman."

Ranulf immediately pulled her into his arms for a quick hug before starting off into the darkness with Kerry tagging along, taking two steps for each one of his.

• • •

The moon had risen overhead, lightening the shadows among the firs. Ranulf could feel Sandor moving off to his right. Judging from his energy reading, the younger Talion was stone-cold ready to fight and die for the cause. That was good, considering the monster who was waiting for them up ahead. Sandor usually did battle with words, not bullets and blades, but he'd stand his ground.

Ranulf had never faced a renegade and doubted his ability to take the bastard out, but Bradan wasn't the typical renegade. Not only was he a Talion with his own enhanced powers but he'd also been feeding deeply on the darkest energies imaginable. Bullets might slow him down, but they wouldn't stop him. And he'd already had hours of time to work on Judith, the strongest of their kind. Guilt burned deep in Ranulf's gut.

Kerry had been right to make them stop and replenish, though. They couldn't afford the handicaps of exhaustion and low energy.

The trees were thinning out. He slowed his steps and gave a low whistle to signal Sandor to wait. When Kerry and the Talion were right next to him, he whispered, "Wait here. I'll scope the place out."

He took off at a ground-eating lope through the trees. Bradan's house was only a short distance ahead, no more than a hundred yards. The forest had been clear-cut in a large circle around the building, but with luck they could get within sprinting distance before having to leave the cover of the trees.

Hiding in the silence and shadows, Ranulf studied Bradan's base of operations. The house had the same abandoned look as the last time Ranulf had seen it. The only difference was that right now it lit up the clearing like the beacon of a lighthouse, warning all who approached of danger.

Did Bradan feel so secure that the labyrinth of false names and hidden payments would have insulated him from discovery? No, that didn't feel right. He'd just wanted to make sure that only the right people found him. Knowing Bradan's ego, he probably had a welcome mat with their names on it laying on the porch.

It was time to end his games.

Sending out tendrils of energy to study the house, Ranulf recoiled at the murky blackness that came rushing back at him. Death had its own flavor that hung in the night air. The brightness of the electric lights did little to dim the darkness of the soul that clung to the house in thick waves.

Ranulf fought against the impulse to go charging in, his weapons drawn and ready to fight to the death with the evil inside. As much as he preferred the role of lone gunman, this time he would be risking far more than his own life. He had Kerry and even Sandor to consider, not to mention the hostage. Judith would most likely be the first to die at Bradan's hands, but not the only one if the three of them didn't attack in concert.

So be it. He faded back into the trees to rejoin his team. Despite his orders, they'd followed his trail toward the house, but at least they'd stayed back far enough to remain hidden.

"How bad is it?" Sandor asked.

"Bad enough. We'll have cover until the last twenty yards. We'll split up and make a slow approach, then run like hell when we have to break cover."

"I'll take the front." Sandor had his gun in one hand, a knife in the other.

Ranulf measured the resolve in Sandor's dark eyes. "Anxious to play hero?"

The Talion sent a burst of disapproval in Ranulf's direction. "No, but I figure you stand a better chance of protecting Kerry."

Ranulf rarely apologized, but he tried this time. "Good thinking. We'll separate when we reach the edge of the trees."

He pulled a smaller version of the gun he carried and handed it to Kerry. "Do you know how to use one of these?"

She nodded. "I took a self-defense class a couple of years ago, but I haven't practiced in a while."

"At least that's something." He checked it over before showing her the safety and how to click it off.

"Sandor, we'll give you time to attract Bradan's attention and then hit the back. Good luck."

He offered his hand to Sandor and was relieved when the Talion accepted the gesture. Kerry immediately hugged Sandor, kissing him on the cheek. The Talion grabbed her up in his arms for a quick hug and an even quicker kiss on the lips. When he set her down sputtering, Sandor grinned at Ranulf in the darkness.

"Watch your backs, you two."

"Watch yourself, Sandor. Don't do anything stupid." Like try to be a hero, which would likely get him killed.

"I won't." Sandor moved out, the night swallowing him up.

As soon as he was gone, Kerry reached up to run her fingers along the side of Ranulf's face, her touch a soothing balm.

He smiled down at her, loving her fierce determination. "Let's go. We don't want Sandor to get all the glory."

She reached for Ranulf's hand. If his touch comforted her, he wouldn't argue. And truth be told, the warmth of her fingers entangled with his felt pretty damned good.

Judith's lungs weren't working without a great deal of effort, and pain had taken over her world. Bradan's face was so twisted with evil that it would have been difficult to recognize him if she'd passed him on the street.

Toward the end of the last bout of torment, he'd kept pausing every so often to listen. When he hadn't heard whatever he'd been listening for, he'd cursed and then started in on her again with more fury and enthusiasm. If there had been a square inch on her body that hadn't been bruised or bleeding, he hadn't found it. Yet.

Death was coming for her, and regrets filled her mind. She should have done better by Ranulf, but she'd tried at the end. She hoped he was smart enough to grab onto the love Kerry Logan had for him.

Sandor would hate that, because he only saw the darkness in Ranulf, not the strength and the honor that went bone deep in her Viking warrior. That was her fault, too. If she'd used Sandor the same way she'd used Ranulf, he would have lost some of that slick polish, but he'd have been stronger for it.

And she should have been up front with Kerry from the beginning. If they'd really talked while they'd had the chance, she could have better prepared Kerry to serve as Grand Dame. There was so much she needed to learn about the Kyth, but at least she'd bring a fresh eye to their problems. With both Ranulf and Sandor to support her, she'd do fine.

Bradan's laughter rang out in the living room overhead. She shuddered, fearing for whoever had caught his attention this time. He'd spent a long time telling her how he'd perfected his art with scalpels and probes by practicing on human victims. He practically vibrated with the energy he'd harvested.

Maybe she could draw his attention back to her. If she succeeded, it would give the innocent human time to escape or give her Talions more of a fighting chance.

Focus, Judith, focus. It took every bit of willpower to shove the pain and the fear to the back of her mind, keeping the last vestiges of her powers at the forefront. She'd never make it up the steps, but Bradan didn't know that. All that was required was the appearance of an escape attempt.

One after another, her restraints snapped. Being able to move again sent a new upsurge of pain ripping through her, but she felt it only at a distance. Death already had her in his grip, her fumbling steps only a short distance ahead of him. She stumbled toward the staircase and deliberately knocked over the metal instrument tray, sending it clattering across the floor.

If Bradan heard it, he didn't react. Desperately, she looked for something else. There were bottles of chemicals in a cabinet with glass doors. The gods only knew what was in them, but if they produced poisonous gases, so much the better. Holding on to the wall for support, she crossed to the cabinet and tried the doors.

Locked. Closing her eyes, she sent one last energy burst to reinforce the strength of her unbroken left hand and slammed it through the glass. She unlatched the lock from the inside and let the doors swing open. One after another, she shattered the bottles, making as much noise as possible.

This time Bradan came charging down the stairs, but only halfway. "You'll pay for that, you stupid bitch, but so will both of your Talions. And when I'm done with them, I'll start in on Kerry. I'm betting I can keep her alive for days, maybe even weeks. So know that your little tantrum is going to cost them."

She didn't have enough breath left to talk, so she let another bottle fly in answer to his threats. They both knew that nothing she did would change his plans.

He started down another step, then abruptly stopped, as if he'd been a puppet and someone had pulled his strings. He struggled briefly, then gave in and backed up the stairs.

"Your friends are here, Judith. I hope you live long enough to greet them properly."

Then he was gone. She wilted to the floor, knowing she'd done all she could. May the gods grant that it was enough.

• • •

Judith's little tantrum was most vexing. Bradan charged back downstairs and hauled her body back up to the living room. She was barely breathing, but she'd served her purpose by drawing his enemies out into the open.

He could feel them sneaking around, thinking they were camouflaged by the trees. He paused in the kitchen to reach out and taste the invaders' energy. Sandor was alone, but there was a mixed signature coming from the back of the house. Ranulf, judging by the strength of the power, but he wasn't alone. He'd brought Kerry right to Bradan's doorstep.

Which one would attack first? Sandor or Ranulf? Not that it mattered. Bradan could take on all of them at once. He was that strong, that deserving of the gods' blessing. Who else had sacrificed so many for the glory of the Kyth? Ranulf, probably, but not within such a short time period.

Ah, Sandor must have drawn the short straw, getting to play sacrificial lamb while Ranulf got to be the real hero.

Bradan turned toward the living room and used a bit of his energy to unlock the door from across the room. A few seconds later, the doorknob started to turn.

"I'm coming for you, Talion. Surrender now or die!"

Bradan smiled. Sandor was so damn honorable

that he actually followed the protocols of ritual combat among their people. How had he managed to live this long, if he'd always warned his enemies he was coming?

Calling his dark energy to full power, Bradan widened his stance and waited.

Chapter 15

Sandor swallowed hard and braced his shoulders. The door lock clicked open, which meant Bradan was expecting him. They had known it was unlikely they'd get this close without alerting him to their presence.

Pulling his gun, he called, "I'm coming for you, Talion. Surrender now or die!"

Laughter was not what he expected as an answer, but then Bradan was crazy. There was no telling what he was capable of at this point. Sandor gave the doorknob a quick turn and shoved it open, bringing up his gun at the same time, his finger twitching on the trigger. The sight waiting for him was simply indescribable in its horror.

Bradan stood over Judith, her face barely recognizable through the bruises and the blood. He spread his hand wide, ready to finish her off if Sandor made the wrong move.

Check and stalemate. Sandor stood his ground and waited for Bradan to make the next move.

The next few minutes would decide who would live and who would die.

Gripping the talisman at his throat, Ranulf sent a silent prayer upward. *Please, Thor and Odin, keep the women safe and give your warriors courage in the face of death!* The hammer burned hot in his hand, his prayer heard.

"Stay behind me," he warned Kerry, making it clear that his word was law now.

The bright glow from the kitchen window cast her face in stark relief as they scurried past. Her eyes reflected her grim determination to do battle against one of the most dangerous foes he'd faced in his long, long life. No one would look at this petite woman and not see her fierce spirit burning bright. He wanted to kiss the hard slash of her sweet mouth and tell her how proud he was of her courage, but time was running out.

He motioned for her to press herself against the back wall of the house. When she'd done so, he looked inside the window. The kitchen was empty, but in a house this small, Bradan couldn't be far.

"Stand back while I kick the door in. Give me a chance to clear the way before following me."

Kerry moved into position, her eyes burning

with energy, her expression determined. "He won't get past me."

Please, gods, don't let it come to that. He kept his gun drawn but didn't expect to use it for the kill. When a Talion killed his own kind, it was hands-on work, up close and very personal. Especially this time.

On the second kick, the lock broke free of the jamb and the door slammed open, banging against the wall. Ranulf was through it with Kerry behind him out of the line of fire, leaving him free to go after their prey.

A short hall led toward the back of the house in one direction and the front in the other. There was no question which way to go, because he could see Bradan as soon as he looked toward the living room.

Sandor was holding the bastard at bay. But with Bradan's fingers splayed on Judith's face, he couldn't do much more than glare at Bradan without further endangering her life.

"Kill . . . dead anyway." The harsh sound of the Dame's whispered order echoed in the room.

Hearing her sound that way was like walking on broken glass. Ranulf wanted to deny her final request, but he'd served her too long to refuse her now.

He dropped his gun to the floor, hoping the clatter would distract Bradan for a second or two. No such luck. The Talion's grip on Judith tightened briefly. She didn't even whimper as he stripped more of her energy. Then in a surprise move, he flung her body aside and brought his hands up, one pointed toward Sandor, the other right at Ranulf.

A blast of energy burst from his fingertips, heading straight at where Sandor had been standing only a heartbeat before, leaving a smoking hole in the carpet. Ranulf sent a return shot of power at Bradan that should have fried the bastard on the spot.

Instead he deflected the jolt, redirecting it right at Ranulf along with a boost of his own energy. It shimmered along Ranulf's skin, burning but doing no permanent harm. Bradan must have been living and breathing dark energy round the clock for days to put that much power behind a single charge.

He felt Kerry moving up beside him at the same time Bradan spotted her. Ranulf would have shoved her back, but he couldn't afford to break his concentration. Sandor saved the moment by going on the attack while Kerry laid her hand on Ranulf's arm, sending her own powerful energy coursing through him to blend seamlessly with his. Where had she learned that trick?

Bradan blocked both attacks again, this time absorbing their energy instead of deflecting it. His face lit up with unholy joy as he taunted them. "Is that the best you've got? If I'd known it was this easy to take on Judith's precious elite enforcer, I would have done this years ago!"

"Wish you had, Bradan. It would have saved us putting up with you for all this time." Ranulf met him smile for smile.

"Ah, but then I would have missed the chance to meet Miss Logan." He gave her a lingering look that made Ranulf see red and then black.

They had to figure out a weakness soon.

Kerry stepped away from Ranulf, making herself into a target while she tried her best to plaster Bradan against the wall. For the first time, Bradan's shields flickered, forcing him to retreat a couple of steps. Ranulf joined and went on the attack while Sandor did the same.

Slowly, inexorably they went after Bradan, but then he managed to tap in to more of his energy and returned their attack with interest. Each blow he landed shorted out more of their ability to retaliate, until he got in a lucky shot and hit Sandor square in the chest. Kerry screamed as the Talion collapsed in a boneless heap. If Ranulf hadn't grabbed her, she would have gone charging right into the line of fire to get to the fallen Talion's side.

Ranulf dropped back a few steps, dragging Kerry with him, hoping to lull Bradan into thinking they had been seriously weakened at the loss of Sandor's energy. He hadn't fought and won such battles beyond count without learning a few tricks.

Reaching down deep, he turned his rage into a burning cold fire, letting the pressure build, knowing this would be his one shot to burn Bradan right down to the ground. If necessary, he'd go down with him, but this shit was going to stop.

Now.

Judith hadn't moved since Bradan had thrown her to the floor, and from this angle Kerry couldn't tell if Sandor was breathing or not.

The air between Ranulf and Bradan coalesced in swirls of energy, arcing and hissing, sometimes bulging toward her lover and sometimes toward Bradan. It was a standoff, one that frightened her more than the earlier blasts of power that had bounced around the room, leaving holes in the wall and smoldering burns in the old shag carpet. At least one had left her feeling a little fried around the edges, but otherwise unharmed.

How could she help Ranulf? She focused on Bradan, studying the monster who had caused so much pain and death.

Her shoulders tingled and stung, the sensation just shy of pain as it radiated down her arms to her fingers. Instinct made her splay her fingers wide, her eyes narrowing as she searched for a vulnerability in Bradan's defenses. There, despite the thickening haze in the room, she could see his lower legs clearly.

She sent the energy spiraling out of her fingertips in a lightning-quick strike at the side of Bradan's knee. He screamed, the outpour of his power faltering and flickering. She sent another burst, alternating with Ranulf's darker blend of power.

When Bradan fell to his knees, Ranulf hollered a battle cry and went charging forward, only to see Sandor scramble to his feet and dive onto his former friend, his face flushed red with hatred and rage. As the two men grappled, Ranulf held Kerry back.

"Don't touch them, Kerry. I doubt Sandor would even recognize you right now, and Bradan wouldn't give a damn if he killed you."

The battle rolled toward the other side of the room, giving Kerry room to finally get to Judith. With Ranulf's help, they carefully carried the Dame to the safety of the kitchen. Her skin was cold and blue, her breathing horrifyingly shallow and infrequent.

Kerry tried to piece together enough energy to share with the older woman. Ranulf's hand came down heavily on her shoulder, sharing what he could from his own reserves before running back to help Sandor. His warmth washed over her, through her, and into his Dame. Though Judith soaked up the healing energy like a desert thirsting for rain, it clearly wasn't enough to free her from death's grasp.

But her pained expression slowly transformed into peaceful repose, the bruises and swelling fading to reveal the elegant beauty below. Kerry gently brushed the hair back from Judith's face as the injured woman's eyes fluttered open. At first she looked confused, but then she smiled so sweetly that it brought tears to Kerry's eyes.

"Don't waste any more of your power on me, young lady. You're going to need all you can muster if you're going to take my place." Judith's eyebrows drew together in a worried look. "You will, won't you? The Kyth will need your strength to get them through this."

How could she deny a dying woman's request? "I'll try, Judith. It's all I can promise."

"Take my talisman. It should be yours." Her hand fumbled at the neckline of her sweater to grasp her necklace. "I hope life brings you joy, Kerry Logan."

Kerry helped Judith remove the necklace. It felt warm and heavy, as if the responsibilities and burdens of being Dame had been absorbed by the metal itself. When Judith closed her hand over Kerry's there was a blinding flash, followed by a montage of images flooding into Kerry's mind, one after another, faster than she could make sense of them. Her stomach lurched and rolled, as if she'd been on a roller-coaster ride. Finally they slowed down and settled into her head as if they'd been her own memories, instead of belonging to a woman whose life had spanned a millennium.

When the imagery finally stopped, Judith smiled again. "My history. Our people's history. Now it is yours, Kerry Logan. May the gods bless you and give you long life."

The Dame's wounded body was wracked with another spasm of pain, clouding her expression once again. "Where's Ranulf? I must set him free of his oath to me . . . served me so well . . . not fair to him." She grasped Kerry's hand in a painful grip, her gaze desperate. "Tell him I was proud to call him friend."

Kerry blinked back her tears. "I'm sure he knows, Judith, but I'll tell him you said so."

The light in Judith's eyes dimmed. "Sandor will have a hard time with all of this . . . Bradan . . . and especially your love with Ranulf . . . Takes a strong woman to convince a strong man that he needs her . . ." She coughed and drew a ragged breath, then tried again. "Needs you more than his freedom."

Then there was silence. Tears burned acid hot as Kerry eased Judith down to the floor, closing the faded blue eyes with a gentle touch. Bowing her head, she prayed for Judith and so many things.

When she whispered "Amen," she sat in silence for several seconds before realizing that the whole house was silent. Had the fight ended? *Dear God, please let my Talions be all right.*

Grabbing hold of Judith's talisman, she charged

to the rescue. As she rounded the corner, she came to an abrupt halt.

The three men were locked together in a battle to the death, so entwined that it was impossible to tell where one ended and the next began. Kerry circled around the tangle, looking for an opening, some way to help her friends without breaking their concentration.

It was obvious that Bradan was on the losing end. Sandor had his hands around Bradan's throat and face, his expression grim. Ranulf had talked of stripping a renegade of his energy, but hearing about it and seeing it happen right before her were two different things.

The skin on Bradan's face had drawn so tight that he looked like a skull stripped down to bone, his lips pulled back over his teeth, his jaw locked open in a silent scream.

"Damn it, Sandor, let me finish it!" Ranulf was bruised and cut, but he seemed unaware of the blood dripping down his cheek as he tried to pry Sandor away from Bradan.

"*Mine*, damn it. He killed Judith!" Sandor shouldered Ranulf aside. "He deserves to suffer like his victims did."

"No, Sandor! He deserves to die, but make it swift and clean. You'll hate yourself for what you're doing."

But Sandor's eyes glowed and flickered with

sparks of deep red. Energy pulsed and writhed across his hands and up his arms, leaving smoking black streaks in its wake. The sight of it flickering under his skin left Kerry feeling nauseated and dizzy.

Bradan's death stretched out for an eternity. His skin slowly lost all color, his bones their substance, until finally all that was holding him up was Sandor's death-giving hold on him. Finally, the last of his breath left his body in a single rush of smoke and air.

He was dead—the enemy vanquished. All that was left was an empty shell that collapsed in on itself when Ranulf finally succeed in prying Bradan's skull from Sandor's grip.

Sandor's dark eyes were wild and unfocused, as if he no longer recognized his surroundings. He held his hands up in front of his face, grief slowly combining with horror across his face.

Ranulf caught him in his arms, holding him close as Sandor's body shook from the effects of what he'd done.

"Get the door." Ranulf muscled Sandor up into his arms. "We need to get him out of here."

Kerry gestured in the direction of the kitchen. "But what about—"

Ranulf shook his head. "I'll come back later, but we need to get Sandor out of here now."

She opened the door. "Go ahead. I'll be right behind you."

"Make it quick or I'll come drag you out." His words were gruff, but the worry was real.

"Five minutes, I promise."

As soon as he hauled Sandor through the door, Kerry hurried through the house turning off lights. The last thing they needed was for it to act like a beacon.

She left the stove light on in the kitchen, not wanting to leave Judith alone in the cold, dark night. After saying another small prayer, she hurried out the front door.

They'd fought the battle they'd come to fight. Now it was time to mourn their dead and move on.

And say good-bye to the one man she'd give anything to spend her life with.

The trip through the woods had been a rough one. The battle had left Sandor weak and sick at his stomach. After stopping twice for him to heave up the remains of his dinner, they'd finally made it back to Ranulf's house. They'd headed straight for the bathroom.

"Damn it, Sandor, stand up."

Ranulf wanted to smack the man, but it was no fun beating up on someone who was already being harder on himself than Ranulf could possibly be. The killing rage that had possessed Sandor had worn off, leaving him badly shaken by what he'd done.

"Brush your teeth and do whatever else you need to do. I'll wait in the hallway."

He was still waiting for Kerry to get back from Bradan's. She'd promised to be only a few minutes, but the five she'd promised had already stretched to double that. If she didn't show up soon, he was going to go back after her.

What had been so damned important that she'd lingered at Bradan's house of pain and death? Judith. That had to be it, because it had damned near killed him to leave the Grand Dame behind. He reached out with his senses, and felt Kerry's approach. Something about her felt different, but familiar at the same time. What was up with that?

The bathroom door opened, and Sandor came lurching out. Ranulf quickly pulled the younger man's arm around his neck and helped him put one foot in front of the other until they reached the living room. He slowly lowered Sandor onto the couch and covered him up with the same quilt Kerry had used earlier.

"Thanks, Ranulf." Sandor covered his eyes with his forearm, shutting out the dim light in the room. "I owe you."

"No, you don't. We were there to do a job, and we did it. Nothing more, nothing less." He fought the urge to pat Sandor's shoulder, knowing the man wasn't ready to accept sympathy yet.

"Bradan deserved to die, but—"

The front door opened, and Kerry stepped into the room. She looked like hell, but just the sight of her soothed Ranulf's soul. Her heart and her courage humbled him.

Sandor rolled on his side toward the back of the couch.

Kerry tiptoed past the couch after giving Sandor a worried look. "Is he okay?"

"Not yet, but he will be. He's a Talion for good reason." Ranulf pitched his voice loud enough to carry. Sandor wasn't ready to talk about the evening's events, but eventually he would have to come to grips not with what he'd done but how he'd done it. Hopefully he would be strong enough to live with that burden.

Kerry's eyes looked unutterably sad, the color in her face washed out.

He needed to hold her. "I don't know about you, but I think we should all get some rest."

Especially with her tucked in next to him. He was almost afraid to ask, because she'd finally seen him at his worst. He'd give anything to know what she was thinking.

She knelt by Sandor. The Talion tried to bat her hand away, but she forced him to accept her gift of healing energy. It didn't take long.

Rising to her feet, she finally came close enough to Ranulf to lay her hand against his face. A surge of healing warmth washed over him. He should've stopped her from wasting her depleted reserves, but right then he needed her touch, even if she treated him with the same clinical detachment as she had Sandor. That hurt, but he understood.

Finally, he said, "Look, you can have my room. I'll bed down out here on the floor where I can keep an eye on Sandor."

Kerry frowned, but all she said was, "Come get me if you need me."

Her words confused him. Of course he needed her. He watched her walk out of the room, ripping his heart out as she went. While she showered, he reestablished his wards and moved around in the kitchen, too skittish to settle down. Dark energy always had that effect on him. After Kerry finally left the bathroom, he took a shower before heading straight back into the living room.

"I don't need a babysitter, Ranulf." Sandor lifted his head long enough to glare at him. "Quit being so damned noble, and go to her. If you let her slip away now, you're a bigger damn fool than I've always thought you were." Then the weary Talion yanked the quilt over his head and curled in on himself.

Sandor was right: he was being a fool. This could be his only chance to convince Kerry that he could never let her go back down that mountain alone. Still, it was her choice to make, and this was the toughest mission he'd ever faced. The bedroom door was closed, but he didn't knock before entering the room. Feeling as if he was about to plunge off a cliff onto the rocks below, he braced himself.

"Kerry, I need you."

She was waiting for him in the bed, with a soft smile and sad eyes. "Took you long enough."

As soon as he took a stumbling step toward her, she held back the cover in invitation. He didn't have to be asked twice. She met him in the middle, with a kiss that healed his heart and inflamed his passion at the same time.

"Will you love me tonight?" Her smile was tentative.

"That's not nearly long enough," he told her firmly. "I'm going to love you the rest of your life."

She blinked twice, clearly not believing what she was hearing. "Judith shared herself with me tonight, Ranulf. I have all her memories locked in my mind, including how she's used you all these years. I can't walk away from my responsibilities, especially now that I know how badly I'm needed."

She took a deep breath and gave him a ragged smile. "Looks like I'm going to be the new Dame. You've already served our people for a thousand years. I won't ask you to do that again."

Once again, this little slip of a woman was trying to protect him. The beauty of her generous heart stole his breath.

"The difference is that this time I'll be serving my wife, not just my ruler. If you'll have me."

There was hope in her eyes, however tentative. "But I thought you wanted to live up here on the mountain?"

"I do, but I figure we can add a few guest rooms and spend weekends and holidays up here." Then he kissed her, deepening it until they were both breathless with need. "Now—we can talk some more, or we can find something else to do in this bed. Your choice."

"That's easy. I choose you."

And she did.

Epilogue

Kerry held her hand out to Sandor. "Dance with me?"

He clearly wanted to refuse her, but she would have none of it.

"Must I remind you that it's my wedding day, buster, and everything has to go my way? So I'm sorry, but you can't say no. It's just not done." She gave him her haughtiest look, but spoiled it with a giggle.

He gave her a ghost of a smile as he swept her up into his arms. Even depressed, he could out-dance almost anyone else she knew.

As they made their first turn around the floor, Sandor asked, "And what about your new husband? Doesn't he object to you dancing with other men— especially me?"

"Probably, but he's going to have me all to himself up on his mountain soon enough. For now, he can share."

The band played a waltz as she had requested, giving her a chance to talk to her Talion warrior. Sandor had changed drastically since the night Judith died; he never laughed and rarely smiled.

When the music ended, she led him from the floor and out into Judith's garden. "We need to talk."

"Now? Maybe I should remind you that it's your wedding day. Surely you have more important things to do than worry about me."

"No, I don't. You're my Chief Talion, Sandor. I need you. Our people need you."

His face twisted in pain. "I don't know if I can do it, Kerry, even for you. How can I face Ranulf, day after day? How many years did I misjudge him? We both know Judith sent him after all those renegades not just because he was strong enough to do the job but because he could do so without compromising his honor. I don't have his strength, and I have no honor left. Not after I let Bradan get to Judith, and then took pleasure in killing him. That makes me no better than he was.

"And do you know what's worse?" He turned away from her. "I still feel the black energy curled up deep inside of me, just waiting for a chance to take over. If that happens again, I could turn renegade myself. What if you had to order my death? I won't risk causing you such pain."

"The answer is simple: It will never happen." Ranulf strolled in the door, looking every bit the warrior even in his tux. "If you were like Bradan, you wouldn't feel the way you do now. That awareness proves the strength of your honor. I would be proud to fight with you at my side again any day."

Kerry beamed up at her husband as he wrapped his arms around her from behind. She was counting the minutes until they could start the honeymoon, but she still had business with Sandor.

She gave him a stern look. "Here are your first orders from me, Talion. When I return, I want you to have a plan drawn up for training more Talions. No single person should bear the burden of policing our people."

She waited until he reluctantly nodded. "And I had to come from somewhere. I want you to track down my family. Find out if there are more like me out there."

He shook his head. "I appreciate the faith you have in me, but I don't think I'm the best one for the job."

"I *know* you are, Sandor." She gave him a teasing smile. "Don't argue with your ruler at her wedding. Now tell me you'll do it, so I can have one last dance with this handsome Viking."

Sandor bowed slightly. "Very well, Dame Kerry; I'll do as you ask. Now if you'll excuse me."

As he walked away, Ranulf squeezed her tight.

"That was well done. At least now he has a purpose to his days. That will help."

She turned in his arms. "And what can I come up with for you to do?"

He laughed down at her. "Don't worry, I have plenty of ideas about how to keep both of us busy tonight. Now, wife, let's go have that dance."

Turn the page for a sneak
peak at the next book in
Alexis Morgan's Paladins series,

DARKNESS UNKNOWN!

**Coming in February 2009
from Pocket Star Books**

Consciousness came burning back, jerking Jarvis out of the deep sleep his body demanded for healing. With it came the familiar surge of anger, coupled with a heightened awareness of being alive. His skin burned and hurt, as if it were too small to contain him any longer. Old habits had him twisting and turning to break free of his bonds; he hated being tied down, and hated the need for it even more.

But something was different. Waking up unable to move was hardly a new experience, but he was used to the cold stainless steel under his back, not soft, sun-dried sheets. He tried to move his sword arm, but couldn't budge it more than an inch or two. Same with his left.

His legs were bound, too—but with rope rather than the security straps and chains his Handlers used. What was going on? Keeping his eyes shut, he reached out with his other senses.

There were other heartbeats in the room, two of which weren't human. The good news was that they weren't Others. The third heartbeat was definitely human, and from the faint scent of floral perfume, it was most likely a woman's.

Where the hell was he, if he wasn't dead and he wasn't in the lab?

His last clear memory was the nightmare realization that he was about to die at the hands of a rogue mob of Others. Everything after that was a complete blank.

He opened one eye to assess his situation. A ceiling fan whirred softly overhead.

To the right was an old-fashioned oak dresser and a wall covered in floral striped wallpaper. Careful not to make any sudden moves, he slowly looked to his other side and hit pay dirt.

A woman lay sprawled in a chair in the corner. She couldn't possibly be comfortable with her neck bent like that, but it clearly hadn't interfered with her ability to sleep. Who was she?

He'd always been a sucker for redheads, especially the ones with fair skin and a few freckles thrown in for extra interest. He grinned, willing to bet she hated each and every one of them.

He studied her face, liking what he saw. What color were her eyes? He was betting on green, or maybe a rich chocolate brown. Her hands looked strong and capable, and she wasn't wearing a wedding ring—although that didn't always mean anything. Not that it mattered. Once she cut him free, he'd leave, never to darken her doorway again. And that was a damn shame. He wouldn't mind a romp in this bed with her.

Then he noted the rifle within easy reach of her chair. She'd been smart enough to tie him down, and he bet she knew how to use it. A bullet from a twenty-two wouldn't kill him, but it would hurt like hell. And if she hit a vital spot, it would definitely slow him down.

He shifted slightly, causing the bed to creak. Immediately there was the sound of claws scrabbling on a wooden floor, and two furry heads popped up over the edge of the bed. The dogs were well-mannered enough not to jump up with him, but they whined and looked back at their owner as if trying to figure out what to do next.

The woman went from sound asleep to wide awake in a heartbeat. She jerked upright, her eyes wide and a little scared. Then she reached out to reassure her guardians.

"Down, boys. He doesn't need you in his face."

The animals immediately disappeared from view.

If she'd been pretty while asleep, she was stunning wide awake. And he'd been right the first time: her eyes were bright green with flecks of gold in them. And right now they were focused on him with sharp intelligence.

"Good morning, Mr. Donahue."

How the hell did she know his name? Then he spied his wallet on the small table next to the chair. She'd rifled through his things?

He let a little temper show in his words. "You seem to have me at a disadvantage, Mrs. . . ."

"Gwen. Gwen Mosely, and it's Miss."

That pleased him far more than it should. "I would offer to shake your hand, but I'm a bit tied up at the moment."

When she made no move to untie him, he tried again. "I won't hurt you, Miss Mosely. If you'll just untie me, I'll leave and never bother you again."

Preferably without answering any of the questions she was likely to start asking, ones he couldn't answer.

"My dogs found you last night, and my brother and I brought you up to the house."

He could imagine what shape he'd been in when they found him. After a fierce fight, he'd managed to escape from the Others, but he hadn't expected to live through the night.

"Thank you."

"You were a bloody mess." Her eyes darkened. "I don't suppose you'll tell me how you came to be in that condition."

"You suppose right." With the toll healing took on his body, he simply didn't have the energy to think up a believable lie. "You don't want to know the details."

"Well, yes, actually I do." She leaned forward, as if to encourage him to start talking.

He went on the attack. "Why didn't you call

the authorities? Or are you in the habit of taking in wounded strangers and tying them up?"

Her fair skin flushed. "I thought about calling Sheriff Cooper, but he would have insisted on calling an ambulance. I didn't think you'd want the local medical authorities to get their hands on you. A man with your particular abilities could end up as a lab rat somewhere."

His stomach clenched. She was right—but her reaction to his ability to heal didn't make sense. Unless she knew more about Paladin physiology than any civilian had any business knowing.

"I would have survived the experience." Short of a head shot or amputation, he could survive almost anything, but she didn't know that. Or shouldn't.

"My mistake, then. Next time I find you cut to shreds and half-drowned, I'll save myself a lot of work and call 9-1-1." She had a redhead's temper, all right.

He tried his most winning smile. "Did I forget to thank you? This is a far more pleasant wake-up than I expected to have."

She wasn't buying it. "Save the charm for someone who might fall for it, Mr. Donahue."

He couldn't help laughing. "Okay, but the gratitude was sincere. I really do appreciate what you did for me." He tugged at his ropes again. "Now, can you cut me loose?"

She gave him a slow nod. "On one condition. You stay for breakfast and meet my brother."

That seemed like a simple enough request, but was it? What difference did it make if he met her brother or not? Maybe he should find out.

"Deal."

She smiled. "Good." She began working on the ropes before she spoke again. "There's a bathroom down the hall on the right. I'll lay out towels and a toothbrush for you. Your clothes are clean—well, your jeans and socks are. I'm afraid your shirt was beyond salvaging. My brother is about your size, though, so you can wear one of his shirts."

So her brother was full-grown. If he was an adult, though, why would he let his sister stand guard rather than do it himself? They had no way of knowing whether he was a good guy or a bad guy, and he'd give her brother an earful on the subject.

He remained still until she finished untying him, not wanting to startle her with any sudden moves. When she stepped away from the bed with her two dogs flanking her, he slowly sat up. Other than a few sore spots, he was well on his way to mending.

When he swung his legs over the side of the bed, she actually blushed and backed farther away. He grabbed the sheet to cover himself up. In the lab, he was used to waking up stark naked with a serious woody and thinking nothing of it. But from the way she kept her gaze strictly on his face, she wasn't used to strange men walking around her house in their underwear, aroused or otherwise.

"I, um, I'll go get your things." She beat a hasty retreat.

Once she left the room, he picked up his cell phone from next to his wallet and called headquarters to check in. They sounded relieved to hear from him, but he didn't fool himself that they really cared. His permanent death might even come as a relief to some of the Regents, considering how often he was in their face over how they treated the local Paladins.

The good news was that the barrier had finally stabilized during the night. The mop-up campaign was nearly complete, and everyone had orders to stand down for the next couple of days.

Jarvis hung up, then headed down the hallway to the bathroom. After a hot shower, he'd ask his hostess a few pointed questions of his own.

Gwen heard the shower shut off. She flipped the pancakes on the griddle and decided she should make half a dozen more. Chase ate like a bottomless pit lately, and considering Jarvis Donahue's size and that he was coming off a night of intense healing, cooking three times the normal number of pancakes, scrambling a dozen eggs, and frying a pound of bacon should be enough. Maybe.

The coffeepot had stopped perking, and a pitcher of orange juice was already sitting on the table. She wiped her hands on a dishtowel, then caught herself patting her hair to make sure it was tidy.

What was she thinking? Granted this guy was good-looking, but he wasn't the kind of man for a woman like her. Even if he did make her hormones sit up and take notice.

It had been a long time since she'd enjoyed the company of a man, in bed or out of it. She'd been responsible for raising her brother ever since she was twenty and he was ten. Keeping a roof over their heads and meals on the table had taken most of her energy; she'd had very little left over for something as frivolous as a boyfriend.

Keeping the farm had been a wise choice; now it offered Chase a sanctuary from the outside world that sometimes felt too small and confining for him. He was becoming increasingly aggressive and short-tempered, especially around boys his own age. Keeping him buried under a stack of chores all summer had drastically reduced the number of complaints about his behavior, but she dreaded what would happen when school started up again.

She listened to the sound of her unexpected guest moving around in the bathroom. For the first time, she might find some answers to the question of what made Chase that way. If this stranger shared other characteristics and had found a way to master his volatile nature, then there was hope for her brother.

The footsteps overhead meant Chase was up and moving, too. Good. It would be interesting to see how the two males reacted to each other.

The bathroom door opened, and she quickly added the pancakes to the stack in the oven, then set the warm platter on the table.

Jarvis walked into the kitchen and instantly the room seemed to shrink in size. Although there was no aggression in his stance, it was like watching a large predator establishing its territory. He had to still be hurting from the worst of his injuries, but there was no sign of it in the flex and play of his muscles under Chase's shirt. And Jarvis filled out that T-shirt in a *whole* different way than her brother did.

Had the temperature in the room just jumped up twenty degrees?

Jarvis came to an abrupt stop when he saw the table. His dark eyes lit up, and his mouth curved up in a slow grin. "Maybe I *did* die and go to heaven. Tell me you didn't go to all that trouble for me? Although I'm not complaining a bit."

"I have a teenager in the house, Mr. Donahue.

Cooking for him is almost a full-time job." Still, his reaction pleased her no end. Chase blindly ate anything that she set in front of him; having a more appreciative audience was an experience to be savored.

"Please have a seat while I pour the coffee."

He pulled out the nearest chair and sank down into it, moving a little gingerly.

"Would you like a couple of aspirin or something?"

"No, I'm better off without taking anything. I should be back to normal in another day or so." He added three teaspoons of sugar to his coffee before taking a big gulp of the scalding liquid.

"Go ahead and serve yourself. Chase should be along shortly."

"Aren't you going to sit down, too?"

He made no move eat until she took the seat opposite him. She'd chosen it because it was the farthest away from Jarvis, not trusting the way she was reacting to his proximity, but now she had no choice but to look straight across the table at him.

He was already pouring a generous amount of maple syrup over the huge stack of pancakes on his plate. Adding a sizeable serving of eggs and several strips of bacon, he looked like man intent on doing some serious eating after a long, lean period.

The two of them ate in a companionable silence for several minutes until Chase came pounding down the stairs. When he entered, Jarvis stopped chewing and stared at the teenager with something like shock before he quickly schooled his features to a more neutral look.

He definitely knew something, and she wasn't going to let him get by with keeping it to himself.

"Chase, this is Jarvis Donahue. Mr. Donahue, my brother Chase."

Jarvis immediately set down his fork and stood up. He held out his hand to Chase and smiled. "Make it just plain Jarvis. I've already thanked your sister for taking me in last night, but I know she couldn't have done it without your help. I appreciate it."

Chase's eyes flickered in her direction, waiting for her slight nod before accepting Jarvis's outstretched hand. "You look a helluva lot better this morning than you did last night."

Jarvis grinned. "I'm sure those hounds of yours have dragged in better looking specimens than me." He sat down and picked up his fork again. "Sorry for starting without you, Chase, but it's been a long time since I've had home cooking."

He was a charmer all right, but his remark still pleased her. Once again silence descended on the table as the two males concentrated on stuffing their faces. Oddly, it felt very comfortable to have this total stranger join them for a meal.

As usual, Chase was the first one done eating.

He pushed his plate away and stood up. "Nice meeting you, Jarvis. Glad you lived."

She sighed. "Chase, I swear, one of these days . . ."

He just grinned. "See you later, Sis. I promised Mr. James I'd help him load the hay in the back field today."

"Okay. Be home for dinner by six."

"Will do." Then he whistled for the dogs and tore out of the house, letting the door slam shut behind him.

She loved her brother dearly and enjoyed having him around. However, that didn't mean she wasn't grateful that he'd found part-time work with the neighbor for the summer. It kept him in spending money and gave him something constructive to do with his time and overabundance of energy.

Jarvis finished his own meal. "That was terrific, Miss Mosely. If I ate like that every day, I wouldn't be able to fit through the door."

"Please call me Gwen."

He nodded as he picked up his plate and headed for the sink.

"I can clean up in here later. Please sit down."

"Let me earn my keep, Gwen. It won't kill me to do a few dishes."

He cleared the table with quick efficiency, leaving her nothing to do but sip her coffee and enjoy the view.

• • •

He hoped Gwen never took up poker for a living. She'd starve to death, because every thought was right there on her expressive face. Right now, she was working herself up to ask him something important.

When he'd been in the shower, he'd tried to figure out why she hadn't gone to the police when she'd found a half-dead stranger in the woods. Especially one whose wounds had closed up and healed in a matter of hours.

But one look at her younger brother had answered that question. He was a dead ringer for a Paladin who'd served in the area just about the time Chase would have been born. Chase might not know it, but one day soon he'd be picking up a sword and learning to fight. If he didn't, his life would be hell, and his pretty sister would suffer right along with him. It was obvious that the two siblings were close, and Gwen wouldn't like hearing her brother was a born warrior destined to die over and over again, fighting the same secret war that Jarvis did.

It was a bitch of a way to live, but it was written in their blood and their bones. Somewhere in their past, alien beings called Others from a dark world had crossed into this one and left their mark on the human gene pool. It was ironic that those distant ancestors had helped create the Paladins, whose job was to drive the Others back into the darkness of their own world.

While Jarvis kept his hands busy drying dishes, he tried to decide how much he could safely tell Gwen about her brother. Not much. He would also have to insinuate himself into their lives long enough to get Chase started on the path to becoming a fully trained Paladin, without his sister realizing what he was up to.

Being around Gwen certainly wouldn't be any hardship. The problem would be to avoid any messy emotional entanglements. He was too old, too tired, and too close to the end to get involved with a woman, no matter how tempted he was to find out if she had freckles all over that luscious, creamy skin. The mere thought made him harden.

Great—how was he supposed to hide his erection now? He turned away from the sink and dried his hands on the dishtowel, keeping the terrycloth in front of him until he was safely seated at the table. Stretching out his legs, he leaned back and waited for the inquisition to begin.

It didn't take long.

Gwen's green eyes looked troubled. "You were pretty badly hurt last night," she began.

"Yeah, I was."

"Bloody and cut to pieces." She worried her lower lip with her teeth while she waited for him to respond.

"I don't remember much about it, but I'll take your word for it." He wasn't about to tell her that he'd been fighting a pack of ravening monsters within spitting distance of her backyard.

"Yet here you are, no more than twelve hours later, with barely a scratch on you."

"True." He reached behind him to snag the coffeepot and refilled his mug. "Want some?"

There was a small flash of temper in the way she shook her head. She suspected he was toying with her, and she was right. Maybe he should just answer the question she was dancing around.

"You and your brother had different fathers, didn't you?" He dumped sugar into his coffee and stirred it.

She looked puzzled. "Yes, but how did you know that? Other than hair color, we have many common features."

"Because Chase is the very image of an old acquaintance of mine. He had that same black hair and bright blue eyes. And I'd guess when Chase finishes filling out that frame of his, he'll be as big as his daddy was."

Just as he'd intended, he'd shocked her.

"What did your mother tell you about Chase's dad?" he asked.

Sadness settled on Gwen's shoulders. "Not much. She never told us even who he was, but he hurt her pretty badly. I was just shy of ten when she met him. For the first time since my father died, she seemed happy. She would get all dressed up and go out to meet him somewhere, so I never even saw him. Then all of sudden, Mom quit going anywhere. She'd just stare at the phone as if willing it to ring, but it never did. Then a few months later, she gave birth to Chase."

The dates fit. "His name was Harvey Fletcher, and he was a good man. It wasn't that he didn't want to call your mother; he couldn't. He died almost exactly eighteen years ago."

To his horror, Gwen's eyes filled with tears. "I wish someone would've let my mother know. At least she could've grieved for his passing, rather than spending the last years of her life waiting for him to walk back through the door."

"I'm sorry, too. I'd guess no one knew about your mother's involvement with Harvey. But from what I remember about him, he would never have willingly abandoned his son." He leaned over and put his hand over hers in comfort.

She stared at their hands. "Did this Harvey person heal like you do? Like Chase does?"

"Yes, Harvey had that same ability."

She nodded as if she'd already guessed that would be the answer. "Were you and he related?"

Now there was a question. He couldn't very well tell her that they shared alien DNA. "Only very distantly."

She ran her hand over the table, smoothing a couple of wrinkles in the tablecloth. Evidently she had another question but wasn't sure how to go about asking it.

"Gwen, just spit it out, whatever it is."

"Chase gets into a lot of fights, especially with boys his own age. The trouble is, he's so much bigger than most of them that folks are afraid he's going to kill somebody one of these days. It's better in the summer, when he's not shut up in school all day, but he's getting less able to tolerate crowds of any kind."

Boy, did that sound familiar. If the Regents hadn't found Jarvis when they did and brought him into the Paladin organiation, he had little doubt that he would have ended up in prison. Chase's sister was smart to realize the boy needed help.

"Have you thought about getting him involved in martial arts? The discipline helped me learn self-control." Coupled with weapons training, the Regents had honed his innate urge to fight into a lethal combination designed solely for killing Others.

"Is it expensive?"

Here was his in with the family. "To get him started, just to see if he likes the sport, I'd be glad to work with him."

She considered the idea for all of two seconds before shaking her head. "I couldn't ask that of you, but thank you for offering."

"Why not?"

Her fair skin flushed with embarrassment. "Because I can't afford to pay you, and charity doesn't set well with me."

Pride was something he could understand, even if it was misplaced. "I wasn't asking for money, Gwen. Someone did the same thing for me when I was about Chase's age. It saved my sanity, so I'm just passing along the favor."

Pursing her lips, she slowly nodded. "All right, I'll talk to him and see if he's interested. If he is, how can I get in touch with you?"

"I'll give you my cell phone number. It's good day or night."

At least he'd planted the seeds. If they didn't take, he'd have to think of some other excuse to return to the Mosely farm. A new Paladin wasn't something to be wasted; there were too few of them as it was. He had a duty to the Regents organization to recruit a new warrior. It had nothing to do with the boy's sister, much less her red hair and those adorable freckles.

Yeah, right.